Author Vanessa Wrixon

Book Title Iberville

Vanessa Wrixon

© **2020**

Self-published

(devilvness@yahoo.co.uk)

Thankyou for buying my book.
Hope you enjoy reading it

Vanessa

IBERVILLE

I am unsolved, I am a statue in mortality, my smile has had an impact on society but my life has never been absolved

All I wanted to do was entertain, but instead, someone betrayed me and let my blood fall like rain and with nothing to gain

Before and after, my eyes have always been open so while you figure out who's the killer, I have to wait invisible to the world.

CHAPTER 1

My name is Jasmine Tormolis, but everyone calls me Jaz for short. I am a Journalist with big ideas and a huge enthusiasm for travel.

Ever since I was a little girl I loved the tabloids, I enjoyed reading all about the private lives of the rich and famous. Every Sunday the newspaper boy would arrive with the latest gossip in my father's newspaper, I would swoon over it for hours, writing my name in some of the columns as if I had written them. My parents laughed at me when I announced at the age of seven that I was going to be a reporter.

After finishing college, I started my dream job as a junior reporter for a local Sussex Newspaper, it was near to where I lived so an easy commute on my bike. It was an online paper, dedicated to covering all of the news and features in Sussex. We tried to make it more uplifting with inspirational and motivational stories, often asking our relatively small cohort of readers to send in stories of their own which we then adapted, making them more interesting for our readers.

I had lived in Henfield, a village in the Horsham District of West Sussex, for as long as I can remember, but I was actually born in Burley, Hampshire, we moved when I was two years old. Henfield used to be a thriving little village, but has become quieter of late, as the younger generations grow up and move to bigger towns and cities for work. To this day although modernised it still retains a lot of its rural character. It has the guide books boasting about old fashioned high streets, old haunted inns and many interesting stone-built houses that take you back to the Restoration period. According to the local village historians, Henfield was once home to Colonel Henry Bishop, the inventor of the very first postmark to be used on British mail. He was appointed Postmaster General to King Charles II, but within a year of taking office he was accused of abusing his position and was dismissed or whatever the term was back then, however his legacy continued and remained in use until 1787, when the square postmark was replaced by a new double circle type. Henfield is also home to one of the oldest cricket clubs in the world, dating back to 1771, not that I ever got involved, it was such a boring game with little sense of purpose, much the same as rounders which were made to play at school.

I had lived in Henfield as an only child with my parents and childhood sweetheart John, who was in fact the boy next door. John and I used to play together, go to school and our respective parents got on with each other, so we all grew together as one, sounds kind of corny I know. We even went to the same college, so probability was that one day John and I would become lovers.

As an adult I found life in Henfield really quite mundane, there was nothing much to do unless you were over the age of sixty-five, as I have said previously, most of the younger generation left as soon as they could to follow their dreams, leaving the village for the 'Saga' generation. Initially, I was in no rush to leave, why should I, my mother and I got on well, dad spent most of his days snoozing in his armchair and I was actually quite happy being spoilt by my parents. I wanted for nothing and paid for very little, which meant I could save for my future.

However, having said all that, there comes a time when you reach your mid twenties and feel enough is enough, there is a need to spread your wings and fly off into the unknown and find your new career. Luckily for me, this happened, to this day I am still not sure how I managed to get my first big break, but I landed myself a reporting contract with a well known paper overseas. My parents, although sad at my departure (naturally)! Were pleased for me, they could have their home to themselves at last and their only daughter was going to make something of herself.

The contract was for the Alise newspaper in the Caribbean, unlike Sussex it was the second most dominant daily newspaper throughout the Caribbean. It was first established in 1895, and to date was the longest continually published newspaper in the country. Printed in colour, it covered a wide array of topics including business, sports, entertainment news, politics, editorials, and special features. In addition to this, the local teams did a little investigative journalism and covered all local, regional and international news on a daily basis. You can tell I researched this, well I had to, it's a big decision to leave the comfort of your home in England and fly four and a half thousand miles to start a new job and life!

This all happened as a consequence of me moaning to my boss in Sussex, that I was bored and needed something more to get my teeth into, he apparently knew a friend of a friend, who he contacted and helped me to seal the job through a telephone interview, it made me wonder if he was actually glad to see the back of me, as it happened all so fast. Just me being paranoid! I was one of his best reporters, or so he told me at my appraisals. So, I relinquished my Sussex job and with some excitement and anxiety, flew off into the unknown.

However, little did I know when I left my childhood home and started work here in the Caribbean as a reporter, that a turn of events was about to change my life forever. So this is where my story begins.

Four years ago, I stepped off a plane onto the island of St. Kitts, the larger of two Caribbean Islands that make up the nation of Saint Kitts and Nevis, it is well known for lush rainforests, huge mountains and beaches of pure white, grey, and some black volcanic sands. The capital is Basseterre, situated on the southwest of the Island. It has a vibrant Caribbean vibe with mock Georgian buildings dating from the colonial era and a plaza called 'The Circus' which is supposed to be modelled on London's Piccadilly Circus, it comes complete with a Victorian-style clock tower, which has never worked since it was installed many years ago.

The place is full of character and has a great street food and spice market each day, however, it is slightly let down by the cruise terminal right in the town centre, where visiting ships tower over the beautiful old buildings and disgorge thousands of tourists a few times each week!

On this Island, everyone knows you and about your lifestyle, so your business is by no means a secret. I'm still not convinced that knowing the in's and outs of everything and everyone is a good idea, but it definitely works if you need something doing, you scratch my back and I'll scratch yours ethos. The main problem here is, nothing gets done quickly as the Island runs on 'Turtle Power'. As long as you are happy to go with the flow all will be fine, nothing is ever written down but everything is well remembered.

Looking across the bay from the village where I have now made my home is Mount Liamuiga, a dormant volcano dominating the skyline, wisps of white cloud rise from its peak each day and the rainforest continues to grow up its sides. For adventurers with an athletic ability there are organised hikes through the rainforest to its top which stands over a thousand metres high. Something I was not about to try, even though I did consider myself to be reasonably fit, or in good shape at least.

I was given some money by my parents as a 'well done' gift when I first moved here, so I rented a tiny room in a house until I could afford to buy my own shack right on the beach, which if I didn't stay could then become a holiday home as an investment. I set to work as a journalist for the Alise newspaper, enjoyed every minute of it and have never looked back. Not only did I love the work but I loved the Island, it's people and the lifestyle that came with it. So, here I am today, now classing myself as one of the locals.

It's 8.30am in the morning and there is a chicken in my shower, how very Caribbean! I casually glanced at it drinking some of the residual water puddled on my shower floor. I'm completely fine with this as long as it doesn't then want my feet as a meal. This is not the first creature to make an appearance in my shack since I moved here, doors left ajar often lead to spirited encounters with all sorts, and that does not just mean the locals, creatures such as scorpions, tarantulas, lizards etc, all visit on a regular basis, but a chicken, now that was a first! I chuckled to myself before shooing it away with my towel, funny creatures, red head, orange eyes, funny little bearded beak and it's odd little strutting movements as it clucks it's way outside fluffing it's feathers, what a sight I must have looked if anyone was watching. However, nothing got anyone flustered here, 'limin' and 'chillin' were the norm.

I made myself a breakfast of some fruit and two leftover readymade pancakes and did a quick tidy through, the heat was beginning to make its way into my shack, so now I was in need of a long cool drink. The mornings always started out warm but it then got hotter as the day progressed, not until late evening did it start to cool down a little. I poured myself a drink of cool juice from the overworked fridge, better not start on an alcoholic beverage too early I thought to myself, after all I was supposed to be working. I meandered onto my deck as by now a few hours had passed and the morning was turning into the early afternoon. In no mood to over-do it too much, I decided to chill on my deck for a while longer. Apart from looking at couple of e-mails quickly, work could wait for a bit, I was now given the responsibility of managing my workload, so I could catch up later.

CHAPTER 2

Sitting on the deck of my beach shack staring out to sea, the sun beat down its warm rays, which lovingly stroked at my pale skin, I soon became lost listening to the rhythmic percussion of the waves plummeting onto the shoreline like wild horses, rearing up before crashing down onto the beach, pounding the sand with their white foam hooves, and in the distance Mount Liamuiga sat still, a low lying mist covering its head like a sombrero. It definitely hadn't erupted since 1843 but it's tall peaks were a reminder that it could if it wanted to and I find that quite a scary thought as I would be right in its line of fire.

It had been an unusually quiet day, minimal e-mails from work and nothing much for me to report on. I had spent the last month reporting on Haiti and their struggle ten years after being hit by a severe earthquake. Despite billions of dollars being spent in the country, the magnitude of the disaster and the disorganisation of international aid, together with local corruption meant they were still in a place of poverty and destruction even today. I found it an extremely challenging report to do. Not only because there were other journalists from across the world that also arrived on location to do their spread, but having to witness the long term impact on those who have experienced it first hand, some of the people I came into contact with were still extremely vulnerable, so I had to handle it with sympathy and sensitivity.

Such reporting plays an important role in helping the public understand how the disaster happened and informing them of any new emerging developments. If it's done correctly it brings everyone together to share their feelings of grief or compassion and to hold the authorities to account for their failures to respond appropriately. I had done a good job getting my point across, especially on the economic and political front, but I felt exhausted, you are not supposed to let your job get to you, but it does affect, you, you wouldn't be human if it didn't.

I had decided today, rather than go into the office I would work from home. Of late I had been disorganised and had not really got my act together, but I often did this and as long as I was able to produce a good story my boss didn't seem to mind. Trouble was I was not being very disciplined on this particular occasion and I did not have a good story to report on.

I meant to get down to some serious research and speak to my contacts to see if there was anything developing, but instead I remained 'limin' on my deck lounger watching the world go by with a glass of red wine which had made its way into my hand. This was very bad news, it meant nothing would get done least of all written today.

My usual tipple was Red Label, a delicate red wine, with a hint of cinnamon usually served on the rocks, it seemed to quench my thirst in the sun, not that I'm an alcoholic you understand but I do often consume more than I should. (Note to self to drink less alcohol in future, especially in the heat of the sun.)

Just to the right of my shack, I could see Blot the local fisherman was waist deep in the sea, using his net to catch bait which he then sold on to Mogsy, who was as usual lazing in his boat, near the shoreline, waiting for his small bait so he could go out to deeper waters in search of tuna. Mogsy was very adept at doing nothing, but seemed to get by on what little he did do. At this moment in time only the pelicans were hard at work circling above, diving splat, into the water, fishing for their meal as Blot caught bait below them. The only difference, I thought to myself, was the pelicans didn't do this to earn money but in order to survive. Isn't nature a wonderful thing I thought to myself.

Continuing to people watch, I noticed a woman strolling along the beach, very striking in appearance, she was covered from head to toe in a bright red striped material, very coordinated, funny how her dress and headwear matched, she reminded me of a raspberry ripple ice cream. I laughed out loud to myself as that thought came to me.

Suddenly a scream echoed, I thought it came from the nearby shoreline, but I couldn't be sure. I looked up to see Blot up to his waist in the sea, which was gently lapping at him as it made its way back to shore before being pushed out again, he was waving frantically and shouting at the top of his voice, "Bird speed, bird speed," this was the local dialect for quick, quick. I sat up on my lounger and pushed my head forward, my ears becoming radars, straining, to see and hear what the all the fuss was about.

I couldn't really get a good enough view, so I shuffled my feet into a pair of flip-flops which were lying empty next to me, placed the now empty glass of wine on the deck, picked up my phone and strolled over to see what all the commotion was about. I wasn't in any great hurry, as I said, no-one moved fast over here, it was well known that everyone in this village was on the famous 'turtle power'.

Blot was trying hard to pull in his net, but having trouble doing so, every now and then you could see something large and long bob to the surface which he kept pointing at, whatever it was, it was definitely entangled in his net. "Shark, shark" he kept shouting and due to the commotion quite a few of the locals had now gathered to see what the noise was all about.

They all stood on the beach, chattering to each other and pointing at Blot's catch, but no one seemed remotely interested in wanting to help, that meant getting wet, so ever

Page 14

the adventurer, I removed my flip-flops and placed them on the sand along with my mobile phone and without further thought, I waded in to help Blot, after all, a shark this far in could make a great story, especially if it bit someone! I know it's macabre, but when in the media and all that. Blot pointed to the other side of the net "Du you ting, Du you ting," which was his way of telling me to take some action. I grabbed one end of the net and started to pull hard with Blot holding on to the other side. After a lot of exertion in the heat of the sun we somehow managed to get us and the net much nearer to the shoreline and as the water lapped back out to sea it became clear that the long bit in his net was in fact part of an arm.

We both looked at one another, "Mi hab ketch ah riva muma." Blot stated very matter of fact. Now that would make for some news finding a mermaid. We heaved even harder as the net felt like it was hooked on something and the more we pulled the more it tightened beneath the ebb and flow of the waves. "Come on help us" I shouted to the gathering crowd who were still stood around dry, chattering and finger-pointing. After a lot of encouragement and cajoling, I managed to get some of them to join in and together we eventually managed to haul it a bit closer to the waters edge. In doing so, it became very apparent that this was no shark but in fact a person's body. Then without any warning, whatever the net had been caught on suddenly gave way and the whole net with its entangled human catch lunged out of the sea and lay motionless on the sand. We all fell awkwardly backwards onto the beach after it, the chatter now changed to gasps and screams at what lay before us.

My journalistic instinct wanted to take over immediately, my head, a whirling concoction of words and titles, reporting on this for the Alise, wow what a fantastic story! I can see the headlines now, my boss would be totally amazed, nothing like this ever happened here. There had been almost no crime in the last five years, well, any that had been investigated, most crime here was covered up very quickly. However I knew that despite the Islands notorious corruption, I had to do the right thing and report this to the local authorities. I reclaimed my mobile, shook off the tiny grains of sand that it had become dusted with and dialled 911 for the police, local authorities and ambulance.

Despite making the call there was no certainty of any response at this time of day, most of the Islands police would be playing cards by now with a joint in their hands, even if they were still on duty, if I was lucky and there was someone to answer my phone call , this crime would not be investigated at any great speed, that was for sure.

Unfortunately our local police were well known for their cheating at card games in Ziggy's bar and their corrupt ways, but no one was brave enough to challenge them, for fear of any repercussions. There was still an awful lot of corruption here in the Caribbean, but new training programmes and more investments from local governments to help the police meant it was hopefully starting to decline but it would take a while to become non existent.

Eventually a man's voice at the other end of the phone spoke, "Yo Police." I introduced myself but left out the reporter bit and then explained the current situation as best I could with several interruptions from the locals trying to get in on the call and add their slant on the situation. Blot came close to the phone and yelled in my ear "Wi ave pulled ah bady fram di sea Eh a a lie pan St Thomas beach Yuh cum mon" "OK ma'am." The phone went silent then clicked off, they had hung up, probably swinging into action, and racing to the scene with great gusto, sadly I fear not. "Thank you Blot, I did have it under control," I said with a grin on my face, not sure why.

Luckily for me, the police did take their time, so I was able to get a couple of illegal snapshots of the body on my mobile phone. There was so much arm waving and commotion going on amongst the locals that I don't think anyone noticed what I was doing. I carried on managing to get close enough to the body to get a quick 'recky' and see if there was any ID or a clue that would help determine who the person was and how their death occurred, long before any police activity happened. As I touched the decomposing corpse, Yuk, I shivered and felt a wave of sickness come over me, She was cold, so cold, her blood and limbs had become stiff, it is a ghoulish thing.

From what I could make out the body was that of a female, she was ghostly pale, her lips already bluish. I wouldn't like to guess her age, as judging by the state of her, she had been in the water for sometime. I could however make out that she had brownish grey long hair that was matted and dull, possibly Caucasian of origin. I think she had been in the water fully clothed, a long sleeved print dress, ripped and torn clung to her lifeless body, this was very unusual here for this time of year as the locals often bathe daily in just their vests and pants due to the heat. On her wrist she wore a tarnished charm bracelet, her fingers and toenails were painted red but chipped in places.

This was definitely a women who once took pride in her appearance, in my non-expert opinion she did not go into the water aiming to die, was this an accidental death or even a murder? How good would this look on the front page of the Alise. Mystery woman's body ensnared by fisherman, but I must remember the reporters code of conduct to be sensitive to this trauma.

My thinking and image taking, was cut short by the sudden screeching of tyres on the dirt track leading to the beach, it caught all of our attention and signalled the arrival of the local police force, bursting out of their truck as quickly and as dignified as they could manage, no one wanting to be last out and miss anything. Our local police team were a funny bunch a complete mishmash of personalities, the team consisted of a tall and well-groomed man in smart attire, clearly he had pride in himself. He was Sangerman, the Inspector and his colleagues, Sergeant Bordeaux, a Rastafarian, of equal height, in uniform but looking slightly dishevelled, his dreadlocks hanging like strands of thick rope around his unshaven face, a gold medallion gleaming around his neck, he looked quite scruffy and out of place, they were followed closely behind by two very overweight women constables, Ruby and Tanice who seemed to be in competition with one another adjusting their hair, pulling their uniforms straight and putting on lipstick, chattering and holding on to each other as they made their way unceremoniously across the sand to where we were all gathered in modest awe!

Both the Inspector and Sergeant were gesticulating and jabbering on about how this could have happened here, when there had been no crime in the area for fifty years, l think they meant five years, but everything was over-egged here, "This was 'gonna take some sortin," they remarked as they scratched their heads, but at least the Sergeant took his cap off in respect, I had to smile at the shenanigans.

The woman's body was quickly 'fleeced for evidence' this form of policing consisted of the Rasta peering over her and signalling to one of the police constables to come forward with her camera and take some snapshots. A lot of huffing, puffing and brow wiping was very evident, apparently something to do with the heat. The Inspector was now questioning Blot and some of the crowd, whilst the other police constable seemed to be taking samples from the sea, who knows why? What on earth could this large expanse of water reveal in a laboratory?

I laughed to myself as she tried desperately not to get wet, it was proving to be an impossible task, it resembled a Monty Python comedy sketch. Eventually I was beckoned forward by the Inspector for questioning, it didn't really take very long as he seemed most disinterested by what I was explaining and at one point lit up his cigarette. The sergeant tried to keep up jotting my explanations in his notepad. Suddenly, the Inspector waved his arm in the air and the woman's body was then lifted unceremoniously and dropped into a black body bag by two more men who had arrived on the beach both wearing red T-shirt's and brown trousers both smoking joints, very dubious characters, presumably they had been summoned from the local morgue by the police constables.

I felt for this poor woman as the thud of her dropped torso was then rolled into the body bag and awkwardly dragged up the beach by the two men, it was just like they were pulling a cart behind them, the black body bag was picked up then dropped swiftly onto the floor of a black van which then vanished into thin air as quickly as it had appeared, presumably taken for further investigation and possibly a postmortem. I made a mental note to myself to touch base with the morgue about this in the morning.

I looked around, what had I missed? Everything had gone back to how it had been previously, as if nothing out of the ordinary had happened. Blot was back in the water carrying on fishing, obviously with a different net, Mogsy still limed in his boat, and the raspberry ripple lady continued her stroll along the shoreline picking up shells and looking at them, before discarding back onto the sand, whilst the rest of the locals were dispersing and going back to their business without saying another word to each other, just the odd wave of the hand or nod of the head was enough.

I slid my sandy feet back into my flip-flops and I too, strolled back to my shack, running through the details as best I could remember, to put in my report and thinking through what I was actually going to say to my boss at the Alise newspaper to make her believe me.

CHAPTER 3

The contract with the Alise was initially only going to be a years secondment, to see if I liked it and they liked me sort of thing, but after a relationship break up with John my childhood sweetheart, I took some time to visit different places on the Island and it's funny way of life and I reached the conclusion that this was definitely going to be my forever home, the Alise was of course, over the moon with my decision to stay.

John and I had been together since childhood, but with my posting to the Caribbean we both found that the long-distance relationship didn't really work. We both wanted different things, I wanted a new challenge, excitement and freedom. John was committed to travelling the world with his job, as part of the UN Peacekeeping organisation. After some deliberation we came to a mutual decision that it would be better for us both to go our separate ways, but we vowed to stay in contact, always remain friends and be there for each other if we ever needed help.

The Alise newspaper was my first big break, and I loved being part of it! It is well known for having plenty of punch and has a surprisingly significant impact on the world's view of events in this part of the Americas. Before I came to the Island I used to sit in my office in the UK reporting on local mundane news, so it was initially quite hard for me to believe that a Caribbean Newspaper could play such a key role in influencing the World News and Media.

Our current newspaper team consists of the boss and senior editor Petra, she has overall responsibility for the newspaper, quite a fierce woman but with a heart of gold if she likes you, she has the biggest Afro hairstyle I have ever seen. My line manager, sub editor, Tilly, reports directly to Petra and ensures that I meet my deadlines and schedules to her specific requirements. She is blonde and very glamorous, everything a woman would want to aspire to, she is quite shy in nature but there is a side to her that I wouldn't like to cross. Then there is the assistant, Marigold known as Goldie, she adorns herself in big gold-effect jewellery which shines so bright against her dark skin, you end up squinting as an initial protection to the brightest of lights, but once accustomed you can open your eyes fully.

In the print room is Colby, an ancient part of the furniture with over forty years at the paper, who peers over his half moon glasses and grunts a lot. Winston is our express courier, very thin, athletic build, dark skin with long sexy dreadlocks. He manages to turn his hand to any odd job going, I have never come across anyone who can ride a bicycle as fast as Winston can, its like he is going to take off and fly. Finally, there's me Jasmine, known as Jaz, slim, reasonably fit but nothing much to look at, pretty ordinary really, however, I do consider myself to be a good reporter, I enjoy the work and have struck up a good rapport with everyone. My ambition is to take over the paper one day when I make the Island my permanent home. Why shouldn't I aim high?

I got back to the shack and rang Tilly to get the go-ahead to run with this spread, she answered the phone almost immediately and screeched. "Glad you phoned, have you heard what's going down," before I could get a word in, she squealed at me again, "well get on to it Jaz what are you waiting for, this is a big, big story." How did she even know? Eventually when she did let me get a word in edgeways, it transpired that Blot had spilled the beans at Ziggy"s the local bar, he had gone there after giving his bait to Mogsy, news travels fast on a small Island, unlike the people. I was quite glad that she seemed as excited as me to run with this headliner, could this possibly be the story that would lead me to the top?

After replacing my mobile into my jeans pocket, I meandered over to the computer and pressed the power switch, an orange light glowed dimly on the front, followed by a flashing white arrow appearing on the screen awaiting its instructions. I clicked the mouse and started to search the web beginning with the missing persons database, but this drew a complete blank, maybe it was still too early to notice she was missing, so instead I put out a plea on social media, this was always a good place to start, I could check after a few hours to see if it had sparked any interest. The woman must be missing from somewhere and someone must know her. I stared at the photo on my mobile, did I recognise her, no, I don't think so, but I couldn't be absolutely sure, she vaguely resembled someone who was once part of a higher social circle that I may have done a feature spread on a few years back.

By now it was getting late and everywhere was closed, this was the norm here, I remember thinking it quite odd when I first arrived on the Island. Having come from England where trading does not cease until 10pm and we even had access to some stores twenty-four hours a day, here we are lucky if local stores are still open at four in the afternoon. If the locals have to serve more than six people in a day, they class themselves as 'being busy,' in the Caribbean 'limin' takes precedence over working. Living on the Island for a while now, I have managed to adapt to the culture and way of life.

I couldn't stop my brain from its explosion of thoughts, hundreds of ideas keep whirling around in a buzz of electricity, this could be the calling card of an adventure, of unknown paths waiting at my feet, my climb to the top, to stardom even. Whatever lay ahead could be a great challenge, imagine what might happen if I could solve this! Oh come on, Jaz, don't try and bite off more than you can chew, you do not need to become a private investigator now.

I decided I would resume my investigations tomorrow, having had so much excitement for one day and a gap of at least five hours since my last alcoholic beverage. I decided it was time to pour myself another large glass of Red Label and chill, but with my mind still buzzing and the computer sitting idle, it kept enticing me back to surf the net. I trawled the web for a little bit longer, writing down on a scrap of paper any sites that could prove useful sources of information and give me a head start on tomorrows research.

I got engrossed in a public records search followed by a Missing Persons Database called Craigslist, an American site I had used before which was quite helpful and had various web forums. Unfortunately, after an hour or two, I had to give up, I was just drawing a blank, as much as I was desperate to pursue this story, I wasn't actually achieving anything now.

In a bid to relax, I found myself beginning to shop online, this was bad news, to me it was like eating Pringles, once you start you can't stop. (Note to self, I must not buy anything unless I really need it) I already had plenty of useless items that I had bought but didn't really need. To hold back and not purchase anything would be a first for me, I had very little discipline you see and usually managed to find something to buy, even if I didn't need it. A realisation of how hungry I was came from nowhere, just in the nick of time as I was about to buy a pair of shoes. Purchase not accomplished, I decided it was time to give in gracefully and settle down to an exciting night alone in front of some trashy TV with something to eat. The majority of our TV was dominated by American sitcoms, reality shows and news, there were a few odd Caribbean programmes, but to be honest they were atrocious viewing material, but it all made for some light hearted fun.

I took a frozen meal for one from the limited contents of my freezer, heated it in the microwave for three minutes and hey presto it was ready, how lazy and unhealthy this was. It now sat before me on a tray, as if it had been beamed in from outer space. The kitchen, you see, was spotless, rather than a tell-tale food-preparation mess, if only I could be bothered to learn to cook properly. I could hear my mother's voice in my head "Jasmine, you must look after yourself as nobody else will, if you live on junk food, don't blame me when you feel ready to get carted off to the knackers yard at a young age!" 'arrragh' why are mothers always right?

CHAPTER 4

I decided my only way forward at the moment, was to make my way into town, an uncomfortable twenty minute bus ride from my shack, to pay a visit to the town morgue and see if I could speak with Candice who had worked there as a mortician's assistant for about ten years. She had become a really good friend to hang out with and was often a valuable source of information and fact finding extraordinaire when I needed to know info on the quiet. In return I supplied her with the odd 'tobacco' joints, all legal and above board of course, Mogsey was always pleased with a bit of extra cash for suppling tobacco good to friends!

Our senior editor, Tilly was also a friend to Candice, I use the word friend loosely in this instance, as a journalist's contacts book is their most prized possession. It is these contacts that can provide the heads-up on potential stories, background information and opinions often for a small fee. Therefore, finding her way into a senior editors contact book and becoming a go-to person made Candice feel very important and powerful, "cud be rich one day" well that's what she told me anyway when I questioned her motives. The more trusted and reliable you proved to be as an information source, the more journalists turned to you for contributions, be it in the form of interviews, written anonymous statements, articles and blogs and in return you got monetary rewards as well as a buzz from being involved. Not particularly ethical but it worked.

When I mentioned to Candice about being sure of her friendship with Tilly, she just replied "Mi an Tilly all false Mi ongle tell har sum bits cos shi can git nassy buh shi pays mi criss Eh nah lakka wi Wi a Chue fren dem," translated into English, Candice is happy to be paid for some information but her and I will always be true friends. I know it's a bit of a mouthful to say, but you have to go with the flow, Candice is her own person and makes up her own language at times.

Candice was of medium build with long black wavy hair which she scraped back off of her forehead usually with an orange bandana, but to be honest it could be any colour as long as it was bright. Her skin was a rich brown dimpled complexion, probably from all the smoking, I don't think I had ever seen her without a cigarette of some description in her hand. She had a larger than life personality and was affectionately known in the town as "Dicey," I had never asked her why but I imagined it was something to do with all the scrapes she got herself into.

As per usual she was stood outside the morgue propped up with one foot on the pavement the other on the wall drawing on a newly rolled cigarette. Her distinctive smell wafted in the air, a rich mixture of wacky-bakky blended with Monsieur de Balmain, her eau de cologne with which she doused herself, so you could smell her long before you saw her. "Yo

Boonoonoonoos" she said as I approached, signalling the peace sign with her fingers, the other hand still clutching the cigarette. "Yo to you too, so the body found yesterday, washed up on the beach, obviously came here, got any information to share with me?" I asked desperately trying to take on a laid back local style, but not succeeding that well. She stared at me, then half smiled as she took another draw on her cigarette, blowing out a puff of smoke from the corner of her mouth as she tossed her head back. "Waah ah drag?" I shook my head. "Nah kno nutten bout dat fi mi fren" she replied. "Oh come on Dicey, stop kidding around, just tell me what you know or what you can find out for me, we both know a woman's body was brought here yesterday." Candice sighed "Did tell yuh areddi Boonoonoonoos, Mi kno nutten bout dis," she gave me an unusual glare which I had never seen before, then stubbed her cigarette out on the wall letting the butt fall lifeless onto the pavement below.

She turned and went back inside the morgue, looking back momentarily, as if she was going to say something, but instead became spooked by someone or something, she just snapped "Nuh nutten happened cut out ih empress," with that she disappeared inside, out of sight. This was really weird, usually she was a great source of any gossip in the town and it was difficult to stop her flow of information once she started, either for money or in my case to help out a friend in need, but this time she was not going to give anything away. Was someone or something warning her off? Why was she holding back?

She definitely knew something, but why was she so intent on not giving away any information. This was like a red rag to a bull, I really needed to know now more than ever why this was being covered up, maybe her life was in danger?

I needed to get into the morgue to look through the death records, but there was no way I could get in without Candice and as she was clearly not going to help me. I was running out of options, maybe I could break in after dark? Not an option, it would be far too risky. I was so frustrated at my lack of progress, Tilly would expect this lead article on her desk from me pretty soon and to date all my efforts had been met with blanks.

As I stood in the small queue waiting for the local bus home, beads of perspiration trickled down my forehead, the sun was at its hottest and I had unfortunately had a fruitless journey into town. After a couple of minutes, the half full bus arrived and stopped in front of me with a jerk. Its engine let out a deep sigh, reminding itself of the heavy weights it had been carrying all day. The bus was anything but luxury, its seats dulled by the grime of many years, its floor well trodden and the windows covered in dust, small peepholes stuck to the windows where people had made holes trying to get a glimpse of the outside. I tried to imagine when it first rolled off the assembly line, the seats a brilliant blue, the chrome hand-rails mirroring the sunlight, it would have looked so smart and proud, making its way around. Now it is a dirty yellow faded canister transporting us to our destinations, just pile in, bang the roof once to stop and it will obey your command.

The bus ride back home rocked us from side to side as it tried to avoid the potholes and goats aimlessly wandering in front of it. I looked around, people were chattering, their voices rising and blending together in the sweet ritual of friends, whilst others absorbed themselves in their music. It seemed a quicker ride home than normal, maybe because my brain was working overtime, trying to come up with my next move and work out the answers to the questions. My talents of private investigative work, was living proof that it would not be a good career move. How amazing would it be if only I could solve this case single handedly, then watch my Island status soar, mmmh, I could see the headlines now, English girl strikes gold and solves murder. I put my finger to my chin then said out loud "where should I start? With Murder I think." Realising what I had just said, I looked around but luckily no one had even noticed my loud outburst.

CHAPTER 5

Still dreaming of stardom and my poor attempt at problem solving, I opened the door to my shack jumping with fright as my mobile rang. I delved into my jeans pocket and scrolled the answer button across, it was Tilly. Great I thought, she is going to want this article right now and I haven't even started yet. "Hello" I said hesitantly. "Jaz, Jaz I want you to change tack and go to a Luncheon and tour at Iberville, the Sugar Plantation on Tuesday. We need an article with Lord and Lady Wrexham about the estate's future." "What, I'm in the middle of this beach body article you wanted me to run with, can't someone else do it" I blurted out.

Tilly ignored my interruption and carried on. "They are going to reinvent their home to help the Island's economy. I have booked you a car to pick you up around one, you just need a frock, got it?" I felt completely deflated, "Um yes, I suppose so, but I'm still busy with this murder story, can't Goldie go, I really need to find out about the woman's body on the beach." "No, Jaz, it has to be you, my best reporter, leave the body for now it's not as important, the Sugar Plantation is a much bigger story, think of what it could do for the Island's economy and tourism when we go global with it. I need this article on my desk by Thursday morning so we can go to print and run with it for Friday's edition, Petra is on board with it." With that the phone fell silent and she was gone.

I stood rooted to the spot, completely stunned, I looked at my hands, my knuckles white from clenching my fists too hard, a scream from deep inside me forced its way out of my mouth, as if I had unleashed a demon, I punched the air, I felt so much anger. If anyone called me now, they really would feel the full force of my frustration. I was really cross, why on earth did I not stand up for myself more? Why had Tilly changed tack, she had seemed excited about the woman's body on the beach, it's not like her to want to drop a big story so quickly? If I did the article on the Sugar Plantation, the body on the beach would be "yesterday's news and then forgotten about." This was not right, the dead woman, whoever she was, deserved the respect to find out what had happened to her so that she could rest in peace. I knew there was no arguing or reasoning with Tilly, once she had decided on something we all had to fall in line even if we had differing views. Even if I went to Petra she would take Tilly's side. I sighed, I had to change tack.

I walked into the bedroom and sat down on the bed, Tilly's words still echoing in my head. I felt myself suddenly slouch, I felt let down, I wanted this to be my best story ever, but it wasn't going to be. I stared dead ahead, mesmerised by the sunlight playing on the wall creating dappled shapes as I sat motionless for a few more minutes, I had to do something.

Eventually I found the energy to heave myself off the bed, walk over to my wardrobe and search through my extensive collection of clothes. I tossed them onto the bed scattering them around the room in shear frustration, a bit like a mole digging its hole. Except it was clothes flying everywhere not dirt and moles don't get frustrated, do they?

Luckily, my clothes were quite resilient and took the beating well. Thoughts flew in and out of my head trying to come up with a plausible plan. I'm sure Tilly was thinking of her own benefits, not only could Lord Wrexham influence the paper, but more importantly, Tilly would do anything to rub shoulders with a local dignitary's, she could and would always pull strings to make herself look good. Maybe I could secretly carry on my sleuthing investigation on the side, after all I had read many a detective novel, how hard could it be doing both at once? I was a woman, I could multitask. When I had all the facts and solved the case single handedly, I could surprise Tilly and Petra with both completed articles, surely they would be in awe of their best reporter then, wouldn't they? I may even get promoted sooner! "Pigs might fly Jaz," why am I talking to myself out loud?

My clothes throwing tantrum didn't take very long, I owned absolutely nothing that resembled a dress, I was always content living in my favourites, washing them out overnight, I was so predictable. I looked around, adorning the floor and bed were a couple of pairs of cut-off jeans some shorts and a selection of plain and garish motif T-shirts, a hideous orange and green spotted skirt which Candice had bought for my birthday one year, matched with an orange off the shoulder top, agh, I shuddered, I must throw this away.

I stood amongst the clutter, my wardrobe now completely empty. Maybe if I stood there long enough a secret compartment would open up and reveal a stunning dress, no chance! Great, now where on earth was I going to get something chic and stylish to wear for the Sugar Plantation experience? If I shopped online it wouldn't be sent to me in time and the local stores, well the less said about them the better.

I jumped as the rusted post box in the wall unexpectedly rattled, I really must get around to getting another one, I had said that every year since I bought my place but to date had done nothing about it, I had no excuse, I shopped online often enough. As I headed outside to see what had caused the noise, I caught a glimpse of Winston the Alise newspaper courier, pedalling off like Speedy Gonzales on his bike. He was in his usual attire, black hoodie and brown trousers, his skinny legs working the pedals so hard that in a strong breeze he would have definitely taken off, a bit like ET on his bike.

Enough of the day dreaming, I opened the rusty old box and there it was, the invitation for Tuesday, this I could really do without, another wave of anger hit me, my brain becoming a spinning top once more as I stared at the invitation in my hand. It was printed on a small pale blue card and on its front was an opaque photo of the Sugar Plantation known as Iberville, the edges were embossed in a gold leaf.

On the back of the invitation, written in fancy bold black print, were the words;

Lord and Lady Wrexham formally Invite Alise Newspaper

Tuesday 15th March 1pm — 4pm

A luncheon and Tour of Iberville followed by a question and answer session

Our aim to promote services and the Island's economy

Dress code Formal attire

Oh, what a joy this was going to be, the last thing I needed was to be dressed in some posh frock during the hottest part of the day, drinking, eating and hobnobbing with gentry. To make matters worse, at this moment in time I resembled Cinderella, I needed to come up with a dress, otherwise I would be going to the ball in rags!

Suddenly a brainwave struck, Goldie, she was the one person who would definitely have something, that would be suitable for the occasion, but, it would be colourful. I tapped in her number on my mobile, "Yo empress" came the reply after two rings, I returned the gesture then uttered. "Have you heard, they want me to do a story on Iberville, I have to go there on Tuesday, but I'm lacking anything to wear in the dress department, do you have anything I could borrow that's a bit erh sophisticated." I bit my tongue as I said this, oops, I didn't want to offend her. There was a short pause followed by "sure empress, Mi hab jus di ting fi yuh need any shoes too?" I paused, was this really a good idea. "Yes, please if you have anything, I'm a size five," I found myself saying. "Ok, bi ova laical more empress," with that the phone clicked silent, a couple of quacks sounded, reminding me of the unopened text messages I still needed to address.

CHAPTER 6

I returned to my desk taking a glass of water with me, as it had only just turned eleven o'clock in the morning. I had already made a promise to myself not to drink so much and so often. Trying to stay focused and disciplined, I began to search the web again for any information on persons reported missing or dead in any recent suspicious circumstances on the Island. I also started to trawl through the National Crime Agency, they hold an international database for all missing persons and unidentified body cases. But still, despite all of the names and information listed, nothing suggested who this ,woman was. Why am I consistently drawing a blank, was this corruption at its best?

Still frustrated, I decided that a walk would help me, I needed some air and different scenery might help me think more clearly. My brain was still in overdrive, I couldn't switch off, I really needed it to slow down to think rationally, how is it that thoughts can bring different emotions to the fore and conjure up all sorts of images? I guess that's why people say live for today, not the past, but in this case, the way forward needs the answer from the past? Well, I think it does!

I decided to go to Ziggy's Bar, it was only a short stroll, not for a drink you understand, but I knew Blot and some of the other locals would be there at this time, limin' away the day, smoking the odd joint, putting the world to rights or bird spotting, if you catch my drift! Perhaps they would offer up some information, after all, they would all have talked to each other and the village grapevine was always helpful when you needed information, you just had to do something in return. "You scratch my back, etc."

Ziggy's bar was the epitome of the mellow Caribbean vibe, a distillation of sun, sand, rum and reggae and with it came the untamed personalities that made this Island life simply the best, as Tina Turner would say! The bar started out as just a plank of wood suspended between two oil drums on the beach, but then it grew into something very special with everyone's help. Nowadays, it was an actual shed, constructed largely of driftwood and other odds and ends the locals had managed to acquire and was predominately held together by a collection of donated bras, panties, and other "unmentionables" from guests past and present. Despite appearances the atmosphere was fantastic, it was like a little piece of paradise, somehow it had even made its way into the Hitchhikers Guide to the Caribbean as one of the top ten places to hang out. Not sure it deserved that much accreditation but it was definitely the place to go for us locals, and for tourists, well, a source of amusement.

Ever the dependable, Blot was there, propping up the bar, nodding to the music which filled the air, people were drinking, jumping, singing and dancing to the reggae beats even at this time of the day. I paused for a couple of seconds, watching the spectacle, maybe this vibe is what the world needed and lead us onward to a greater healing. Blot's head lolled uncontrollably from side to side, this was not going to be the most fruitful of ideas I had ever had, he was close to complete inebriation, a glazed look came over him as he turned his head in my direction. "Whad up" he slurred, by now he had obviously downed quite a few rums and still had others lined up ready to be drunk. I wasn't convinced he would know where he was, let alone help me with any information. I strolled over, stupidly I bought him a double rum as way of a bribe, what was I thinking? I propped myself next to him, "Blot what happened at the beach?" "Doh hot yuh head, I not know whad yo talkin bout," came his inebriated slurred reply "What, do you mean, don't worry my head, you do know what I am talking about, don't you?" Blot grinned showing his teeth.

He had the teeth of someone who had grown up in poverty, they were all crammed together as if they were the last ticket holders to some amazing dance scene. "Stop messing with me Blot, why no one will talk about it? It's a cover up." I waited as Blot tried to remember and process the conversation. "shhh, av a drinkz" he slurred, beckoning for more drink to be lined up, "anneda glass." "No, No" I snapped back, banging my fist on the bar in shear exasperation. "What is going on, you were there with me, this is corruption at its best, Blot." "Shhh, ave ah drinkz Jazzy, calm yuh nerves." He beckoned the barman again, "fill em wid rum, mellow it babes."

I was now even more frustrated and so cross, why? Even the locals were refusing to talk, they were intent on going about their business and keeping their heads down. This certainly wasn't the norm, something or someone was in on this incident, scaring them, and I was going to get to the bottom of it. I had to do something, I had to find a way, even if I gained some serious enemies in the process, I had to succeed.

I felt like a volcano, I had to get out of everyone's way before I erupted, it would not be a pretty sight, I would say things I didn't mean and hurt a few feelings in the process. Defeated, I gave up and made my way back home with the scent of Island corruption following me. Something was definitely going on, but being a lone sleuth wasn't going to be as easy as I thought. It was very evident that I didn't have enough knowledge to find the avenues that could lead me to the information I needed and no one wanted to help me, they were afraid that was for sure.

Back at the shack I decided that this poor woman deserved justice, so I would report what I did know and try to persuade Tilly and Petra to run with this, instead of the article on Lord Wrexham and his stupid antics. I knew the story would cause a stir but it might jog memories or urge people to come forward and not be scared, especially if the Alise reported on it. All fired up, I began to tap away on the keyboard, my fingers on fire, not once wanting to pause for a break. I read it back to myself, I was quite pleased with what I had written as a brief synopsis, well it was a start anyhow.

Mystery or Murder?
Unidentified woman netted by fisherman

A mystery woman's decomposing body was netted off the shoreline of St Thomas beach by a local fisherman Blot Camerado. He ensnared the body in his nets whilst fishing in the area. Locals helped him to drag his nets ashore. The woman could be described as Caucasian with brown greying shoulder length hair, her finger and toenails painted red. She had been fully clothed when entering the sea and was found wearing a torn faded blue printed dress, a tarnished charm bracelet was on her left wrist.

There is no further information available at this time. It's a mystery whether she entered the water of her own free will or if there was foul play involved. Current investigations are on going to find out her identity and cause of death. This is a very tragic incident/possible murder. We urge anyone who thinks they might know the woman's identity, or have any information to get in touch with Alise Newspaper immediately.

Any information given will be treated with the utmost confidentiality.

Jasmine Tormolis, Journalist

Just then Goldie arrived as promised with my attire for Tuesday. She opened her shoulder bag, OMG there it was, thrust before me, a bright red very slinky, silk, off the shoulder little number. It was gathered in at the waist with a silver buckle, the skirt flared out in a sort of skater style. I didn't like to ask where it came from, certainly nothing I'd seen on this Island. "Gwaan empress try ih," I paused momentarily staring at the dress I now held before I tried it on. I'm not sure if I was disgusted or just couldn't believe what she had brought, anyway I should be grateful so I tried it on. I could just about tastefully squeeze into it as long as I didn't eat too much between now and Tuesday. If I was honest, at least I had something to wear even if it wasn't to my taste. I glanced down at the shoes that now hugged my feet, they were also red with little silver bows on the front to match the dress buckle.

The shoes strapped around my ankles, with heels that were about three inches in height so I would have to practise walking elegantly in them. If I had the ears to go with this outfit, I could be mistaken for Minnie Mouse. A far cry from trainers and flip flops (note to myself to buy some smarter shoes). I walked into the room where I had left Goldie standing, now wearing her outfit. "Stunning empress, gud fit" she said. "Thank you so much, I love it" I squeakily lied, the dress making me breathe in more than usual. "Peel neck fowl bawl fi life, im nu bawl fi fedda" Goldie replied, roughly translated it means just remember outward beauty isn't the most important thing, it's the person wearing it. Did it look that bad, or was she paying me a compliment? Who knows, what I did know was I had to get out of this dress!

Before Goldie left me, I showed her the quick report I had written ready to e-mail to Tilly and Petra, she frowned "Did tink yuh did did tell tuh figet ih an concentrate pan di Iberville story" she said, "Yes but respect prevails, this woman deserves the truth." "Jaz, Eff enuh wah deh gud fah yuh Cut out ih delete ih an research Iberville as yuh did tell. A no wantin tongue mek cattle can't talk" she added, in other words keep my mouth shut, "but why." "Jaz, jus cut out ih ok, Alligator lay egg, but him nu fowl,Yuh ah gud fren Nuh waah fi si yuh git hat," Things aren't always what they seem is the English synopsis of her speech, with that she kissed me on both cheeks and opened the door to leave. Mmhm, has she been warned off too, she never normally leaves my shack that quickly, she is usually happy to stay and provide non-stop chat about her life.

I never tell her much about mine and she doesn't usually ask, which I don't mind. Her life is much more interesting and glamorous, whereas mine is pretty boringly static, but I need that constant in my life. We're all different, I need boring, she needs sparks, fire, hot energy. "Fulljoy Iberville an tan aweh fram di odda." She said as she descended down the path, waving like the queen as she climbed into her car and disappeared.

I felt quite dejected as I closed the door on the world outside, why had Goldie warned me off, was it that she knew something or was it that she knew Petra could be pretty fierce if I didn't tow the line, maybe I could loose my job. Goldie wasn't that worldly wise, however her eyes did show a gentle concern. Was it fear, were there foolish consequences if I continued, probably, but I have to have a go, I have a greater duty to help this woman's family than sit back and do nothing. I agree with myself that I am worried, petrified even of the challenge ahead, yet I believe I have the ability and drive to solve this. I heard a voice in my head, warning me again but I had to do this for my own sanity, no matter what the outcome would be.

I printed off what I had written, slipping it into a blue file folder on my desk for later use and then pressed the 'save to file' button on my computer, taking heed of Goldie's warning not to upset Petra for the moment.

Story out of sight, I sat in my chair, poised, pencil in my mouth and half-heartedly began my research, making some notes about Iberville and its owners on paper to jog my memory. It was abundantly clear I wasn't going to get out of this event, so if I did this now it would give me a head start for Tuesday and help me prepare questions for the interview I had to do with Lord and Lady Wrexham. And so the research begins.

CHAPTER 7

A few websites later, I sat back in my chair and stared at the monitor, the word document on the screen was still garishly white. I had written nothing, I crossed my arms, frowned and let out a rather heavy sigh, my brain felt numb. I hadn't made any notes as I went along, it would have made life so much easier, I had just speed read sites about Iberville. I put the reason I had not typed a single word down to firstly, complete lack of interest and secondly, I could not stop thinking about the dead woman. I looked at her picture on my phone again, nope still nothing!

I needed a break, so I made myself some lunch and wandered outside and around my deck catching a few of the suns rays before resuming the research. If I stayed out here too long there was every chance that no work would get done and a glass or two of wine would find its way into my hand, so I resisted the temptation and went back to the computer trying to find a new enthusiasm for the task ahead.

Something had clicked inside my head, as I began to type furiously on the keyboard, the soft click-clacking of the keys filled my ears. Here we go, The Sugar Plantation known as Iberville to the Islanders had originally been built in the 1800s. From old photos I found on-line, it seemed an impressive house and estate, well to my eye anyway, but I would need to take up to date photos on the day to do with my report. Over the years it had been restored and brought back to life by its current owners. There were a couple of photographs showing how they had managed to transform it into a handsome villa, whilst keeping a lot of its character and not making it look out of place on the Island.

The main house was of Georgian design, stone built but disguised with stucco on the upper storey. Its lower level consisted of nascent stone walls which looked pale and grey. It may prove more attractive in the flesh, but for now, I can only describe it from an online photo taken a few years ago.

After perusing a few more images, I jotted down on my notepad, which areas I should concentrate taking photos of. For one, the large double teak doors, sheltered by a wide archway supported by stone pillars, very impressive. A tower of steps flow up to the archway and a stone balcony looms above it. The driveway, oh so grandiose, sweeping in a wide curve up to the house and circling an ornate fountain in the centre. These could be my opening pictures, with Lord and Lady Wrexham, if I can get them both to agree having their photographs taken at the entrance.

The entire estate boasts further outbuildings and acres of land which helps it merge with nature, become one with the flora and fauna, as it sits proudly in the hillside. I'm sure the panoramic views of the coast it boasts, would be absolutely spectacularly awesome.

Ok, that should be enough on the actual photos, our readers should be able to conjure up an image in their head from this if they haven't already seen it. But who actually lives there? It sounds like a line from "Through the keyhole," a TV programme I used to watch in the UK. I actually found myself being quite interested researching the owners and their family history, probably because I could dig deeper hoping to find the dirt on them, metaphorically speaking. The current owners are called Lord Edward Wrexham and Lady Amélie Wrexham. Lady Wrexham inherited the estate from her father after his death in 1980, lucky her!

Iberville had been in her family since 1909 when her grandfather bought it for $10,000. Prior to that it had been owned by a sugar planter, Alfonse Hanlon. Alfonse was no businessman or a good farmer, he continually suffered severe crop failures, which in turn resulted in a declining income for him and an increasing amount of debts. The stress from all of this caused his health to fail quite dramatically, which in turn meant he incurred large medical bills which he was unable to pay. Eventually, he was declared bankrupt and ended up taking his own life as he felt a failure and burden to society. How very sad, all the Islanders and slaves who depended on him and the plantation lost their jobs, their income and their homes with no compensation.

Lady Amélie Wrexham was a beautiful American heiress and was affectionately known as Miss Amélie. She came from a background of music and art, as a child she lived in Paris with her parents and enjoyed painting. When she was in her twenties she decided to return to America in order to seek her destiny. "Meh this sounded a bit like me, except I don't have the beauty" I commented out loud to myself. Lady Amélie continued to be an accomplished artist and exhibited her best work at the Corocon Art Gallery in America. She went on to develop a passion for collecting art and antiques, which meant, when she inherited Iberville she lovingly adorned it with all things related to visual arts and her collection of antique toys she had invested in.

They are many online references that suggest she was quite "skittish around strangers," and preferred to keep company with a very small circle of close friends. Nowadays, Lady Amélie, is said to be a loner, spending much time on her own and maintaining her privacy, apparently due to some childhood misdemeanours which led her to distrust people including some of her family members. She never sought help for this disposition, so in the end it became so bad that it affected her psychological health and she believed everyone around her were kleptomaniacs wanting to steal her treasured collections and inheritance.

Lord Edward Wrexham on the other hand was the son of a civil servant, his mother was a descendant of the French Creole elite, in other words she was of Portuguese origin. Edward Wrexham was born and educated in England until his parents moved to Spain when he was eight. After finishing school he went on to study the history of slavery which brought him to this part of the world, researching and eventually publishing a number of well known books focusing on the Caribbean. By 1992 Edward Wrexham had become a successful business entrepreneur, creating new businesses, bearing the risks but enjoying most of the rewards, he was knighted for his financial and economic successes. His many business ventures (or scams depending on how you looked at it) were said to have helped this Island's economy tremendously.

I came across an entire website, devoted as to how Lord Wrexham met Lady Amélie. It shows him attending an exhibition of her paintings in America, a dodgy looking character if you ask me! It states, they fell head over heels in love on their first meeting, he was the only one able to convince her that he was not after her money. If you ask my advice, he looks like a con artist, making up his own rules, sly and cunning becoming his way to survive.They married in 1994 with a lavish society wedding before making the Iberville Estate their home. I wonder if she did have any idea that he was just using his devious nature to obtain money and power?

Unfortunately due to the legal system over here, Lady Amélie had no idea nor was she advised, that when she married, she would loose all her rights to do anything to or with her estate without her husband's written consent. Local gossip says she became very depressed after her wedding causing her to hide away from society, embarrassed by Island gossip. To date she is seldom seen in public, living the life of a recluse and devoting all her time to painting. Since 1994 it looks like there has only been the odd occasion when she has been by her husbands' side predominantly for his business ventures and a couple of reported overseas trips to buy art and sell her paintings.

Lord Wrexham isn't best liked on the Island, he is well known for enjoying the high life, gambling, drinking and making new female acquaintances, he is often photographed in various Island magazines with a beautiful women on his arm. Apparently he decided he wanted to do more to help the Island's economy by renovating and opening parts of the old Iberville plantation site to tourists, renting out the cottages on the estate, sort of like a self catering resort, this would create jobs for the Islanders and build a tourist brand around the history and workings of the sugar plantation, possibly even getting Islanders to like him.

As a part of this 'Heritage' development he had already used some of Lady Amélie inheritance money, installing a fully operational cane-grinding steam mill and rum distillery, making 70% proof rum. This had already boosted employment on the Island and improved the economy, however there had been questions surrounding the health and safety of the distillery, I remember Petra doing a spread on this. The Distillery however still went on to do tours with popular tasting options which feature in most excursion brochures for Cruise Ship passengers.

I had actually been on one of the tours in my first year on the Island, but had never noticed the house or the Wrexhams, I did feel that it was unsafe for the workers as they walked up the grinding machine loading it with sugar cane, not a hat, gloves, goggles or hard shoes in sight! Completely unimaginable that this would happen in England, great rum though! Nowadays it supplies the majority of the bars and restaurants on the Island and can be bought online for sale abroad.

Lord Wrexham's vision, according to local information, had always been to transform the estate into a tranquil paradise, branching into the tourism industry, however the Islanders seem convinced that Lady Amélie did not want this, instead she preferred to keep the estate as a museum of historical interest, keeping alive the history of the sugar trade and slavery, living off the proceeds, and providing opportunities to sell her art to the many tourists.

I remember watching a report on television that Lady Amélie tried to file for divorce because of her husbands' drinking, gambling and philandering ways. It was all over the news for weeks, but due to unknown legal complications, it was never enlarged upon, meaning the case was quickly dismissed.

It was the biggest thing that had happened here in a long time, even the Alise was given special access to report on it until it was suddenly hushed up and instead we had to print an article about Lady Amélie's desperate attempts to seize the love she'd been denied by her husband. Rumour had it that she gave him an ultimatum to stop his infidelities for one year and she would become the perfect wife. All would then be fine, however if he were to fail, he would have to leave the Island for good and renounce all his inheritances, hence Lady Amélie would get everything that was owed to her and more. Maybe this was just a rumour as nothing more was ever heard. It was assumed by the locals that they had reconciled, but this was a troubled lady in a troubled marriage!

CHAPTER 8

I was now beginning to get bored, as much as it was vaguely interesting, I needed something more, why does inspiration never come when I want it to? Wine and crisps might help spark a brain cell into action. I strolled into the kitchen for some sundries but instead made myself a peanut butter sandwich and placed some crisps in a bowl to take back to the computer with me. I sat peacefully, eating and staring at the ocean rather than the computer screen. Today the sea was as still as a millpond, its surface barely managing a placid ripple, the sun reflecting tiny mosaic colours into it. Some way offshore, a pod of orca's broke the surface with their black dorsal fins, how lovely, suddenly one leapt high into the air, twisted its shiny grey topside and whiter underbelly, then still with its body arched and tail flipped it disappeared back down under the sea with a heavy splash.

I needed to get back to the research before I lost interest. I picked up the bowl of crisps, which I then clumsily managed to drop onto the floor, oh well, waste not want not, I could hear my mother say as I scraped the majority back in the bowl, my floor was clean. I pressed the space bar and continued, diving into the bowl of crisps and intermittently sipping my glass of Red Label.

Slavery and the sugar trade, this was going to be riveting stuff. Sugar was the main and most important crop produced on plantations throughout the Caribbean. Most of the Islands still had sugarcane fields and refining mills.

Alongside coffee and rice production, the sugar industry created a unique political ecology throughout the Caribbean. Sugarcane was grown on flat land near the coast, as the soil was more fertile nearer the sea and the ports were close to hand, giving the plantations the added advantage of shipping their crops worldwide. I knew this bit, I had been taught it as part of my history and geography O-level exams in the UK.

The arrival of the sugar culture had a deep impact on Caribbean society and its economy. It not only dramatically increased the ratio of slaves to free men, but it also increased the average size of slave plantations. The very early sugar plantations made extensive use of slaves to cultivate and harvest the crops, mainly for export to Europe and became a profitable industry for the owners. The larger plantations were the most successful. However in terms of the environment they had quite a negative impact, as the sugar industry led to a lot of deforestation in order to create more farmland to grow crops. Then there was the water pollution, freshwater ecosystems became contaminated with silt and fertilisers washed from the farms, as well as plant matter and chemical sludge from the mills.

Most of the slaves were immigrants from Fante and Ashanti in Africa, shipped over and imprisoned to work. Life on the plantations was extremely hard and these poor labourers had no way to opt out of the treacherous work. A third of all slaves died within three years of working on the plantations, this created a constant demand for new slaves to replace them. It is widely documented that in every sugar parish, black people outnumbered white people. They were the labourers, farming the land and mills, alongside women and children who also toiled with assembly line precision and strict discipline, they were under constant threat of boiling hot kettles, open furnaces and grinding rollers.

I poured myself yet another glass of wine from an opened bottle I found on the floor next to the computer. This was bad news, there was no way I was going to be able to read these notes through and make sense of it if I become too inebriated. I sat back in my chair, took another large sip and looked at the ceiling, giving thought to western lifestyles, this is where I get melancholy. When did the past become so insignificant? It has helped us shape the future, globally we all seem stuck in an endless loop of mundane stuff, oblivious to the importance of the past, crippled by a forced dissociation of the mind. European politicians believe that we stopped slavery but actually we haven't, we have simply exported it. We are the beneficiaries of slave labour in our industries from seafood to chocolate plantations, textiles and manufacturing, our modern civilisation is built on the suffering and death of those slaves and their modern equivalents, of which there are at least forty-million people who are still victims of modern slavery worldwide, the Alise did a spread on that a year or so ago, so number could be more by now, so sad.

Oh dear, that was a bit deep, I took another sip of wine and tried to read on. The vast majority of Africans brought to the Caribbean worked as the lowest rung in the social hierarchy but were the backbone of the plantations. Sugarcane production required a rigid organisation, the slaves were grouped based on their physical strength, their experience and the plantation's needs. The strongest and most capable often worked from sunrise to sunset cutting and transporting cane to the mills to be processed, whilst the weakest slaves were sent to cut firewood which in turn provided fuel to the boilers that then processed the cane.

Towards the end of the eighteenth century there became a growing unrest amongst the slaves, no longer were they passive employees of the plantation, but instead, they began to develop a fierce temper, standing up for their rights, this had been unheard of before. Many of them struggled both physically and culturally against an oppressive system so they rebelled. This was an extremely important milestone in the move towards the abolition of slavery. Left behind were the days of glory and luxuries for plantation owners, who had extracted huge profits from the slave trade and sugarcane production. It meant the next few years that followed, saw economic, political and demographic instability throughout the Caribbean Islands.

Nowadays, the sugarcane industry has almost completely disappeared, any plantations left have become modernised factories and in their place are elaborate plans to diversify and create wealth with tourism and financial services. If I think about this for a moment, every positive change in our History, began with a peaceful protest and then moved to mass civil disobedience. Is this the only way people can show that the status quo is broken and we need to change into something that actually works, a healthy culture on a healthy planet?

As I scrolled down the page to read further, the power went out. Thank you Lord, saved by a power cut! I hadn't realised the time until I looked at my phone. I glanced out of the window, I must have been so distracted, I hadn't noticed the sun sinking lower in the sky, draining away the daylight, now giving way to the velvety dark of night, the crickets were chirping along with the first buzz of mosquitoes. Right Jaz, move from this chair, I said to myself as I hauled my body from it like I had really bad arthritis, I had definitely been sat there too long. Tomorrow was the big day at Iberville and I didn't need dark circles under my eyes.

The power went out fairly regularly here on the island, happening at any time and without warning. The quality of the power service here has continued to get worse over the years. The frequent and prolonged power cuts result mainly from a company called Diamol, who have financial problems, unofficially, predominately due to the lack of bill collections, laziness really, as well as this, the population of St Kitts and Nevis has increased, so we are using more electricity more often and for longer, with not enough to go around. The Islands generators tend to cut in for a while but they are antiquated and rarely maintained or replaced, so give up the ghost quite quickly. Often the power can be down for hours, it is a pain, but you just get used to it, it's part of an accepted lifestyle here.

I stepped into the cold shower, my toes flinching as they touched the slightly chilled tiled floor. I turned the dial, old and metallic, it began to release thousands of lukewarm water drops, darkening my hair, as it continued to trickle down my back. My eyes fell closed, reassuring my senses with its water-hug, warmish but still cozy. I would normally take time for myself, to recenter and feel my calm nature which would help me sleep deeper when I eventually hit the sack. However despite standing under my everlasting beautiful waterfall, it would be a quick shower due to the lack of warm water, which was quickly becoming colder.

After I had finished showering, I changed into my PJ's and slumped onto my bed. I lay there, staring into oblivion, hoping that against all odds power would resume and I could microwave a pasta dinner. I was still hungry and dare I say it, I also needed to finish the dregs of that Red Label bottle I found. Well, I couldn't leave it half empty now could I! I knew the no alcohol rule wouldn't last for long. I had very little discipline you see and I considered today to be a bad day, all the research stuff I have had to do, plus the non productive information on the dead woman, I was getting nowhere, but worst of all, I had to present myself at Iberville tomorrow. Well, at least that was my excuse for finishing the bottle and I was sticking to it.

With that, the power came back on, telepathic or what! I moved from the bed to the kitchen, then the sofa, I was a creature of habit, very predictable. I nestled under a blanket, with my microwaved pasta and quickly became glued to the television. I tried to follow the plot of a drama I had become engrossed in. "Top Boy" which is a British crime drama series.

The series follows the plight of Ra'Nell known as Top Boy as he navigates the pitfalls of living on the crime-filled summerhouse estate after his mother, Lisa, is admitted to a mental hospital. Ra'Nell gains a reputation around the estate for his volatile behaviour after stabbing his abusive father and the killings continue as they are investigated. It is a bit way out there, but good watch series. Before I knew it the empty bottle lay next to me, along with the demolished pasta dinner, a bar of chocolate and half a packet of Oreo's and the commercials had come on.

There were quite a few, but at least they were short and required no intellectual effort. Once they were over and the drama was in full flow, my mind turned to the half opened packet of crisps left in the kitchen cupboard. I always feel more hungry when I have drunk too much, well, 'in for a penny, in for a pound.' I stood up and tiny crumb particles dived to the floor in quick succession, I brushed off the ones that wanted to remain clinging to me and returned from the kitchen with the crisps. Potato crisps are a gazillion calories a bite, but on an occasion such as this, they are a necessity and so very good. Hopefully I would still be able to squeeze into the little red dress tomorrow after eating all this unhealthy rubbish, otherwise I was done for!

CHAPTER 9

The early morning sunlight, soft and diffuse, gave way to the first strong rays of the day, bringing true warmth through the open windows of the shack, it was twenty-five degrees but only 8.30am in the morning. I climbed out of bed, ate a light breakfast of just fruit, deciding to start the day healthily after last nights antics. I still managed to have plenty of time before I was picked up, so I thought about all the things I needed to do beforehand to get organised and did none of them. Instead I became preoccupied with a typed note that had been put into my post box overnight. It was laying there staring at me when I checked my post this morning. Housed inside an unwritten long off-white envelope, on a grubby A4 piece of paper folded into three, the note had cut out newspaper and magazine letters of all different sizes stuck to the paper in a random fashion. It read:

A faas mek anansi de a house top. Bucket go well every day, one day di bottom ago drop out!

I felt scared, what is going on? I told myself being scared is normal and natural, an appropriate response to a situation that feels threatening. Translated the note said that it was dangerous for me to meddle in the affairs of others, and if I continued repeatedly to take risks I would end up dead. I stood for a moment completely motionless, rooted to the spot, the note firmly in my grasp, whilst I let the envelope drop lifeless to the floor. My heart was pounding as I walked over and sat down in front of my computer.

I shut my eyes and tried to breath calmly, but every time I reopened them, those cruel, unnecessary words were there. Slowly, I managed to get the panic and anxiety attack to flow away, my clasped hands opened and the note joined the envelope on the floor. Trepidation swelled through me, I bent forward and picked it back up. I read it again, A faas mek anansi de a house top. Bucket go well every day, one day di bottom ago drop out! I felt afraid, my stress hormones and adrenaline surging through me as I tried to remind myself that my decision making ability is temporarily offline and I need to wait before I can figure things out, wait for my brain's usual connections to resume.

Someone out there actually knew where I lived and what I had been asking about, I was being watched, but whose cage had I rattled? I knew nothing was secret in this village, but I never thought anyone would stoop this low, if they set out to frighten me, they had succeeded.

The bigger question was, what should I do now? I needed to conquer this fear before it got hold of me and come up with a plan. It was no good taking this to the police, they had already made it quite clear that nothing had happened and they would relieve me of the note, never to be seen again, I couldn't let that happen it was my only shred of evidence that now proved something was going on. I couldn't go to Candice as she had also warned me off as did my colleagues at the Alise. The solution to this problem wasn't to show or tell anyone, but to deal with it myself, I stuffed the note back inside the envelope and I filed it in the drawer by my bed under a few undies, whilst I decided my next move, no one would think to look here for it.

I switched on my mobile and it immediately sprang to life, ringing for all it was worth, it was Tilly. "Jaz, you all ready for today" she said blaring down the phone before I could get a word in edgeways or even say hello. "Um, um yes, I suppose so, Tilly, I need to find out more about the dead woman, something weird, is definitely going on, no one will talk to me about it," I swallowed hard, as I continued I became aware that I was stuttering more and more, the words just wouldn't come out of my mouth correctly. I tried to slow down, but that just made it sound worse. "I gggot ttthis… What am I doing? I shouldn't reveal anything more.

I managed to stop myself in my tracks. "Jaz, are you ok? What's happened? I'm coming over right now, you can tell me what's wrong while I help you get ready." Was it that obvious? "Um, um, er, Ok" was all I could say. This note had affected me more than I cared to admit. I ended the call and sank down onto my bed, tossing the mobile phone onto it too. I sat staring ahead, my eyes trained on some invisible spectre, it was as if my brain was suffering from a massive short circuit and was struggling to compute, my thoughts were completely blank.

I must have been staring into a far-off planet when a voice called from the deck making me jump, it was Tilly. I opened the kitchen door and let her in "God you look pale, better get some make up on you. What's wrong?" She placed her mobile phone and car keys on the kitchen top and grabbed herself a bottle of water from the fridge. Despite my best efforts to stay in control, my hand seemed to overrule me as I retrieved the note from my undies drawer, thrusting it in her direction. She took it and read it. If I was to describe her facial expression at that moment, it would have to be lifeless, devoid of any reaction at all.

There was a small nano-second of silence before she uttered "Oh," "Is that all you're gonna say" I replied loudly, slightly irked, "I was hoping for some advice at least." "Mhmm, give me a second to think," she cocked her head to one side, I think something flashed beneath the surface of her hardened expression, but I couldn't be sure. She took a deep breath and then in one long sentence said, "Right, here's what we do, I'll keep the note somewhere safe but I think you should ignore it for now, it's a one off isn't it? Probably just a hoax, has it scared you?

I knew it was dumb to be scared, but I couldn't help it. Tilly smiled at me, like a long lost sister, she had tried to conduct herself perfectly.

I was always taught never to trust a person I thought was perfect, as far as I was concerned the greater the perfection, the greater the danger that lay beneath that hardened exterior, I know everyone has flaws and quirks including me! For a split second, a breeze whisked through my brain whispering as it went past,"shh, play your cards close to your chest, Tilly is involved." With this in mind, there was no way I was going to let Tilly see how anxious I really felt. I took a deep breath and sighed,"no not really, just a bit unexpected that someone is watching me and knows where I live, um, yes just the one note." I sighed again as Tilly's mobile bleeped with yet another text message, I remember thinking it must be worn out by now the number of times it bleeps a day.

I peered over to see if I could make out what was on the screen and just about had time to see the name Ed Wrexham as several missed calls, before she grabbed it quickly and slid it in her trouser pocket.

She was always protective over her phone, never leaving it unattended, but when texts or email's came through, she could be occupied for ages messaging back and summoning everyone to go about their jobs with a commanding wave of her hand, a bit like Lady Muck, but everyone responded to it without any questioning.

Tilly looked at me, then the note, "I'll take this back to the office and keep it safe, if you get any more, tell me and we will take it more seriously, but for now just forget about it." "Tilly, wait, I'll keep it here if you don't mind, it will still be safe." I replied as I grabbed it from her perfect mitts. She looked at me scornfully but let go of the note, if she was implicated, she wouldn't want to cause a scene. What was wrong with me? Why did I even open my mouth and tell her? I'm not sure what I expected from her, but I didn't expect that lack of emotion and coldness. I wanted to figure out why she reacted and responded the way she did, but now was not the time. It was as if different thoughts were arriving in her brain from afar, she was somehow completely disconnected. I wanted her to tell me to forget going to Iberville, because I was in shock and hope that she would offer to go in my place, but that was not going to happen.

I tried not to show my disappointment as she followed me into the bedroom and helped me squeeze into the little red dress that reached my lower thighs, clutching my body in a way that was tight but tastefully feminine, "Nice fit, suits you" she said, "is it yours?" "No borrowed from Goldie" "Ah that explains all" she said as she glanced down at the shoes I was strapping around my ankles, I think it was the Minnie Mouse bows that made the corners of her mouth curl up and form a grin. "Lovely Jaz, you look lovely, the belle of the ball." She smirked.

She then made her excuses about having to get back to the office, "Busy, busy, enjoy yourself and don't worry, you're my best reporter, remember that." She was shouting as she reached her jeep and gracefully climbed in. As she started the engine, a gust of smoke blew from the exhaust, then she was gone. I stood for a moment at the door, peering round to see who was about, the usual locals were passing by with a wave or nod of the head, but nothing out of the ordinary except for me in a little slinky dress with Minnie Mouse shoes catching their eye, which I think they found quite amusing, they didn't ever see me dressed like this.

I closed the door, muttering to myself to get a grip on reality, if I didn't get control and sort myself out, the car would be here and I would be nowhere near ready. I walked back into my bedroom, looked in the mirror and organised my hair, it ended up in a sort of up down look with a plait to one side, not quite what I had in mind but it looked ok. I piled on the makeup, then more blusher to bring out the sharp structure of my cheekbones. I applied a bright pink shade of lipstick on my thin lips, probably a bit over the top for the heat outside, but it brought out my more feminine self and helped my self confidence too. Having said that, I knew I would regret it later as the afternoon drew to a close and the makeup had smudged or even merged in the heat, making me look like a clown in drag but what the hell. "Live dangerously," I said to myself as I did the final pucker of my lips finishing off applying my lipstick.

I just about had enough time to hide the note back in my undies drawer, no one would think to rummage amongst my delicates. I grabbed my black shoulder bag, notebook, pen and mobile, before trying to perfect the art of walking in a sophisticated manner to the door in unfamiliar high heeled shoes as the car drew up outside.

My ride was a silver grey Mercedes S600, quite posh for the Island, not that I know much about them, mostly we drive four by fours or cycle everywhere, the roads are so uneven. There is only one main road, in and around the Island, the others are just like dirt tracks, you take your life in your hands driving down them, avoiding the trees growing out of the middle. Apparently according to the driver, it had a 389 horsepower, 6-litre engine and at ninety-six kilometres per hour the engine was only idling. I tried to appear interested as he walked me round the car pointing at it, but really I wasn't remotely interested, I had to stifle several yawns.

It was driven by a guy named Glenmore, an Afro Caribbean man, in looks and nature, he didn't look like the type of person to own a Mercedes, not that I am stereotyping, he had a tiny beard, groomed into a perfect triangle right in the centre of his chin. He introduced himself as "your chauffeur, ma'am" beckoning me to climb inside as he opened the door to the car with one hand, whilst drawing on a joint with the other. Gosh, so much leather but completely in shreds. On the front seat was a take out double brandy in a grotty cup and a couple of half eaten coconut dumplings along with their crumbs. I moved some old newspapers to one side, as I sat in the back, where I was introduced to a caged cockerel, who was going to drive me mad with its incessant squawking. Thankfully he took the newspapers from me and littered them on the pavement. The cockerel went next, but only onto the front seat next to his brandy and dumplings. "Mi best bredren" he said, as it still screeched, making any alarm clock wholly redundant. How sad to have a cockerel as your best friend, but it takes all sorts to make a world, I smiled.

No sooner was the door slammed shut behind me than we were blasting through the streets at great speed, luckily the Island's roads were never busy, they only ever had about four or five cars on them at any one time unlike the roads in England which were frantic rivers of humanity most of the time. Despite being thrown from side to side in the back as he swung around the corners, I was thankful that he kept his eyes on the road and left the food and drink untouched. His incessant chatter, mostly to the cockerel and occasionally to me, was a sort of verbal dance, quite chaotic, talking about everything but nothing if you catch my drift. The cockerel seemed to enjoy it, replying with its irritating little squawks. Luckily for both of them, we arrived all too soon, otherwise I was just about ready to commit hari-kari!

When we arrived at Iberville Glenmore opened the car door and took my hand, helping me out, well pulling me out would be a better use of words. I came out in a very unlady like fashion, showing things I didn't want on show, if you know what I mean."Here wi den" he said as he shut the door behind me, "How much do I owe you" I said, as I tried to stand still on my heels whilst straightening my dress, "its paid fi areddi Tilly dun ih." He replied as he lit another joint and sipped his brandy before climbing back into the drivers seat and roaring off into the distance.

CHAPTER 10

So, here I was, standing alone, my breathing had become heavy, not from the heat or fatigue, but from fear, genuine fear, I've no idea why, but I have been dreading this day. Everything hinges on me and my article, I took two steps to the left and looked ahead, as Iberville's driveway emerged before my eyes. Set on pedestals amid the water of the fountain were stone sculptures beside perfectly manicured hedges resembling animals and birds. A tower of steps flew up to the archway, with that balcony looming above, exactly the same as the online photos I had seen.

No longer just an image on an internet page, this was Iberville in the flesh. I took a couple more moments to soak in the building, the atmosphere and its surroundings, which also bought me a few precious minutes to figure out how I was going to climb the steps wearing this dress and these shoes, I should have practised walking in them more!

Slowly and clumsily I began to ascend, clickity clack, scrape, how embarrassing, with the amount of noise I was making everyone would know I was about to make my entrance! I decided my best option was not to look up as I continued carefully up the steps, watching my feet so I knew where I was placing these shoes, I must make myself look so awkward.

I am sure concentrating hard on placing my feet also saved me from the watchful eyes of those peering at me, I could feel their arrogant triumph, smirking as I neared the top. I paused momentarily and looked up briefly, catching a glimpse of a group of women, pouting their lips as they puffed on their cigarettes, each one stunningly beautiful like princesses from a fairytale, all chattering and laughing, there was no way I was going to make belle of there ball I thought to myself, as finally I reached the top, more like the ugly duckling!

Having made it up the steps, I was now stood in front of Iberville's entrance, two large overpowering open teak doors held up with the most ostentatiously detailed pillars, I inhaled deeply. This is it Jaz, don't stuff it up. I was greeted by a slender middle aged lady dressed in a crisp white blouse, tucked into a dark grey knee-length skirt, on her feet were high heeled black patent leather shoes. Her hair was scraped back from her face into a high pony tail, her skin was the kind of white that could enchant snow and her bright red painted lips stood out from the paleness of her face. She stood tall and strong, integrity intact, reserving her emotions, she was a mast, a measure of her fortitude equal to any male.

In front of her beckoned a tray of flute glasses containing champagne, high end no doubt, Moet and Chandon Brut. She welcomed everyone in turn, gesturing us to the house. I remember thinking that this was something to be admired in those heels as I felt like I was still swaying in mine even when

I stood still. I assumed she was Lord Wrexham's personal assistant, she seemed too austere to be the maid.

I took a flute from the tray and smiled nervously at her, oh God, I was now in possession of a glass, a handbag and heels, all of which needed to be juggled in order to keep my decorum. "A very warm welcome to Iberville, please make your way inside," she said smiling. I went through into a large entrance hall, a quadrangle with a flagstone floor of soft blue hues. I looked up, the ceiling must be twenty feet high. Designs of fruit and flowers carved into the moulding and small fat children with wings looked down at me from every angle.

Also greeting the visitors was the most monumental of chandeliers, it came from a time of opulence and emotional indifference, but now shone in all its beauty. All around, vases of blossoms gave off a cloying scent that made my eyes itch. It must take a small army of servants to upkeep such an abode. This place was a status symbol, superior, untouchable to those without means. I moved towards an open door and peered discretely inside, it too was very ornate in design, a huge stone fireplace dominating one wall, it was as big as my entire shack. In the centre, a grand piano sat proudly, displayed in all its glory, the polished top gleaming as the sun streamed through the windows warming its keys. It was a timely reminder of what once could have been family life. As I glanced back around the entrance hall, I noticed some ornate chaise lounges lazing next to the vases, they were covered in the most sumptuous garish fabrics that could only be carried off in a place full of richness like this.

Still trying to balance my champagne, I extracted the notepad from my bag, as I did, a voice from behind startled me, it was the hard tap on my back that made me jolt forward, spilling some of my drink over me and the floor, great! "Jasmine, good to see you." I turned round, fixing a look that would make any character other than this man shrivel. He met my gaze with a smile of someone who knows they have the upper hand and lit up a cigarette to add to the ambience. "Hey Robin, good to see you too" I lied. Robin was an editor from 'Local Island Magazine'. "There's a fair few of us from the media here isn't there." I said in a professional manner, I had never made small talk with this man and really didn't want to break a habit of a lifetime now. I disliked him intensely, he has a huge self ego, in fact, I would go as far as to say he was ego blind. He only seemed capable of decoding what suited his own primitive sense of self worth, everything else flies over his head. Thankfully, any conversation we had ever had revolved around work and prevalent topics, such as corruption, money, petty crime etc, " Yes, my dear, just a few from local papers, magazines, Island radio and some tourism dignitaries as far as I am aware, probably about thirty or so, of us in total," he replied.

Robin was a well known character on the Island, mostly for his bad editing skills, he complained about everything and everyone and would always rewrite what he was sent instead of just editing and he would always take the credit, despite his lack of involvement. He is unbelievably cocky and extremely sure of himself, confidence just oozing from him, a vibe that says that I'm better than everyone else. I'm sure if push came to shove, he wouldn't hesitate to step on anyone that got in his way. Emotions were something alien to him, he barely understood his own, let alone anyone else's. I once saw one of his colleagues start to cry next to him and he just patted her head like a dog, I kept telling myself that it wasn't that he didn't care, just that he wasn't born without the faculties to understand how to relate to people.

Our conversation was thankfully cut short, as a well groomed gentleman in a dark suit and blue tie proudly stood before us all at the top of the staircase. From where I was stood, at the front, no less, I had a good view. He appeared to be in his mid-sixties, his hair was combed and seemed to be stuck to one side trying to conceal a square imposing forehead, his eyebrows stood out, like bushy caterpillars overwhelming his eyes. He squinted at us through those hardened eyes that looked like they had many unfounded accusations and probably hid many secrets. His most striking feature was his grey pencil-moustache, a visual cue to a self-confident, authoritative man who felt good about expressing himself. He could definitely rock a moustache even at his age, he clapped his hands together, cleared his voice with a sort of throaty gnarl and began his rehearsed welcome speech.

"Ladies and Gentlemen, good day to you all, My name is Lord Edward Wrexham. I would like start by extending a warm welcome to our home, Iberville. Both my wife, Lady Amélie and I are truly grateful to you all for sparing time away from your busy schedules in order to join us today. For the first time, we have been able formally to invite you into our home creating an opportunity to explain what could be the most remarkable venture this Island has ever seen. Working together we can ensure a greater creation of jobs and economic growth for our Island by turning Iberville into a much needed resort.

Your support for this project is vital and we really do value your comments and media coverage which would help us move forward to achieve this goal. There is a small scale working model of how this estate could look in the orangery. I do hope you will all find it sympathetic to the environment and understand how it will improve the Island's economy. I will answer any further questions you may have when you have had chance to see the model. I hope that you enjoy your experience with us today, if you would now all like to join me now on a conducted tour of the estate."

He gave the impression of a natural born leader, his voice was quite deep and he had an air of solid confidence, it was magnetic, well it made us all stop chattering and listen to him. As he conducted himself down the staircase his hand waved, beckoning everyone to follow. We obeyed and with a sudden rise of energy, all surged forward, herded like cattle, not a single brain between us. No-one was polite, we all jostled to be first in line, leaving glasses of half empty champagne strewn around, I kept hold of my glass, there was no way I was going to waste half a glass of the best champagne!

Lord Wrexham continued to wave his arms around frantically, like a demented octopus, as he pointed out the rooms and antiques of Iberville. Family portraits, painted in oils were hung on walls in gilded gold frames, every piece of furniture was very ornate probably handmade. The stair rails were carved mahogany, twisting in a perfect spiral, polished intensely and gleaming in the light. To the left of the staircase was a dining room and on the right, the drawing-room which we were not permitted to enter. To the side of these were old teak doors which apparently led to "other" apartments, I presumed for domestic use as this was not enlarged upon.

The interior of the whole place was very elegant, oversized mullioned windows, almost cathedral-like let the diamond shape sun rays flow through, dappling the walls with glowing rainbow hues. I began to daydream, here I was as free as I wanted to be, in my serene space of infinite potential I could create anything new and tempting, this time Iberville was my home, beyond the pageantry and ceremony, beyond my garments of grandeur, I would become a warrior queen, I would ride into battle to defend the citadel and protect my country. My daydream was a heady potion of chance and excitement, a personal movie with myself as the main character, I could change the plot to move in any direction, dramatic and swift. As I took a deep breath in, "Lady Jasmine Tormolis," I uttered out loud, as I returned to reality, raised voices became apparent once more, each getting more shrill to make themselves heard, thankfully my little voice was unheard.

We were led up the huge staircase, its smooth rounded banister sweeping us ever upwards to the next floor, our voices still babbling like the flow of a mountain river. Most of the women, myself included used the strong balustrade as a pulley to get us up the stairs, well we were all in heels after all, and I was still clutching my champagne glass, albeit empty by now.

Once we reached the top, there was a suite of bed chambers, a study and a huge private apartment belonging to Lady Amélie Wrexham which housed all her paintings. Although the largest, it was the most simplest of all the rooms, walls plainly painted in beige, no ornate gilding or ceiling roses, no chandeliers. A red threadbare rug hugged the centre of the oak floor, upon which, stood an easel and a wooden table covered with paint pots and brushes. What was most striking about this room was the beautiful paintings and artwork, polaroids of emotion, freedom, rising hope, of love and loneliness. A communication in art form that would take volumes of the written word to convey and even then, not nearly so well. Every painting, whether of landscapes, animals or people conjured up its own feeling and story.

Silence fell as we all stared at the glory before us, each composition of the paintings quite curious. My eyes scanned everywhere, trying to take it all in, I have always thought of artists as healers, their art, a story told in the foundational languages of the brain, in emotion and in visual dreams. Lady Amélie must be in a state of shear turmoil if her art was anything to go by. Her stroke lines were bold with vivid colours almost to the point of garish, encapsulating the minutest detail. They are both stunning and head-ache inducing, you can see why people are drawn to her art.

The easel in the middle of the room had a sack like cloth draped over it, a mystery hiding beneath maybe an unfinished painting. By now everyone had moved on, following the sound of Lord Wrexham's voice bellowing about his Orangery and the pièce de résistance, the formal gardens. As I seemed to be alone momentarily I placed my glass on the windowsill and tiptoed as best I could to the easel. I took a corner of the sack like cloth between my fingers and eased it upwards trying to peak underneath.

From what I could see, the painting was a portrait of a woman conveying a vulnerability, a sadness in her eyes, lurking behind such a pretty face, her smile so innocent, so vibrant. A poignant gaze, as if she had the whole world on her shoulders, a sociopathic woman, struggling with society, it unnerved me a little. I wanted to look away but instead I stepped even closer, I leaned my head to one side, trying to get a different perspective, she was beautiful, but also familiar. Something clicked, I removed my mobile from my bag and looked at the photo of the woman's body, OMG, it has to be her, it's Lady Amélie Wrexham, isn't it?

Suddenly, the sac cloth disappeared from my hands and was placed over the painting once again. A stern female voice came from behind me, "Please rejoin the others ma'am, you should not be in here alone." I turned to face her and frightened by her hard expression, I stumbled backwards jamming my heel into a crack in the floor.

As I managed to regain my composure and stand up again, I noticed she was now standing at the door arms folded waiting for me to vacate the room. "Out, please," she uttered in a severe way, I think this may have been the housekeeper, but whoever it was I had annoyed them. As I left the room I looked at the photo again and then glanced back at the easel, there was a strong resemblance, but in truth, too much champagne was probably making me delusional, I must expel these notions from my thoughts as quickly as they had entered. I made a mental note to ask Lord Wrexham about his wife, her paintings and so far her lack of presence. I would have thought that she would have liked to talk through her paintings with us, but after all if she was a recluse she wouldn't like all of us rabble invading her space or relish the media coverage.

I hurried as best I could to catch up with the others, wobbling and staggering all over the place on my heels, as I caught up just in time to rejoin everyone in the orangery. Gosh, it was very bright and warm, the suns rays burning through the tall windows, which were each surrounded by carved stones, pitted by weather and age, funny how it contrasted against the rest of the smooth walls.

The back of the orangery was very plain except for two large ornate double doors revealing the dramatic centrepiece of Iberville yet to be seen. In the corner as promised was the scale model laying out the proposed new accommodation, gardens and spa facilities at Iberville. Lord Wrexham felt it was important that we should see what the new facilities would look like once finance was secured and the work was finished. It seemed the model was very well received by everyone, or should I say they were too scared to say anything else. I had to walk away as Lord Wrexham was at the front "pushing" his ideas onto all of those listening intently. He continued, "Changing this Island for the better was never going to be a task for one person or one type of mind, creative minds dream up new possibilities, new futures, new technologies together and turn our visions into realities, so we all thrive because we support one another."

According to Lord Wrexham's spiel, there were about 650 acres in total. Those of us that wanted some air ventured into the gardens, at last we could roam free, albeit with a timescale to adhere too. I bent down to remove my shoes, there was no way I could negotiate the gardens in these heels, they had become a second skin so it was good to get them off, my feet did hurt. I put my other champagne glass, I had acquired along the way on the patio just behind the doors, I was sure someone would eventually find it and with my shoes held by their straps dangling free by my side, I took on the challenge barefoot.

The formal gardens were absolutely beautiful, Bonsai trees in little wooden boxes lined the perfectly mowed lawn, slightly brown in colour, parched from the heat I shouldn't wonder. In the centre sat a lake shaped into a figure of eight with flowering lily pads and a 'Monet' style white bridge across the narrowed middle. The flower beds, which at this time of year were a riot of colour, stretched up trying to warm themselves in the sun. A circular path lined with rose bushes led to a wild garden, where there was more moss than grass, every now and again clusters of defiant flowers native to the Caribbean broke through, rearing their golden heads amidst the gloom of the weeds. There were smallish stone outhouses dotted about that seemed to be devoured by the shrubbery, their doors hung on the last few threads of their hinges groaning in pain at every gentle breeze. They were a curious contrast to the cheerful aspect of the gardens, abandoned they stood, a crumbled beauty of an era long past. Pieces of timber lay across the top, roofs long gone, letting thousands of dust particles dance and swirl as each ray of light shines through and in the distance I could just make out an area of rainforest, probably leading to his own private beach no doubt.

Walking back towards the lake, there was another field segregated by a gate made of rough wood. Weeds cascaded over it, growing tentacles which spread in every direction forcing their way through holes and tearing it apart revealing an overgrown path beyond.

At the end of the path stood a two-story structure standing in defiance of the people who once worked there. It had outlasted the civilisation that created it by centuries, but now its grey walls had given way to a jungle of green. I did a quick web search on my phone to find that it was called, an 'overseers house,' apparently a crucial residential structure on the plantations, like a watch tower, keeping an eye on its workers, the occupants being responsible for the success or failure of the estate.

I wondered if Lady Wrexham was right to want to keep this as a piece of history, something that our future generations could discover and perhaps piece together how the people here once lived. Its a shame to not remember our past, here we are today with all our labour saving devices, whilst the slaves of days gone by, would barely get six hours sleep, they were completely exhausted and would welcome any small opportunity to have some rest.

Lost in my thoughts reminiscing for a moment, I could hear a bell ringing, it sounded distant, but it wasn't. I looked towards the house where a sea of very noisy people were being herded onto the patio outside the orangery. I watched two of them fighting angrily, one of them pushing the other, they looked like they made the best of battle companions.

It had now become extremely hot as it did at this time of day in the Caribbean, I felt as if I was in a sauna, beads of perspiration were trickling down my face. I needed a cool drink and to plunge my feet into cold water. How I wish I'd brought a wide brimmed hat with me. Suddenly I jumped as an arm grasped mine, I felt a wave a panic come over me and turned ready to defend myself, only to find it was the butler, who had come to escort me towards the patio, to rejoin the others. I obliged without saying anything, I couldn't be bothered to make small talk, it was too hot and I was feeling quite apathetic.

CHAPTER 11

I now stood barefoot, the soles of my feet red from the sun heated patio, staring at the vast array of wooden tables laid out in front of me. A feast for the eyes and soul, artistry for the memory, a ridiculous amount of food and drink. I started to wander around each table in turn, I don't ever remember seeing this amount of food and drink all in one place before. Millions of children and their family members die every year from malnutrition, no wonder parts of the world are starving, it's all here, there was enough food here to feed the five thousand, let alone thirty people!

The scene was quite unbelievable, shocking really. My mind was reeling, unable to comprehend or process what my eyes and senses were experiencing. I looked away, then looked back to see if it was still there, it was. There was a whole stuffed roast goat with sprigs of herbs threaded through its body still turning on a spit, whole marinated chickens, grilled trout with lemons, smoked sausages and pineapple glazed ham, huge platters adorned with mounds of rice and beans, sweet potatoes, diced pumpkin and a variety of salads ready to be gorged upon like some medieval banquet.

Countless cheeses with little flags stuck in them displaying their names, accompanied by baskets of crackers and bread rolls shaped like seashells, very clever. Basically everything you can think of and more, there were things you have never dreamed of eating that lay in wait.

Just as I thought I had seen enough, another elongated table beckoned me, OMG! Desserts, lemon tarts, rhubarb crème brûlée, orange blossom cakes, minted fresh strawberries, meringues so huge and beautifully shaped it was a pity to eat them, they were all neatly placed on beds of ice to keep them cool. But best of all were the most decadent chocolate bonbons that oozed rum cream on your first bite. I can guarantee this as I had already eaten five.

I continued to fill my plate as I did a second loop of the tables, the rich aromas wafting in the air beckoning me. I was unable to resist these delightful sensations. Not the best idea I ever had and I was now feeling a quite sick.

Still with my plate in hand, I stood at the end of one of the tables and looked around, hearing my mothers voice, "Chew with your mouth shut, take small bites, make pleasant conversation, don't talk with your mouth full, finish your plates, use your napkin, etc."

People seemed to be congregating around the champagne fountain that glistened in the rays of the afternoons sun. Between mouthfuls, they were talking, laughing, reminiscing, socialising. How lovely, warm, flat champagne, I could just do with a refreshing glass of Red Label right now. Say what you want about alcohol, but sometimes it becomes necessary to create that buzz which raises the soul and I also needed something more to relieve the boredom.

The butlers stood stiffly, hands behind their backs, in their starched white shirts and black bow ties, all clean-shaven, neat, with matching black hair, until they were summoned to refill glasses and plates, manners are not for feasts! I hope Lord Wrexham is aware that this is a modern form of slavery, These butlers has been trained to serve, obey and be loyal.

Glass in hand, Lord Wrexham mingled amongst us, talking to each in turn, either independently or in groups. Staring isn't quite the word for what I was doing, although it would fit the dictionary definition to a tee. It was as if my eyes were trained on some invisible spectre, my heavy eyelids a fraction too slow to blink, my brain was suffering a massive short circuit and was struggling to compute. Lord Wrexham moved into my line of sight, his lips forming a pensive grin. My head tilted towards his face, my eyes following, sliding into focus.

He seemed a pleasant gentleman on the surface, with a friendly face and welcoming body posture. I extended my hand towards him, shaking it as gracefully as I could, I tried to smile but a twitch was all I managed. I tried desperately not to ask too many cutting questions, but I did need to be clear in my minds eye on certain issues. I kept my questions as short sweet, and unassuming, one of the rules of journalism I had learnt.

We discussed his plans for Iberville, how it would turn the Islands' economy around and how he might stand to gain from it. He explained that he would like to be involved in curbing the environmental impact of tourism, making his resort more green and climate friendly, he wanted to integrate Eco-tourism into his products by implementing policies to protect terrestrial resources. I frantically scribbled down his every word in my notebook as, typical me, I had forgotten to update my voice recorder app on my mobile, so it now didn't work. He continued by saying that, despite investments there were also negative impacts on climate change that would increase unavoidably over time. Global warming would probably increase the severity of our weather events, and the local hurricane season might bring more damage to the Islands. Carbon taxes would increase the cost of air travel, a potential disaster for the tourist business. For Islands heavily dependant on air travel this could spell disaster.

We continued to talk about Iberville becoming a resort and how he planned to make it work, as some of the resorts on neighbouring Islands were beginning to struggle. Lord Wrexham, explained that as a businessman through and through, he would continue to promote and sell his rum distillery tours using local labour in order to keep them in employment, he would invite local craft vendors to sell their wares and promote local music artists for nightly guest entertainment. "this sounds very well thought through and organised," I remarked, he nodded before continuing the conversation about how he would ensure lessons were conducted in local schools, teaching children about environmental and tourism related matters. His main point seemed to be that he would always use and help local people whenever possible.

At this point, he turned on his winning smile, (probably reserved for interested journalists), as he explained how he expected the media coverage would promote his plans and the Islands economy. He also talked about the rooms being refurbished in some of the guest houses situated in the grounds next to the main house.

Apparently a number of the stone huts, guest houses as he called them, were to be converted into two-bedroom cottages. The suites within the guest houses would be styled using antique four-poster beds and heavy, canopied drapes and dark wood furniture. Within the grounds for the guests there would be an array of amenities, a large swimming pool, a golf course and also an arboretum by the lake. It felt like I had been talking to him for ages, but he obviously wanted a good spread to be written, after all this was his 'dream'. Blah, Blah, he said that the estate was surrounded by a rainforest, which he had wanted to use for hunting events, but the Caribbean Government had put an end to that idea, preferring to protect rainforest's ecosystem and the species key to its function.

I continued to listen intently and to reply politely, writing my notes as best I could, I was never any good at shorthand. He definitely craved money and power. "Motives matter, Integrity and intention is everything." He explained. "You can dismiss the intention to see the basic motives of the primitive brain, then layer on top the motivation, control the former and encourage the latter, there's your true power, all will fall before it because they want to." I'm not sure I agreed completely with this, but I didn't need to indulge in a too deep a conversation for this spread.

There was a short pause, it's now or never, I bit my tongue and then asked the ultimate question that I had been longing to ask since my arrival, where on earth was Lady Wrexham? "Lord Wrexham," as I spoke I noticed my mouth became dryer than a sandbox in summer, I swallowed hard. "You have great plans here, but there is no mention of your wife in any of this, in fact she has not made an appearance today. How does she feel about your plans? Could we get her viewpoint as an alternative side of the Iberville resort?" Lord Wrexham listened intently, head cocked to one side, then his nostrils seem to engulf the delicate hint of food still in the air, he was momentarily silent, his eyes became narrowed, angry even. He seemed to switch gears to a cold emotional indifference, like this is part of full-on protective mode.

He ran his hands through his hair, "Jasmine, isn't, it?" I nodded, pen poised at the ready. "Please excuse me," something or someone seemed to catch his eye, so without finishing the sentence, he strolled off in the direction of one of the butlers.

This was just plain rude. He could be very forthcoming about his plans for the estate and our economy, in fact he revelled in it, but actually, when it came to my questioning him about his wife, why was he so dismissive? There are times when a retreat from certain questions can be brave, but this was cowardice. After all, leaders are only leaders if you follow them, and respect their orders. Unfortunately that was not me, I didn't get to where I was today by doing as I was told even if it got me into hot water, although I had obeyed Tilly.

I followed him, he was not going to get away so easy. "Excuse me sir, that's very rude" I shouted, my new found confidence fuelled by the warm champagne consumption I'd been knocking back, "Where in Gods name is your wife?" It worked, he turned and walked back towards me once more. "Where is Lady Wrexham? I said again, I would like to speak with her." I felt a coldness envelope me as I became aware of the silence in the air and all eyes were focused on me.

He took a punt, said nothing, but slid his arm around my waist, patted my bottom and guided me back towards the tables, summoning a butler to refill my glass. I glared at him, I could feel the anger in my chest waiting to take over. Perhaps it only wanted to protect me, but it sat there like an angry bull propelling me towards an outburst I just don't need. Calmly I removed his hand from my person, this was an injury to my soul and spirit more than to my body. We each have the right to choose what does and does not happen to our own body, there was no heat in my voice, I just calmly and simply said. "You Cad! If you know what's good for you, take your hand off my rear." Lord Wrexham didn't show any emotion, but instead ignored my outburst completely.

I hung my head down feeling quite embarrassed at my outburst, it was then I realised that I no longer had my Minnie Mouse shoes, worse than that, I did not have a glimmer of hope of knowing where they were. I shrugged, Oh well never mind they were bright enough to be spotted by someone hopefully, and returned to me, although I was not the only female to have given up on her shoes, there were several littered, kicked off at random under the tables.

I glanced quickly but still couldn't see mine amongst them, perhaps they had gone forever, but who would want such garish attire. Only trouble was with the heat of sun now at its hottest, I really needed them, the ground was beginning to burn and eat its way into the soft flesh of my feet. I began jigging around like a demented animal trying to stop my feet from being scorched.

CHAPTER 12

I headed to the lawned area in the hope of getting some respite, warm grass was not as bad as hot patio slabs. I flopped down onto one of the benches fashioned from a wind-felled tree and tried to make some sense of the scribble in my notepad. My head was beginning to swim a bit, my brain felt slightly fogged and my dexterity with a pen was not what it was. As long as I could get the gist of my scrawl, I could write it up properly tomorrow on the computer when I would be less inebriated but supporting a headache.

Haphazardly, I put the pen to my mouth, to make it look like I was thinking. I read my jumbled notes, "Iberville Resort" on one hand its former life as a plantation brings to mind past horrors of slavery and white masters, on the other side, was its future role as a symbol of refined living, hospitality, telling the tales of how we were all wooed today. So many things seemed to have happened on plantations, adventure, romance and some mysteries. Money, power, spread of feast, tour of Iberville. In capital letters, I had written, WHERE IS LADY WREXHAM, he refused to answer, definitely hiding something?"

I crossed my legs and leaned back, sipping more flat champagne from a half filled glass which I found on the bench, I also took advantage of a few leftover nibbles that were on a plate next to it, 'waste not want not'. My god, I had drunk far too much fizz too quickly and with the sun radiating down burning all of my bare skin, I felt very hot and very drunk. It felt like my brain had switched off and a fool had taken over full control running my current situation, my thoughts and my mouth.

I tried to continue with writing and reading my notes. "Dismiss the intention to see the basic motives of the primitive brain, then layer on top the motivation, control the former and encourage the latter, there's your true power, key today is the way we choose to remember history, there's nothing wrong with plantation tourism, as long as we move forward."

I could feel my head beginning to swoon even more, yuk, I felt a bit nauseated, I daren't move too quickly in case I was sick. Ehh, I was definitely the worse for wear, so all that was left to do now, was let the side down. I stared aimlessly ahead at nothing in particular and waved my notepad unceremoniously in front of me, catching the edge of it on my nose at times, it was a poor attempt at trying to cool the air without much success, everything was becoming slightly out of focus, I felt numb, a form of zombie-state.

I must have shifted myself suddenly, because the plate that was cradled in my lap, accidentally fell to the ground with an almighty crash, smashing into small pieces, bits of plate and food remnants were sent flying across the grass, scattering fragments far and wide.

I could feel my face turning very red, maybe even purple. I fell forward and slumped onto the ground, my eyes squinting as the sun hit them. I felt the surging pain of a million knives dig into my knees as I tried to gather the shards of plate with my hands, but all I could see were slithers of red, staining the grass. Butlers seemed to arrive on mass from all directions, trying to clear up the mess as discreetly and as quickly as possible. They helped me back onto the bench, ouch! Bits of grass had become enmeshed in my raw pink flesh, it really hurt as they removed small pieces of glass from my cut knees and dabbed them with some water from an ice bucket.

I winced every now and again as the pain seared through my body, I felt so sick, my stomach ached as it kept tightening, again it lurched and gurgled. I swallowed hard but I could not stop the warm feeling rising through my chest, then I could taste it at the back of my mouth Yuk. It was at that moment, I managed to embarrass myself completely by vomiting onto the butler that knelt before me.

"I'm so very sorry, I want to go home now," I slurred and beginning to let tears form in my eyes, my embarrassment was immense, I wanted to hide myself away as if my inner child was taking over, but I was more grown up than that. I apologised profusely again and found a new strength to inch my way off the bench with help from the butlers. I tried to maintain as much decorum as possible, but my dishevelled hair fell forward and was now hanging listlessly around my face. "What a dirty mess you are lady!" The butler commented, I think I just smiled, what I really wanted to say was, "Ok, so call my appearance dirty if you require such a cheap ego boost, all this washes off, and beneath it I'm as clean as you." Good job, I can hold my tongue when I need to!

As I eventually managed to stand up, I wobbled a bit but tried to remain focused on the task ahead, walking, I seemed to find the momentum as I staggered towards the main house, desperately trying not to make eye contact with anyone, although by now I had become the entertainment for the other guests. I stumbled over something but was not left to fall completely flat on my face as I felt a grip tighten around my arm, I looked up, it was Lord Wrexham. He held on to me tightly, steering me into the main house and ushered me towards a washroom. This time, I did not object but instead held onto his sturdy frame hoping for stability, I remember him smiling but not a word passed our lips.

I attended to my ablutions, I was so sick, I thought it would never stop. As I came out of the toilet I caught sight of a girl in the mirror, her clownish make-up, all smudged, staring back at me, her red dress dotted with spots of wine down the front, accompanied by some food debris. I splashed cold water on my face just to feel something refreshing, instantly wishing I could wash my brain free of the toxins too, I needed coffee for that.

My head felt like a balloon, slowly being inflated, the pressure mounting, I felt like I was going to be sick again. I looked in the mirror once more, this girl was still staring back at me, oh no, it was me, what a mess, no longer the glamour girl from when I first arrived. I had bloodshot eyes, pale face, smudged mascara , etc. OMG, look at me, an inebriated tramp, what a great role model I was for the Alise. I splashed my face with some more water, then dried it on a pristine white monogrammed towel which I then left in a crumpled mess next to the wash basin, luckily most of the make up had now come off on it.

I staggered back out to the entrance hall, I felt like I was falling sideways and backwards at the same time and was thankful to end up landing in a large high-backed red cupcake chair. I really needed to rest my head, so I would wait here until my ride came to collect me, hopefully this had been organised for me, and that they would be able to find me, as I seemed to merge with the chair, everything red! Anyway, I stretched and yawned as I felt the chair snuggle me in. I must have then passed out as I don't remember anything more.

When I came to, my head was throbbing so violently it felt like it was about to crack open, nausea overwhelmed me and I felt like I was going to be violently sick again. I felt grubby and really cold, my body felt numb, the only way back was to feel the painful re-ignition of feeling, of my nerves firing up once more.

I moved my head as slowly as I could, I felt so dizzy, I squeezed my eyes tight willing the pain to go away, but it didn't work. I opened my eyes once more, my heart was pounding, but my mind felt devoid of anything. I tried to gather my senses, rubbing my head and eyes with my hands, they were dirty, remnants of my makeup dotted on them along with green grass stains and a little of my blood.

As my eyes became more accustomed and my body slowly returned to life, I realised I was no longer sat in a chair but I was lying down. I tried to prop myself up on one elbow, dizziness, thirst and sickness made me lay down quite quickly again.

I felt around me as I opened my eyes once more. I was lying on a lumpy mattress on an iron framed bed with pillow and a greenish scratchy blanket covering me. As I acclimatised my eyes, I began to focus more on my surroundings. I was in a small room, resembling a square concrete box, walls and floor were of a greyish stone. A dim ray of light made its way in from a small slit in the stone wall, masquerading as a window, silhouettes bounced off them like stars trying to reach the moon, whilst tiny dust particles reflected the light taking on the appearance of glitter, or perhaps pixie dust.

I tried to move again, more slowly, my head still possessing the urge to explode at any given time. A heavy set wooden door adorned with huge black hinges stood proudly closed, sealing me in to await my fate. I sniffed, ouch, that made my head hurt more, then the smell hit me, a whiff of a sweet, musty odour, straw maybe, with undertones of animals mixed in with old oily machinery.

I listened, all was silent except for the distant sound of water dripping, possibly from a drainpipe, but why, it hadn't been raining had it? There wasn't anything else in the room except for the bed and a metal bucket, it was completely bare. Where on earth was I? I could be absolutely anywhere and certainly no idea of time of day or how I got here. I felt totally disorientated, my thoughts were chaotic, I didn't know where I was or why was I here, what the hell was I going to do? I didn't understand what was happening, was I now a hostage waiting for a ransom to be paid, but why would I be that?

I lay there all alone, nothing but sadness and confusion mulling around, wanting to grow and send me into a frenzied state of panic. This is my worst nightmare, I could be a captive waiting to be eaten by some cruel hungry beast, maybe I was to be taken before a firing squad or die a painful undignified death by starvation. I would wake up soon, this wasn't real, how could it be! The ability of my mind to create a nightmare world or dream up various horror scenarios made me feel worse, I had to switch my brain off.

Suddenly my stomach snarled and howled letting me know it needed food, accompanied by a not-so-subtle wave of pain. I clutched and kneaded my hand on it, in an attempt to silence it but to no avail. It objected even louder, I felt drained and empty, as its grumbling echoed around the stone walls, I don't know right at this very moment, which is worse my stomach, or my most almighty humdinger of a headache banging away.

In an effort to stop the pain from my head and stomach, I rolled myself into a ball and fell back onto the bed. If only I hadn't drunk so much, if only I hadn't passed out. Yes, we can all look back in hindsight, but that was not going to help me now. Regret washed over me like the long slow waves on a shallow beach, each wave was icy cold and sent shivers down my spine. I longed to turn the clock back and take a different path, but that was impossible, there was no way back, I had to go forward, there had to be a way. As I rested my head back on the lumpy pillow I stared at the tiny shard of light from outside, it was my ray of hope. Maybe I could try and dismantle the stone if I scratched out the cement with my nails, or if I screamed loud enough someone might hear me, wouldn't they? I had to have some hope inside this prison box, even if it wasn't realistic.

CHAPTER 13

Panic began to overwhelm me, I now felt a different pain, as a cluster of spark plugs started to fire off in my abdomen. The tension began to mount as it reached my face and limbs, the air felt so brittle it could snap, and if it doesn't, I might. My breathing became more rapid and shallow, my own personal hurricane was taking hold. Oh my God, I am going to die in here. My chest tightened, I opened my mouth to scream, but no sound made it out, my senses and muscles were heavy and unable to move, my eyes, wide with fear and dread, this must be what pure unadulterated terror feels like.

I needed to get a hold of the situation and do something practical rather that let my inner self in panic mode take over. "Right, get control Jaz, sit up, get your mobile phone, hopefully there is a signal, call Tilly, then she can come and get you, and this silly mistake will all be over." I told myself as I fumbled around, but couldn't find my phone, to be honest, it was then I became aware that none of my possessions were with me. What was going on? My fear continued to unleash itself, my breaths became gasps, desperate for oxygen, I felt like I was about to pass out, in fact the sensation of tightness in my chest and fast heart rate became so pronounced, it was as if the final bars of Ravel's Bolero were being played beneath my breastbone.

The room began to spin and I swallowed hard trying desperately not to be sick. I laid back on the bed, taking deeper breaths, trying not to let the panic grow any stronger, however, my mental faculties gave way to my emotions. I wanted to jump right out of my skin and join the ether, I was shaking, absolutely and utterly terrified. As the constricted feelings continued to take hold, I couldn't stop the feeling of being strangled by the air around me and then it won as blackness engulfed me.

I woke suddenly, as if there was an emergency, as if sleeping had become a dangerous thing to do. My heart was still beating rapidly and my brain still buzzing, trying to complete a marathon of erratic problem-solving despite just awoken. I then became aware of footsteps approaching the door, listening to them, it sounded like they were coming down a passageway and were probably from someone of a heavy build. I listened more intently, the approaching footsteps were uneven, like someone who had not learnt to walk properly and instead relied on shuffling, they sounded quite chaotic. They become louder and louder echoing as they approached, announcing their arrival. The noise resounded in my ears like a booming heartbeat, this was it, I was going to die.

I squeezed my eyes tightly giving the appearance I was asleep, whilst actually trying to peek in the hope I would be able to see who it was. I waited, trying to hold my breath so as to stay still and quiet, but this just made my head throb its constant rhythmic beat even more and my heart rate echo in my ears. Finally the footsteps stopped, followed by a deathly silence until the door creaked open. From what I could make out, it was a tall lanky person, a bit muscular but covered head to foot in black with their face hidden, I decided that from their build and stance that it was a male.

A metal tray was pushed forward, no words were spoken, it crashed and clattered as it came to rest on the stone floor, then as quickly as they appeared they vanished just as if there had never been there in the first place. As the door groaned as it was slammed shut, there was a grating sound of a bolt as it was slid into place sealing me in once more. I felt isolated and numb, I rubbed my eyes again, as if the whole thing had been a visual joke, then there was complete silence.

Clumsily, I hauled myself off the bed and tried to open the door, my bare hands pushing against the rough surface, it was all in vain, the door stood stubbornly in its place. A shiver ran through me, a shiver that said I was in deep trouble and should be afraid, deeply afraid. Here I was trapped, confined within the walls of this room, with nothing but my own heart beat and rancid breath for company.

I felt claustrophobic, I feared for my life, my world was about to come to an abrupt end and my family won't ever find out what happened to me. I was going to die a horrible death alone! I know that if I even let out a fraction of how I feel, a never ending torrent of grief will follow and what I really needed to do was be strong, keep calm, think rationally and get myself out of here.

Slowly I bent down and picked up the tray, staring at its contents. My stomach growled like a bear, as I took a sip of the thick black liquid in the cup, aargh, I assumed it was coffee but it was disgusting, it tasted like black treacle. The small bowl of gloopy porridge was equally inedible, the spoon had already decided to stand itself upright like a proud solider. It was a cross between styrofoam and leather, a texture even my molars couldn't grind down into something swallowable. I still felt very nauseated, but perhaps if I really tried to eat a bit more, it would help keep my strength up and help my sanity.

I managed to choke down a couple more mouthfuls but that was all I could manage, as nausea clawed at my throat even more. I tried to force down the bile, but it was too late, I lurched forward sinking onto my sore knees, as my stomach began to contract violently. I grabbed the pail and wavered over the top of it before my stomach rejected its contents, I clung on to the pail as if it were my life raft, my stomach feeling like a set of bag-pipes being vigorously squeezed. Ehh, I wiped my mouth with my hand to get rid of the acidic residue, my head really throbbed, my knees hurt, they felt as if tiny pins remained embedded in them. I shivered violently in the humid room, my stomach felt bruised inside. I sat back on the stone floor, cradling my knees, tears pricking my eyes, my hands trembling with fear and sadness. With a lot of effort I managed to push the tray with the uneaten food back near to the door then slowly clambered back onto the bed to rest, I felt exhausted.

I pulled the green scratchy blanket over me and began to cry, as I blinked briny tears began to fall, my eyelashes felt stuck together in clumps from the remains of my mascara. My tears continued to fall, making wet tracks down my face towards my quivering lips, I felt so ill and at this moment in time, I really needed my mum to hold me and tell me that it will be ok. As much as I tried to hold it back, my frustration of the situation I was in, began to bubble up into my throat, eventually releasing itself in the form of a scream, that did not do my headache any good at all. Beads of water started falling down one after another, I couldn't stop. My muffled sobs wracked against my chest and my head throbbed more and more. Everything seemed to begin turning fuzzy, my consciousness, floating through an empty inky space until everything darkened into nothingness, I must have passed into the oblivion of unconsciousness yet again.

I felt my body jump, hopefully from this nightmare back into reality, as the door creaked open once more, this time another tray of food and a second bucket clanked onto the cold stone floor, in exchange for the used one. Then the door was banged shut once again. Nope, this situation was definitely for real, how long had I been here, this couldn't go on much longer could it, what did they want from me? Why was I here? What had I done wrong? Despite racking my brain, I could not come up with the answers.

Hauling my aching body off the bed once more, I began to feel the stone walls for a way to escape, pushing on them, but they were so thick and cemented together, my only way out was going to be through that door and that was not going to happen anytime soon. The slitted crevice in the wall used as a tiny window was the only way in for the sun light, unless I transformed into a mouse, that was not an exit for me and as far as I knew I did not possess magic powers, so the mouse thing was not an option.

My prison is a perfect cube, the sides just about reachable if I try to extend my arms like a starfish. I have to escape, I have to find another way out, it's just a matter of thinking clearly until I find it. I listened intently, the room now bereft of all noise, as if every murmur and rustle had been stolen away, no birds singing their songs, nothing.

I tried to stretch, my shoulders stiff from my tense muscles, my eyes becoming glazed once more with a layer of tears. As I blinked, they dripped from my eyelids and slid down my cheeks, I bit my lip tightly in attempt to hide any sound that wanted to escape from my mouth. I needed to stop crying, it would not get me anywhere, least of all out of this room. I slumped down onto the floor picking at a piece of limp, lifeless bread and blackened plantain that sat before me, what had I done, why me? Whoever my kidnappers were, they definitely wanted to make sure I had no contact with the outside world. I was in complete solitude, with unmeasurable time, a torture to my mind, body and soul. There is no love, no hugs or kind smiles, no-one to tell me everything will be okay. Why do they feel the need to take away my freedom?

My head fell into my hands, I felt numb, sick and filthy dirty, as I touched my hair, it felt completely tangled and matted. I looked down, Goldie's beautiful dress was now shredded, torn in lots of places and very grubby, my poor knees still red with bits of congealed blood, my feet were bare, sore from the heat of the patios and filthy dirty. What a complete wreck, I looked up, the thin stream of daylight was beginning to fade plunging the room into a darkening cool eeriness. It must be the evening I thought to myself as I climbed back onto the bed, my palms felt sweaty and my whole body ached. I had never felt so ill, my tongue was dry, my throat felt as if someone had thrust a handful of itching powder inside, maybe thirst related. I curled on my side, I was scared, more scared than I had ever been in my life, petrified even. I was at my most vulnerable, in my moment of fear my logic, my self control centre was completely offline.

I can't escape this fear, no matter how hard I try, then it came back again, a panic attack, my psyche wouldn't stop sending messages of fear to my brain. My thoughts became so scattered that any normal rational function is rendered impossible. I needed that reassuring presence of someone loving, calm and stable to tell me I would be ok, or even to just hold me.

My tears made no difference, no matter how fast or how long they stayed for. I was utterly helpless, I tried to slow my breathing down and get control of my thoughts, thinking of happier times, unfolding memories and turning them into a beloved story book. I wanted to feel good, nourished and even supported, as I thought about my family, friends, and colleagues back in England and the Caribbean, the Alise newspaper, I want my life back the way it was.

Surely by now, someone would have noticed I was missing. The Alise would have noticed that I hadn't made contact, well Goldie would at least! My parents, they would know something was wrong as I always called them. Maybe they were doing their research, trying to work out the timeline of events, then they would do the leg work. Tiredness washed over me, until I could no longer keep my swollen eyes open, I lost my battle and fell asleep once more.

Realising I had fallen into unconsciousness again as I woke up, my brain started back up into overdrive, like I was hooked up to the mains, wired for sound, I had to somehow stay awake and alert if I was to get out of here, I couldn't just sleep. By now my headache was receding into a gentle throb rather than a nauseating pounding. I had to get a grip if I was going to escape, then I had to come up with a plan, after all, at this present moment in time, it was only me that could make this happen. I turned onto my back placing my hands behind my head, staring at the stone ceiling for some divine inspiration, I just had to find an escape plan. I played out every idea and notion in my mind, hoping for answers.

Thinking quietly was not a good outcome, it made my eyelids feel heavy, I felt a blackness come over me, more like a blanket, but not one of snuggly and warm but a blanket of coldness making me shiver. Defeated again, I closed my eyes and fell into an oblivion of dreams.

Dreams are your own personal world, your desires living in your own fantasy, the 'you' who you wanted to be, the things you despair and the everything you want to have. It's sad to think that at the moment you open your eyes, everything that is just perfect is lost again as reality brings you back to earth with a bang.

I awoke suddenly, every thought in high definition, my eyes scanning the room, my heart is pounding, but my mind is empty. I heard the door open, its creaking noise bringing a chill to my spine, it sounded like some dying animal, crying out in pain with its last breath. I peered from underneath the blanket as another tray clanked onto the floor. Whoever was behind this must have a conscience, otherwise they would let me starve to death before secretly disposing of my body! As the door creaked shut again, I mustered enough energy to climb off the bed and move the tray away from the door, I couldn't be bothered to eat but I did remove a butter knife, hiding it under the pillow for later use. It wasn't the sharp knife I'd been hoping for, but if I put all my force behind it I could probably wound enough to escape whilst whoever it was fell to the floor injured.

I shaped my simple and only plan; when the person came into the room to retrieve the tray, they would leave the door open, I would knock them to the ground by swinging the bucket at them and then using all my force, stab them with the butter knife, making a run for it as they lay bleeding, in pain and dazed.

I know my plan was a wild stab in the dark, if you excuse the pun. But I had to try something, maybe I could even catch them unawares as they bent down to pick up the tray? Anything could be possible, I just had to put my mind to it. Anyway, in the words of Bob Marley, "Life is worth much more than gold, neither can be bought or sold." There was no way I was going to be exchanged for money, if that was what was going on.

CHAPTER 14

It seemed ages before the sound of trudging footsteps echoed again, this time they were still heavy thuds, evenly placed, as if the person carried the whole world on their shoulders. The hairs on the back of my neck bristled and a gaggle of goose pimples grew on my frigid skin. Right this was it, I sat up and swung my legs to the floor trying to be as quiet as possible. I slithered to the side of the door and was now standing upright pressing my entire body against the stone wall which was beginning to warm a little, my heart was pounding so fast I thought it was going to explode, leave my body and fly across the room, I clutched the bucket tighter against my chest, holding the butter knife by the handle in a downward position. I was really scared, I was no assassin but I had to do this, it was the only way.

I heard the bolt slide across then slowly but deliberately the door opened. The person covered from head to toe in black entered the room, this time I noticed the balaclava and mask covering their face. They bent down to pick up the tray, there was a stillness, if hatred was visible the air would have been scarlet. Then with a sudden purposeful movement, I held onto the handle of the bucket tightly and hit them as hard as I could several times, swinging it as hard as I could, so much anger in every blow.

At first I hit their flank, their body language showed that it hurt as they were put slightly off balance, then as they straightened up, I went again, this time the bucket smashing into their cheekbone, flaying their neck backwards, like a piece of willow caught in the wind. The tray crashed to the floor and they stumbled backwards breaking their fall with their hands. Faster than expected, they caught their breath and stood up again, there was a frozen second between a stand off and fighting as I saw their eyes flicker towards me.

I needed to catch them off guard, so with all my strength, I quickly went again, lunging forward, pushing the knife into their stomach, I never knew I had so much brutality or force within me. The knife met flesh, it felt soft and pudgy and made a squish sound as the blunt blade managed to sink through their clothes and into their skin, deep enough to make my victim scream out. I held on tightly to the knife and began to twist the blade pushing it deeper, enjoying every minute of wounding, barbaric I know. As I removed the knife now covered in blood, the persons cry turned into an agonised roar followed by a few guttural chokes. I was petrified, what had I done! The person held their hand against the wound, as blood oozed between their fingers. It was slowly spreading onto their black hoodie, the bright red quickly darkening, taking on a brownish hue. "Oh my God Jaz, run, what are you waiting for," a voice kept echoing in my head "run, run" but my feet wouldn't move, I was rooted to the spot, frozen solid.

Confusion took hold, I'm sure this was simply anxiety in a different cloak, my brain defocused in an attempt to allow me a moment of distraction. Yet there was a job to do, I needed to escape right now, this was my one chance. When focus and attention matter, I need to teach my brain how to retread back to the pathway I started on.

Eventually my feet did start to move, but it was too late, I wasn't quick enough, I felt myself being grabbed firmly around the waist and then rugby tackled onto the floor. "Shhh!" came a raw male voice, brutal against my ear, I tried to struggle against him, but my movements were too slow. I could feel him wince from his own pain as he moved his blooded hands from my waist and took hold of my arms, trapping them by my side. As I tried to get up, he pushed me roughly, I tumbled back onto the stone floor, letting out an almighty scream, convulsing and trembling like a rabid animal as blood flowed freely from his stab wound. I looked up, pleading for my release, he brought a fist to my face, I felt it smash against my cheekbone as my face turned to one side with the force.

A sudden rush of pain jolted throughout my body, my arms seemed to loose tension and I could feel my legs begin to weaken. "He will not get the better of me," I laid in a crumpled heap, my tongue tasting of blood, I had to do something. My head was pounding, the sweet tang of blood tingling in my nostrils, I grabbed his foot and pulled him to the ground almost letting him fall on top of me. "What the hell are you doing woman?" he yelled, as he rolled towards me holding his wound, but managed to push me hard once more, as I fell back onto my side banging my elbow in the process. For a nano second we both lay on the floor panting, the contents of the tray strewn amongst us.

Realising that I could retaliate at any given moment, he sat and then stood up, wobbling, groaning in pain and holding onto his stomach. Standing over me, he shouted "Do you want to get yourself killed, you stupid woman?" with that he made his way to the door rather like Quasimodo and slammed it shut.

As quickly as it started, it had ended, my ridiculous plan had failed, I was still here, why did I ever think that was going to work? Well, it may have worked if I had run rather than loose my opportunity but just standing there. I have never felt so much rage as when I have been pushed into passivity against my will, all my frustrations and anger a fuel ready to explode."COWARD! I screamed like an unleashed banshee. "How dare you leave me here to die!" I screamed again. "Get me out of here." My scream was primal, with a raw intensity to it that told of urgency, of a desperate need, it was the only form of communication I had right now as I banged my fists on the floor.

I was so stupid, "Ouch," I rolled onto my back with some trepidation, pain throbbing throughout my body, deep and warm, but not in a nice way. It felt like someone has their hand inside me, squeezing my organs as hard as they can. I lay still trying to take slow deep breathes hoping the pain would ease as I surveyed the scene, the floor was a mixture of blood splats and the tray, plus its contents strewn in no particular order, what a mess. I decided it was not for to me to clear up, so it could stay as a reminder of my poor attempt at battle, I was never going to make a warrior queen. I put my hand to my head and felt a wetness, trickling down one side, I looked at my hand, it was sticky with my own blood and that of my opponents, my nostrils sensed the smell of liver and my stomach lurched. Oh God, I was badly wounded and going to die in pain and alone.

I clasped my red covered hands and pointed them toward the ceiling saying my final farewells to my loved ones and asking God to keep me safe on my journey to him. "Remember me as I lived, remember that I have always loved you guys and that I loved life, creation and the happiness that comes of simple pleasures. God if you are listening, I don't ask for much, but please keep me safe until I reach your strong arms" With that I closed my eyes accepting the looming darkness coming towards me gathering speed.

I came to sometime later, pleased that I had not died but aware that I was quite cold, I shivered realising I was still laying on the floor. I had no sense of how long I'd been here, but it was long enough for my legs to have cramp, I put my hand to my head once more, thankfully the blood felt like it had congealed into a thick lump, I ached quite badly but I had to move, maybe if I did it slowly it wouldn't be too bad!

I managed to get myself into a sitting position, my heart hammering, my brain trying to short-circuit with anxiety. I hadn't volunteered for this, I wasn't one of those brave people who relished danger I thought to myself as a wave of sickness came over me, I managed to swing round quickly and grab the pail before I was violently ill again. I couldn't stop, my throat hurt from retching, my stomach was cramping and my head throbbed so much more, I really did want to curl up and die.

At that very moment the door reopened and the man dressed in black hobbled in closing the door behind him. He took a step towards me in slow motion his head hung downwards a little. He thrust a small make-up mirror and a pack of tissues towards me, then placed a bowl of water and a towel by my side. I looked up wiping my mouth with a sweep of my hand, I felt drained of any energy, but was taken a back by this development or was it a guilty act of kindness?

I took a short intake of breath, gosh it even hurt to breath, "Please help me," I said in a pathetic voice before I threw up again, I held onto my stomach, it felt as though it was being pinched in a vice, tears filled my eyes from where I was straining so much with the sickness. "I'm so sorry Jaz, I didn't mean to hurt you," he grabbed my ghostly pale arm, as if to make amends, I pulled it swiftly away, he's deluded if he thinks he can make things better like that, he tried to harm me. "I am hurting too, you actually stabbed me" he uttered, as if he could read my mind. "Wash yourself I will be back later." With that he was gone and I was alone once more, completely and utterly alone not only in my mind, body, soul, but most of all I felt entirely alone in the world. I sat still clutching the pail, utterly terrified, what was going to happen to me now? Wait a minute, he said my name, he knew me! And it almost seemed as if he cared for my well being, he knew me, I repeated to myself in my head.

The more I thought, the worse I made things, I became very overwhelmed, I felt empty and tired, I was being held captive against my will, taken away from my place of comfort. My skin was all blotchy from where I had cried so much, I realised my tears solved nothing and I needed to get a grip to focus my energy on my escape. I sniffed then wiped my nose gently with the tissues, specks of blood had attached themselves to the soft paper, I wanted to close my eyes, but if I did that how could I figure out what is what and find a solution.

I let go of the pail and stretched across to where the mirror was laid, gently I picked it up and looked at what was reflected back, what a shock I got. A scarecrow, clothes are utter rags but my face, my eyes were red and swollen, bruises spreading purple with yellow blotches, there was a cut above my eyebrow, housing congealed blood, the same to the corner of my mouth, my nose felt smashed. I ran my hand over my face in the hope nothing was broken, I tugged at my matted hair, I was almost unrecognisable, I looked as bad as I felt.

I placed the mirror back on the floor, and began to bathe my skin gently in the cool water. I winced as I dabbed over my cuts and bruises, my skin was so sore, even more so with the scratchy towel that had been left. I ached all over, no matter how I tried to move, I was completely exhausted, my mouth was bone-dry, I licked my fingers, a few drops of my bathing water at least wet my tongue, and helped to ease my thirst, even if it was dirty, it was my own dirt anyway.

With a lot of effort and wincing in pain, I grabbed the corners of the iron bed frame and pulled myself up. Clumsily I climbed back onto the bed, the storm playing in my head showing no signs of relenting, I needed an aspirin badly. As I laid down, curling my body into something primeval, the foetal position, to try and ease the pain a little, his voice played in my head. Low, with a trace of huskiness and a hint of more power than his body frame suggested, it was not an educated voice, but it was familiar, I was sure I had heard it somewhere before. My eyelids grew heavier and without any hesitation I felt myself drift off into unconsciousness once more. Falling asleep was the best part of the day, it was as easy as letting the dreams begin leaving reality behind.

I became aware of the door opening again, I opened my eyes as he entered the room with another tray of food and a hot drink. "Here, I brought you some aspirin, thought it would help ease the pain, I have also brought a book for you to read, help pass the time."

With more effort than you can ever imagine, I managed to prop myself up on the bed, I felt so fuzzy and dizzy. He handed me the cup and the aspirin, I took a sip and plopped back onto the pillow. The aspirin was a godsend, it would help things, at present I felt too ill and weak even to say anything. "Try to eat, it won't be for much longer, I promise." He said, pulling the blanket up over me, I flinched, thinking he was going to hurt me. "It's ok Jaz" he said, patting the top of the blanket and placing the tray on the bed beside me. Then he walked slowly back to the door, almost robotically with an odd gait, slightly lurching, leaning too far forwards, probably from where I had stabbed him, then it closed behind him.

I managed to turn on my side and began to pick at the food, rice, beans and fish by the look of it, but I really wasn't hungry, I had to force myself to eat something to get strong, I knew all this, I had to listen hard to the part of me that wants to stay alive to fight. I put the spoon to the plate and scooped up a small mouthful, I chewed a little then managed to swallow it down. I didn't realise that I was actually hungry until I looked at the half eaten food and funnily enough, my headache was beginning to ease slightly. I had an odd satisfying feeling, this was the most I had eaten and drunk since I've been here. I owed it to may body to show it that it was worth the effort of good nutrition, in fact it didn't complain but instead felt rested, releasing me to float through an empty space and continue on to the oblivion of more rest.

I dreamt that I had been in a jail cell for so long that I never even checked to see if the walls were solid. I heard screams from other cells which stopped me from pushing on the door for fear of what might come. Then one day when the brilliant light of dawn shone in, I stood and put my hand on the bars, with a prayer I pushed with all my might and despite a brief flash of pain the walls and bars moved and the prison cell itself was left behind me on a hill.

Looking back at it, the outside looked a tiny, pathetic, lonely building. I straightened up, I had been crouched in the dark for so long, it felt odd to be standing tall. I let the light warm my skin, my hair flowing in a gentle heavenly breeze. Upon the outside walls written in paint were the words "Fear" and "Guilt." I tossed my head towards the sky with relief, at last I had the answer, all I had to do was overthrow and conquer these bullies and then I would be free, I needed to be smart yet sneaky.

As my dream came to an end and I came to, it was getting light and the food tray had gone. I must have slept deeply this time as nothing had disturbed me. I had also stayed in one position too long and could barely move, every muscle seemed to have seized up, my body was struggling to repair itself, it had been through a lot in a short space of time, especially if I include my over indulgence with alcohol. The only saving grace was that my headache had actually gone and I no longer felt nauseous. Ok, part one conquered, now all I have to do is muster the energy to relive my dream, overthrow my abductors, push the walls of this place so they tumble down and then I would be free.

In place of the tray, there now lay the book that was left earlier, my pen and notepad. Very strange! I picked up the book noticing it was called "How to kill your wife," would this give me the answers of how to get one step ahead of my abductors? I picked up my notepad, scrolling through it, as cautiously I rolled onto my back, it still contained all my scribbles about Iberville, nothing had been deleted, no pages removed. Were these clues? Or did he just feel really sorry for me and want to appease me? Wait a minute, a light bulb moment occurred, I was still at Iberville, maybe I was in one of the stone huts yet to be converted. Surely if I had been bundled into a car and driven away to pastures new, I would have known about it, even in my inebriated state. Right I need to think clearly and fathom this out, the answer was here, staring at me.

Suddenly there was an explosion in my brain, a good sort, a type that carried ideas and more possibilities than I could be conscious of. These hundreds of ideas and thoughts started to buzz, spinning in a way that appeared without any design or logic to them. Something was telling me that there was a link to my abduction and the woman's body on the beach, but what? One thing was for certain, whatever path lay ahead would be a challenge, this was not going to be without conflict.

CHAPTER 15

I picked up my note pad, turned to a clean page and began jotting down the sequence of events, trying to remember as best as I could. As I wrote I tried to think of possible solutions without much in the way of success. This was a lucky dip, all I needed to do was have the courage to reach inside and pluck out the answers, from a fine tangle of threads in a velvet bag. My brain became more and more frazzled and instead of erasing the obstacles, all I managed to do was create more.

Time for a new approach, but what? I had so many paths to explore, minimal clues but absolutely no solutions coming to mind. Explanations of aspects of life can only make real sense if there are intelligent solutions, therefore my logic needed to be consulted, however in this very moment neither of them wanted to play ball. Ok, I turned to another clean page to start again and stared at it, waiting for some divine inspiration. I drew squares and then began to write down the order of events in them, drawing arrows, connecting one another.

I started at the very beginning when Blot the fisherman first discovered the body, I felt sure this was all related, I just couldn't prove it or even piece it all together yet. I needed a brainwave or miracle whichever came first. I felt lost in a tide, swept away by my own fears, well I am only human after all. I had to solve this, I had to find my inner strength and courage and keep it alive, not go all pansy again, that would help no one

The footsteps returned, this time sounding very different, short little strutting steps like the persons' shoes were too tight for them. I quickly stuffed the notebook under the pillow and rolled onto my side facing the door, knees curled to my chest, wincing a little as I did it. It was just in the nick of time before the door opened, slightly ajar and only another tray was squeezed through, no one entered. As the door was closed, a strong smell of eau de cologne wafted through the air, it was so exotic yet odd, it represented freshly cut timber, like a damp forest after a rainy day, with a hint of scented pine and honey, intermingled with the outlandish aroma of charcoal flames and cinnamon.

Wait a 'god dam picking minute' I know that smell, 'Monsieur de Balmain,' the same cologne Candice always douses herself in. No, surely not, it can't be her, why would it be? Now I'm really confused, what the hell was going on here, my plan of trying to piece it all together had now been thrown up in the air, nothing made any sense, no matter how hard I tried, I just drew blanks at every corner.

I tried to come up with different options, however, none of them seemed even remotely plausible, this was ridiculous how on earth could or would Candice be mixed up in this. I know she was known as Dicey for her precarious exploits, but not this, she would never stoop this low, we were good friends, she wouldn't let any harm come to me, would she? I think I must have used up all my energy reserves racking my brains, I felt exhausted. My brain hurt, I hung over the bed and grabbed the tray, quite a surprise, beans and rice with an omelette. I just had to be at Iberville, there was no other explanation.What and why would an abductor would serve a meal like this to their hostage.

What was the green stuff? I thought to myself as I poked at the omelette. I didn't want to be poisoned, but then why would they? Poison me, I mean. On closer inspection it looked not dissimilar to stinging nettles, chives or dandelion leaves. They use a lot of natures green stuff in the Caribbean, I took a bite of the omelette, it tasted quite cheesy with these dark leafy greens. I came to the conclusion that they were stinging nettles, Goldie used to say. "Git rid addi stems fram dem Bwile all di rest togedda fi ah few minutes Cole wata squeeze chop Dat a ih sting all gaan." It put me off slightly, but I ate as much as I wanted, I still had very little appetite, I pushed the tray to the end of the bed.

I lay back on the bed, pummelling the lumpy pillow, making it a bit more comfortable for my head. Sleep came over me again, like a falling axe, it always seemed to happen when I had had the comfort of eating or drinking. This time, I had to fight it, I had to stay awake and solve this. If I was asleep I would be defenceless, also every time I had fallen asleep since I had been here, I still awoke to this nightmare. I could not fight my thoughts anymore, it was as instantaneous as it was unwelcome, my eyes closed and I fell asleep.

My dream this time, revolved around, Candice as a killer, she needed to get her own back on Tilly for the way she had been treated over the years. The best way of getting to Tilly was through Tilly's mother. Candice came across a vial of poison producing bacteria which was deadly once it was dissolved in liquid. Tilly's mother would then die suddenly leaving her corpse to be moved and pecked by crows, Tilly would be full of remorse and change her ways.

The murder took place in the toilet at Ziggy's bar, Candice followed her victim, offering to get her another drink, her victim being an alcoholic was not going to refuse. Candice returned from the bar, smoothed her black hair back and removed her hair piece which housed the poison. In seconds the contents of the vile was swirled in glass of bourbon, her smile, truly vivacious as she handed it to Tilly's mother. The drink was downed in one gulp, she barely had time to register her death and probably never felt her collision with the floor as she slumped down dead. Candice knew I had witnessed everything and began to walk towards me. She knew that for me, every murder was a story, but also the start of many tales.
I woke up suddenly t before the outcome of the dream could come to fruition, there was a chilly presence in the room, what a very odd dream and fancy remembering it, did it have

some hidden meaning? I jumped as the door swung open, I opened my eyes wider and in one painful move, hauled myself up on the bed, as the tall lanky person placed yet another tray of food at the bottom.

Adrenaline kicked in and surged through me, he had startled me, I knelt up higher on the bed, fists up ready to swing a punch at him, but his reflexes were too quick, he caught both hands before they hit him and held them tight. "Jaz, Jaz, calm down, it's ok, you will be ok." He winced as he bravely sat down on the bed next to me, the baritone of his voice reverberating through my bones. I calmed down a little and he let go of me, he stood up." You see, you will be okay, how are you feeling?" This time the low rumble of his voice made me feel somewhat comforted, it seemed to wrap around me, giving off the kind of power that could change the world. I still couldn't see his face, but I was sure I knew the voice,

As he made his way back to the door, I noticed a small ray of light beaming through the slit in the wall, it bounced off the wall causing a shadow to fall on the floor. All shadows really do is mute colours, soften the volume of the daytime orchestra, they are my guest, letting me know the sun is shining outside this box, I wanted to be out of here and see the light, feel the light for real.

I needed to beg now, I really wanted this to be over "Don't go, stay and talk to me, I'm scared, please get me out of here" I begged. "Can't, not just yet" he replied. "Please,

please, help me," I squeaked again, letting a lone tear roll down my cheek, that was just the start of the floodgates opening. "Jaz, please don't cry, I will try to come later, I promise it will be all right." He sounded quite genuine and sympathetic. He had a conscience, I should at least be thankful for that. I looked up at him once more with my sad wet eyes hoping to provoke a reaction and make him stay or take me with him. Unfortunately he was not going to be won over that easily, he just sighed and then disappeared once more, bolting the door shut behind him.

Alone once more, sealed in this room of hell, I was being eaten alive by loneliness, swallowing every ounce of hope, leaving behind an empty carcass, full of despair and memories I can't seem to hold onto anymore. I wanted warm hands to embrace me, lend me a shoulder to cry on, make me feel safe. I looked at the plate of food, my lips trembled and my shoulders heaved with emotion, unwilling to back down, I can't stop... I can't stop. Why can't I stop crying? I placed a tissue under my stuffy nose and blew hard before squeezing it into a ball and tossing it to one side.

Through my red swollen eyes, the food before me seemed reasonably enticing, it was still rice and peas but with a small piece of chicken and a slice of cornbread on the side, accompanied by a hot drink of lemon tea. I sighed, a resigned and weary sigh, signalling the beginning of my passive deterioration. I began to pick at the food, followed by forcing down larger mouthfuls. I picked up the now empty white ceramic plate, and turned it over, not sure why, instinct I suppose. Despite my body asking for the easy way out, my brain was wired, I couldn't give-up, I had to find my inner strength from somewhere.

Printed on the back of the plate was a coat of arms, two gold lions clutching a yellow and red shield, a green ship sailing in its centre. Underneath were the letters LLW engraved in black Italic print. These were Lord and Lady Wrexham's plates, I recognised them from the luncheon, I had thought then, how very upper class to have your own crockery marked with the family crest. I was definitely still at Iberville. I turned the plate back over, noticing the gold swirly gilding around the edge. I placed the plate back down on the tray and took a gulp of the warm tea as I retrieved my notebook from under the pillow.

I began to tear out the squares from the pages, one by one, I littered the bed with all the torn bits of paper, trying to rearrange them in the hope that the answers would jump out at me. John my ex lover, had done this before when he was trying to compose a piece of music for a school project, I became fascinated by it, so he let me help him. It was amazing, just by juggling all the compilations around, different sounds appeared and we actually composed a song together. I digress, sorry. I stared at the mess, nope, still no inspiration, nothing made any sense, why was this so hard, I was always good at problem solving.

Without any warning, the male voice popped into my head again, "Winston!" I said out loud, I knew it was familiar. It was Winston the Alise newspaper, courier, but then if it was, this whole mess made even less sense, why would Winston and Candice be mixed up in this? Why did he hurt me? Oh my God, I stabbed him! As far as I was aware, they didn't know who Lord and Lady Wrexham were, but at this moment in time, nothing would surprise me.

I let my brain became a ballet dancer, leaping and twirling, full of silly thoughts. Perhaps they were secret villains, with a desire for power and money so much, they thought nothing of making others suffer. I really couldn't see Winston and Candice as villains, it didn't suit their personalities, although it takes all sorts to make a world. Maybe they were the heroes, working with a sense of love, a duty, a desire to protect others, a willingness to take on suffering if it keeps others safe, they had developed self control and an ability to do the hardest thing when it is the right thing to do. What twaddle I do think, I'm losing the plot!

CHAPTER 16

My thoughts were akin to driving around the block over and over, faster and faster, utterly pointless. I still had no explanations as to why this was happening, or any concept as to the events which led to my abduction, I just couldn't fathom it out, it was so frustrating.

I needed to stop, I must have been at this a while as the room was beginning to get dark, and I couldn't really see to read or write any more notes. I put the empty tray back on the floor and fell back on the bed, stuffing bits of note paper back underneath the pillow for safe keeping and a vague hope that they would send a message to my brain as I tried to rest. I placed my hands behind my head and closed my eyes, just in time to hear the trudge of footsteps becoming audible once more.

The door creaked open, this time as I took a deep breath, I didn't feel scared with him stood at the entrance in a trance. "If you know who I am, then please help me, get me out of here, let me see who you are, you owe me that much." I blurted out, almost in a single breath. Silently he moved towards me and cautiously sat down on the bed. "I can't stay long" he said with his hand in front of the balaclava, obviously trying to disguise his voice, I definitely recognised the voice, it was all or nothing, I would say his name and see what happened. I took another deep breath, blew my inner demons away and took command of myself. I looked at his covered face and calmly said."Winston." There my mission was completed.

It was followed by a deathly silence, a stillness in the air, he fidgeted uncomfortably on the bed before taking a sharp intake of breath, followed by a sigh. It was soft and deflated, as if a sudden tension had been lifted and left him with a melancholy sense of relief. He turned to face me, "I know it's you, you can't hide, let me see your face," I blurted. Somewhat hesitant he reluctantly peeled off the balaclava and flopped back the hood of his sweatshirt awkwardly. He didn't have to hide behind a mask anymore, he could be honest, a release of stress let a fake smile emerge from our lips, enabling us both to let each other know we were scared and uncomfortable. After a moment of silence he spoke softly "Jaz, I'm really very sorry about this," he was sincere, making eye contact as he spoke, his eyes were shameful and vulnerable, "Winston what the hell is going on? I never thought you could be involved in anything like this."

From his body language, Winston was really nervous, constantly on edge, his eyes scanning. A muscle in the corner of his right eye twitched involuntarily as he grimaced, then folded his arms tightly across his stomach as he leaned forward, he was about to whisper something but instead became spooked by something. He got up from the bed and nervously uttered. "Jaz, I've got to go now, you will be ok, I promise, no harm will come to you. I will come back tomorrow." As he moved towards the door, he replaced his balaclava and hooded sweatshirt, I grabbed his hand, "Winston, I'm so sorry I hurt you, forgive me, I didn't know it was you before, are you ok, does it hurt much?" he turned his head away from me, shaking my hand loose at the same time as if he was cross with me. Not another word was uttered as he disappeared once more, swiftly bolting the door behind him, he didn't even glance back at me, a deathly silence had fallen yet again. I lay there listening for a few minutes, secretly hoping he would have a change of heart, that his conscience might get the better of him and he would return. But no, the silence remained and I was all alone once more.

I replayed the last few minutes or so in my head over and over. Winston was an introvert, always preferring solitude over company, if there was a party, he would prefer to stay home rather than go to a bar, he only ever invited his close friends to share a drink with him. This was why it was so weird, what he was mixed up in. Was Winston's father an employee of the Wrexham's, or even an embezzler? Was I to be exchanged for a ransom in order to leverage money from Iberville? What a ridiculous plot Jaz, now I really was just clutching at straws. I just didn't understand, I could feel the frustration building to the point of an explosion. I wanted to shout, have a tantrum and beat my hands on the ground like a toddler, but what was the point, where would it get me.

How long had I actually been here, days, weeks, months, who knows, it seemed like I had been trapped for so long that I had lost all faith that there was a world beyond these walls. There is something about unmeasurable time that tortures my mind, body and soul. Perhaps, as I have said many times, it is because there is no love, no hugs or kind smiles, no one to tell me everything will be okay. I had to do something to get free, but what, and here lies the problem, I still did not have a clue.

Feeling completely demoralised, I hauled myself off the bed and walked over to where a small ray of light was shining. Cocking my head from side to side, I tried to peer through the tiny hole, hoping to see something familiar. Alas, it didn't reveal much except for lots of bindweed, but the glimmer of light felt warm on my face, I placed my hand on the wall, it was semi warm, I have be outside somewhere, the gardens of Iberville? Perhaps I was right in thinking my prison was one of the stone huts waiting to be renovated.

The door came ajar again, I had missed the footsteps for a second time, the smell of the eau de cologne engulfed the air once more, I turned, "Candice, wait" I shouted, but there was no reply. I moved in her direction, but not fast enough as the door slammed shut before I could reach it, and the bolt slid across again. Nothing was left, maybe she was just checking on me, or did I scare her?

My whole body still had a gnawing ache which refused to leave, at least the bruises were subsiding and didn't feel so sore to touch. A craving for water which had been with me for some time was becoming more evident, I noticed by the side of the bed, a glass of water had been placed and was sat being gently warmed by the small glints of light. I picked it up, it tasted like a clear mountain spring. Instead of savouring it, I gulped it down in one, I can't say it eased my thirst completely, but it did help.

Before flopping back onto the bed, I found a half drunk cup of cold lemon tea which I finished off, wiped my mouth with my hand and decided that as I couldn't make sense of anything, I would read the book Winston had brought me, to help break up the monotony and try to calm me.

As I mentioned earlier, the book was called 'How to kill your wife' It was about a man called Marcelo who had a good life, until his wife threatened to leave him as a result of his infidelities. His whole life then went into a tail spin, his business crumbled, his home was broken into and trashed, along with his beloved Aston Martin. Marcelo thought that his wife had conspired against him, emotionally scarred, his first thought was to seek revenge. However, he instead began a course of anger management therapy in the hope that it would help him to deal with the situation he which he had found himself in. He visits a therapist and confides in her about his darkest thoughts to kill his wife, his therapist recommends that he keeps a journal of his thoughts for them to explore together at future sessions. Marcelo thinks this is a good idea, but then becomes embroiled in a night of unforgettable passion with her. His life begins to take on a positive slant, his affair with his therapist becomes intense, he is head-hunted for a new job and everything is just perfect, that is, until his wife is found dead and he becomes the prime suspect. He is falsely accused of her murder. The book is quite a good read, a devious tale of psychological suspense involving deception and encounters that lead to murder.

I started to relate this story to my current situation, well, sort of. I sat forward pulling out the bits of paper from under my pillow. Then placing the book open on the bed, I rearranged the pieces of paper in a different array beside it. I thought that, by following the plot in the book, perhaps I could make sense of what was going on and come up with some answers. I picked up my notebook from the floor and with pen poised at the ready began comparing the book and my notes.

I knew this much, my ordeal definitely had to have something to do with Iberville and the woman's body on the beach. I had got too close, I was warned off but ignored the warning and kept digging, I had to be silenced. What I didn't understand was how and why Candice and Winston were involved. I stared at the scribbled notes for what seemed like ages but I still could not get my brain engaged enough to be able to know what was going on.

CHAPTER 17

I stared at the ceiling, waiting for some burst of inspiration to fly my way. It definitely has to have something to do with Lady Wrexham, she has not been seen by anyone lately and why did she not make an appearance on such a prestigious occasion, she would have been there if she could surely, so where is she? Ok, let's just say for arguments sake, it was her body on the beach and why would I be abducted and no one else? Well, only me that I know of. Hang on a minute, yes, I think I have it, the letter warning me off, yes that was it, I had definitely got too close to the truth and needed to be silenced, but by who? Was this why I was here? Why had no one come looking for me? I couldn't prove anything as I had no concrete evidence, but it could be remotely plausible.

I let out a slow controlled breath and attempted to loosen my body movements, I felt like a clockwork soldier. I gave my shoulders a wiggle and lolled my head in a circle, my eyes moved with an alertness that comes from heavy stress, I felt something was going to happen, I hated not being in control, I hated surprises. I clenched each of my hands by subconscious demand as the door opened, I had been trying to concentrate and had become unaware of any approaching footsteps. In hobbled Winston, removing his balaclava and hood as he entered. "You okay" he uttered, I nodded, "you" I asked returning the formalities. "I've been better, it's quite sore when you get yourself stabbed," he replied with an awkward grin. "I'm really sorry I did that, I didn't mean to, I didn't know it was you, will you be ok?" he nodded. Before he could say anything further, I interrupted his train of thought, "Winston, please tell me what the hell is going on, I am so scared and I can't stop playing my own death in my head.

Winston sat down on the bed and took hold of my hands, both of us trembling together. "I can't tell you everything, as even I am confused by it all, I just do as I'm told, I will tell you bits and pieces." I stared into his eyes, eyes will let me know the truth whatever society permits. He was always honest, I will give him that. I guess the mystery would be from what he didn't say, from what he lacked the courage to express and that's what I had to figure out.

I changed tack, trying to help relax him, so he would feel more at ease "What day is it" I said, "Thursday, you have been here for just over a week," came the reply. "But why?" I asked, as the question fell on deaf ears and Winston began to change the path of the conversation. "Jaz, I really want to help you escape, but I need to come back after dark to do that. Ok." I nodded, stunned into silence by what he had just said.

This past week had dragged like thousands of camera frames all shown one at a time in slow motion. I felt like I had been bitten by a vampire and all my lifeblood had been drained, rendering me weak and unable to trigger any defence. I felt sorry for myself, the world and everyone in it is behind fifty feet of glass and completely inaccessible, I felt indifferent, a nothingness. Winston must have sensed this, "Jaz, I promise you, I will come back later, tell you as much as I know and we can plan our escape. Right now, I need you to rest and stay focused, Jaz are you listening to me?" He retrieved a small torch and a pocket knife from the sleeve of his sweatshirt, and handed it to me as I nodded. "Hide this, and don't hurt anyone with it" he smirked, with that he got off the bed and headed to the door. Just before he closed it, he glanced back, "It will all be ok, I promise, trust me," with that the door closed and the bolt slid across, all was silent again.

The pieces of paper were now all crumpled from where Winston had been sitting, I hadn't been quick enough to move them. As I smoothed them over, one became highlighted by a small ray of sun that gleamed through the slit in the wall, was this some divine intervention? It was then I heard what he had just said in my head, my brain was just about catching up. I replayed the conversation. Did he just say plan our escape? This was crazy, why would he say or do that? If this was for real, it was going to be the scariest and smartest thing I had ever done and most probably my only chance of survival.

I yawned and slowly stretched my arms in the air, this time it didn't hurt so much. Surely I can't need to sleep again, that's all I seem to have done. But my body felt like it was hanging limp, similar to wet laundry on a cold still day, I could feel every muscle trying to give in to gravity being warmed by the light streaming in. However despite my certain level of tiredness, my brain wants to keep on going as if it were on some Olympian over thinking sprint, but my body is already complaining that it wants to enter the world of dreams.

As I closed my eyes to rest, fear and anxiety begin to grab me, I try hard not to panic again, I've been there before, I know the feeling, and knowing it makes it a little less scary. I breathed slowly, convincing myself that I am all the stronger for my battle scars. Instead of letting the anxiety take me down, I propped myself back up on the bed and tried to imagine some good memories, to calm my nervous system, then my feel-good brain chemicals can be released and I can start to make my own natural medicine for my anxieties. As I tried to control my breathing, I keep telling myself, I was once lost in a storm, but I'm now in a lighthouse, shining out to sea my freedom not far away.

I definitely couldn't sleep now, of an evening when I was in my shack, I would try and read a book before going to bed. Usually I would fall asleep after only reading one chapter. I decided to pick up Winston's book and continued to read, I am sure this would help me to sleep if not help relax me.

So, the next chapter began with an overnight flight from London to Boston, Marcelo was trying to escape and take on a new identity. On the flight he met a stunning but mysterious woman called Lily. After sharing one too many martini's, the two strangers began to play a game of truth or dare, revealing the most intimate details about themselves to each other, even I knew this was not going to turn out well.

Marcello told Lily about his failing marriage, how his wife, found out about his infidelities through boredom and how he was framed for a murder he didn't commit. Intrigued, Lily began to question him more, Marcello revealed his tempestuous night of passion with his therapist, who promised she could help him rediscover himself, freeing him of the confusion he felt. Marcello said he and his wife were a mismatch from the start, he wondered why he ever married her in the first place. He was the rich businessman, turned undercover agent, she the artistic free-spirited actress, a complete contrast to each other, he needed passion in his life and she was devoid of all feelings. He was sent to investigate reports that a local woman was dealing drugs, it turned out that this woman was actually his therapist.

It was all a bit of a confusing read, Marcello was all logic and feigned cool detachment until she touched him and managed to seduce him, causing something not only to stir in him, but take over his logical thinking. In that moment, his world became an unimportant blur, banished into the far recesses of his mind. The only thing that mattered to him was touching this woman more and inflaming their passion for one another, what a cliché!

However he now wasn't sure about mixing business with pleasure incase he was found out, his life was in a complete mess. He told his therapist, that they should stop seeing each other, despite a few difficulties Marcello managed to escape the clutches of his therapist. However he now believes that it was her who murdered his wife and then framed him to get her own back after their break up.

Lily and Marcello's dangerous game takes a darker twist when he jokes to Lily that he secretly wanted to kill his therapist to hush her up then get revenge for being framed for the murder of his wife. Lily, is quick to assure Marcello that she could help him accomplish that. She could tear down his therapist's empire of money and filth, creating a world of total misery for her. She wasn't bothered about rival gangs involved in drug dealing, her and Marcello could become masters of their own world and do so much better for themselves. After all, some people were the kind worth killing for, like a lying, stinking, cheating, murderess therapist.

Back in Boston, Marcello and Lily's twisted bond grows stronger as they begin to plot his therapist's demise. There were a few things about Lily's past that she hadn't shared with him, namely her experiences in the art of murder and contract killing, a journey that began in her precocious teenage years. In Marcello's eyes, she was just an average person you would see on the street, perhaps a little odd, though. Lily seemed to have a lot a friends, that would come to her aid at the drop of a hat, maybe this should have been a clue as to who she was! She took a perverse pleasure in attaining positions of public trust and respect, she was charming and socially intelligent. But she didn't play by the same rule book as the rest of society, she had no morals, no restraints. You would be invited into her home to be wined and dined but you would be completely unaware that this could be your last connection with the outside world, a psychopath, a murderer.

I found myself immersed in the book, to the extent I couldn't put it down. As I read on, my thoughts kept reverting back to Iberville and me, this was so similar. I turned the page over to reveal these co-conspirators becoming embroiled in a chilling game of cat-and-mouse, a game they both couldn't survive. A shrewd and very determined detective then comes on the scene and is hot on their tail.

The next couple of chapters revolved around a car chase involving Marcello, Lilly and the police, weaving dangerously in and out of traffic. Half blinded by the glare of headlights, an onslaught of bullet sized rain drops thundered onto their car windshield, wipers frantically moving over the never ending sheets of water as it begins to rain hard. They chased smudged red tail lights, skidded wildly around corners, tyres squealing, at times the car was pushed to its limit, gathering speeds of over 100 km/h as it ran red lights. The chase was exhilarating but nerve-wracking, adrenaline pumping, risk-taking, until it ends up with Lily and Marcello escaping to a secret hideout, but then a twist is added. Marcello receives an anonymous letter which reads: All my life I have lied. I lied to escape, I lied to be loved, I lied for placement and power; I liked to lie. It's my way of living.

Before I could read on any further an idea came to me, a wild stab in the dark here, but is this was why Winston left me this book, is it a clue? I sat up on the bed, leaned backwards onto my arms and dangled my feet over the edge and let more thoughts evolve. Candice and Tilly were friends or should that be acquaintances, well, Alise informant to be precise. Tilly always kept Candice dangling like a piece of string, sweetening her up for information when she needed it, rather than the true friendship that I thought Candice and I had. We had always enjoyed each other's company, laughing, discussing men, the way of the world etc, whilst sharing the odd joint and drinks together at the bar.

Tilly initially introduced me to Candice at a Mortuary open afternoon, not your usual run of the mill thing to report on, but when in the Caribbean, anything is possible. Visitors were able to enter the viewing area and take a look around the newly refurbished building, which then housed three post-mortem bays, all empty, I hasten to add. We were given special dispensation to talk to staff about their day-to-day work and claw from it any juicy details we could. The spread was supposed to capture controversy, local drama and something grim to keep the cynics 'happy.' The actual article we wrote, well to be honest, when I look back now, was meaningless fodder.

For those keen to get a closer insight, I remember a consultant histopathologist was flown over from America, spending her entire time performing virtual autopsies, making 'incisions' with marker pens instead of the real scalpel blades, on willing volunteers to demonstrate how and why they were performed.

Unfortunately for me, this was one of the first events I ever went to. Tilly took me along to show me the ropes, introducing me to the locals as the new up and coming Alise reporter from England. I remember her swanning off, rubbing shoulders with management and local dignitaries, whilst I stood alone like a lemon, feeling very uneasy and unsure of myself. Luckily for me, Candice noticed and took me under her wing, instantly we clicked, she took me to places I never knew existed and probably shouldn't have been witness to. From that day forward, we were always there for each other, she was hot on my heels wherever I went, sometimes I found it quite spooky, she just laughed when I told her so.

Yes, it's all flooding back to me now, Lord and Lady Wrexham were both there along with the local Police Commissioner, "Mr Corruption" himself, allegedly they were going to inject even more investment into the morgue and bring about a positive change.

With more development planned on the Island, the idea was to help drive up the economy and drive out corruption, much the same as Lord Wrexham's recent plans for Iberville. Tilly spent most of her time with them, I can recall watching her at work, her charm and charisma fascinated me. She certainly knew how to conduct herself, she was one of the finest diplomats I'd ever seen. She put everyone at ease, drew them into liking her so they were like putty in her hands. If only I had the personality and looks that would get me noticed, maybe I could go far. Knowing what I know now, it was all a ploy, it doesn't take much to worm your way into a billionaires business as a journalist, work your magic, gain their trust and their hearts and hey presto, you want for nothing more. After all, if you choose the right career, that make the most of your skills and personality, it can give you the flexibility to do anything.

CHAPTER 18

Winston reappeared, frightening me a little, I hadn't heard the door open, I had been too focused on the book and preoccupied with my thoughts. Looking at him, he has the appearance of a sumo wrestler on a diet, his build slightly bulkier than usual and he had brought another tray with him, laden with enough food to feed a small army. Bread, chunks of cheese, bowl of rice and prawns and two warm drinks. He smiled, "You look like you might have worked it all out, here you are, we will need this to keep our strength up if we are to escape." I was about to speak, when I was stopped in my tracks by Winston stripping off.

Gosh, this was a new one on me, he removed a pair of dark trousers and a dark hooded top, which then revealed his own apparel underneath, " Phew, thank goodness," I said, "I was in for the Full Monty experience." He frowned but said nothing. I watched, intrigued and not sure what to expect next, as like a magician, he pulled out a pair of trainers from underneath his top thrusting them in my direction. "I didn't want to get caught, thought this was the safest way" he said.

We both sat on the slightly warm stone floor and started to pick at the feast before us. "Winston, I have worked some things, I think, but I still can't piece it all together, can you tell me what's going on, you can't keep me in suspense anymore. Why would you now want to help me? I tried to get it all off my chest between mouthfuls of food and drink.

Winston smiled, "I'm really surprised you haven't fathomed it all out yet, you being a bright journalist and all that, I brought the book to help you and I managed to retrieve your notepad, thought it would be useful, couldn't get your phone though, it was too dangerous." I stared frustrated at him, "Why can't you just explain it all?" I uttered in an irked manner.

Winston drew a deep breath and then started to tell spill the beans, he did know a fair bit, but he was also afraid for his own life as it transpired he was being blackmailed. He didn't have the money that was wanted, so his punishment was death if he was caught disobeying orders. I sat there, listening intently and trying not to interrupt, despite having quite a few questions. I couldn't believe what I was hearing, I was finding it all a bit hard to take in if I'm honest.

Winston paused long enough to take a breath, "Jaz, I have made a terrible mistake, it has led me down a wrong path and I don't know how to make it right. I chose not to analyse the situation at first, instead I did as I was told for my own selfish gain, I didn't think about the pain it would cause. I know we make our own independent choices, but please believe me when I say that was taken away from me, please understand I never wanted you to come to any harm." I made eye contact with him and took his hand, gripping it firmly, "It's ok Winston, I believe you." I said just about managing a smile.

Winston stared back, his eyes slightly glazed, watery even, he sniffed before continuing. Apparently it all started when Tilly took me on my very first assignment to the mortuary, I thought as much. Shamelessly, she had hobnobbed with Lord and Lady Wrexham and I had watched on in awe of her and with aspirations to be just like her one day. From that day on, Tilly set up secret but regular liaisons with Lord Wrexham, firstly to help him with getting his business ventures accepted around the Island as she "knew people" but then as time went on, their fondness for one another grew and quite quickly developed into a passionate love affair. Allegedly, on Tilly's part it was, well at least initially, all money driven. The power of love turned her into a warrior, giving her the strength to defend and develop a healthy distain for those who dared attack Lord Wrexham, now she had claimed the sole rights to his heart strings. Apparently she was by his side so often, she was given the title of 'Lord Wrexham's Close Advisor,' by him in order not to cause suspicion amongst the locals or from Lady Wrexham herself.

You know Tilly as much as I do, she loved being the centre of attention and enjoyed attending expensive gala dinners, meeting royalty and celebrities. She always wore the finest designer clothes, no doubt bought for her by you know who.

She regularly had her nails done and hair cut, whether she needed it or not. She wore beautiful diamond jewellery, and when we all commented on it at the Alise, she would smile and say. "No cubic zirconia for me, I will only accept the best." When she attended these social occasions, her demeanour always changed, she would speak with an upper class accent, and she would look at you as if you were something dirty she just trod in. I always felt quite intimidated when she did it. I only ever said something once about the way she treated people, that was a bad move. You could see the tension in her manner, a tightness in her face and her eyes began to move robotically. It was as if she's got some clock ticking in her head, a countdown to her next explosion.

It was common knowledge on the Island that Lady Wrexham preferred her own company and would take any opportunity to stay at home with her paintings rather than attend formal functions, if she could stay out of the limelight, she would, hence why it all seemed to work well for Tilly and Ed.

However, Lord Wrexham was a complete con-artist, he could put on an act and be a Jeckyl and Hyde person, depending on who he was talking to and what he needed to get out of the conversation and his victim. He could be everything from very nasty to gregarious, to vulnerable, an ever changing disguise for each situation. He would tell infinite lies and never flinch, a sort of survival skill, no-one ever seemed to cotton on.

Lord Wrexham also loved being the centre of attention and was more than happy to be photographed with beautiful glamorous bunny boilers on his arm, it gave him a huge thrill and sense of power. All the locals thought he was a dubious character, that's how he obtained his position in society. Rumour has it that he could defend or attack, be hero or villain but his only real con was conning himself out of a chance to develop an honest soul, but he was not going to admit to that.

Over time Lord Wrexham fell deeper and deeper under Tilly's spell. Tilly is a very strong willed independent character who can manipulate people easily. She found herself enjoying the high life so much and didn't want to lose it, so she made herself fall in love with Lord Wrexham. Do you remember that she used to boast at the Alise, about the new man in her life, but no-one ever got to meet him or find out about him, he was a closed book, we weren't even sure it wasn't a made up character. I nodded, I do remember that, as when questioned further, she just used to say, "Falling in love with him was the easy part, but admitting it to myself, well that's hard. You see, I've had these very efficient defences for so long, I'm not sure I can let the barriers down." What total rubbish she spoke, in truth, what was really happening was that she could get everything he could offer her at the click of her fingers, financially and romantically, she was feeling totally secure and wanted for nothing.

This carried on for a year or so until Lady Wrexham decided to attend one of her husband's functions as a surprise guest. Unfortunately, surprise isn't an emotion that is always taken well and most of the time someone always gets hurt.

Anyway Lady Wrexham decided to go along, predominately because it was an art exhibition and two of her pieces were to be on show. Lord Wrexham had put on this function for a talented street artist he had come across and instead of letting him continue to project his living dreams onto bricks, he persuaded him to turn out his art work onto canvas and get some money. Lady Wrexham became interested in this new culture, she was introduced to the artist by a chance meeting, he was also interested her type of art. Hence the reason she was able to exhibit a couple of her paintings.

Both paintings consisted of the same theme, but were a variation of each other in different colours. They were of a leaf skeleton with its green flesh eaten away, leaving only a lacy cellulose. The critics wrote; "A sublime, fragile yet natural, beauty in its own way."

Lady Wrexham knew her husband was going to be there but wanted to see his response when he realised two of her paintings were being exhibited. She arrived alone and unannounced, apparently not to be conspicuous, she wore a well made grey trouser suit, classic, figure flattering, feminine and made for natural movement. Tilly was already there, hanging off Lord Wrexham's arm, gazing into his eyes, their closeness clearly on show, then the very public and humiliating kiss happened as Tilly made her move. A kiss that revealed a sweetness of passion, a million loving thoughts condensed into a single moment. Lady Wrexham happened to catch sight of them as the kiss was exchanged, it was then that Lord Wrexham became aware of his wife's presence almost at the same time!

For those around the couple, it was like watching an action movie, as the shock registered on Lord Wrexham's face, followed by a delicious moment where his face washed blank with confusion, his brain cogs couldn't turn fast enough to take in what had just happened. Every muscle of his body momentarily froze before a grin crept onto his face. An almighty showdown followed in full view of everyone and with tensions high Lady Wrexham turned into a screaming banshee. "When you cheat on a relationship, you cheat yourself and everyone else, you risk a foolish vortex of pain my girl." She yelled and from there it grew into a tornado, apparently, despite her rage, it was really nothing more than a shield for her pain and humiliation she felt.

She became a little cornered soldier randomly throwing out grenades, scared for her life, lonely and desperate. She stormed out, her husband close on her heels, grabbing her arms, being tactile, trying to make amends for the situation. But Lady Wrexham was not about to be appeased. Tilly was mortified, initially frozen to the spot, allegedly feeling quite traumatised. She couldn't believe what had happened, and in front of everybody too, it was only a kiss, quite harmful, or so she thought. She was seen sloping out of the back door to avoid the glaring eyes and suggestive comments from the gathering masses, which included several of her fellow journalists.

Unfortunately the media reports that followed this outburst, did not help the situation, it showed pictures of the actual kiss, Lord Wrexham running after his wife and Tilly, captured with her, head hung low, with a small smile playing on her lips as she left escaping out of a back entrance. It made the front page of most papers, except the Alise, the best headlines being Prince to Pauper, Frog kisses Butterfly. The media had a field day with it as you can imagine. Petra, at the Alise was absolutely furious, Tilly was severely reprimanded, and nearly lost her job. But then it was all hushed up, as if nothing had happened and everything eventually went back to normal, it was never spoken of again, Petra always had a short fuse as regards to Tilly after that, but knew she still needed her for good stories.

Poor Lady Amelie Wrexham was unable to cope any longer and refused to tolerate her husbands behaviour, she filed for a divorce and was adamant that this time he would not get away. A court case was instigated, she hired the best lawyers on the Island, who were like loaded guns, armed ready to take Lord Wrexham to the cleaners.

As much as Lady Wrexham hated the limelight, she wanted as much publicity as possible, then publicly she could claim back what was rightfully hers. This meant that Lord Wrexham would loose everything, his title, his land, Iberville, his credibility, etc. To stop this from happening the devious villain in him set to work and secretly bribed all Lady Wrexham's legal advisors who then set about to persuade Lady Wrexham to give her husband another chance, as had happened previously with a caveat that, for one year, he would be devoted to her, showing her the love she yearned for and his infidelities would stop. But this time she was not going to be persuaded. They had to change tack, telling her that legally, as everything was transferred into his name, even this far down the line, it would remain rightfully his and she would lose everything, including her title.

She didn't want her husband to get off lightly or with all that was rightfully hers, so she agreed in principle and the case was dropped. She went back to being a recluse, however some say, she started to devise a cunning plan in order to overturn her husband and make it awkward for Tilly to remain on the Island.

Local gossip said that both Lord and Lady Wrexham took a siesta away from the eyes of the world, they stayed under an invisibility cloak until they were ready to re-emerge as 'new butterflies'. Lord Wrexham allegedly, spent more time with his wife, tending her every need, although I doubt that. Meanwhile, Tilly was put on probation, so sunk herself into the paper becoming quite short tempered with the mundane articles she was given, I think Petra kept her on a short leash for a while.

The gossip chain then reported that after just a few months Lord Wrexham found life unbearable without Tilly, he needed and wanted her. He contacted the Alise, telling Petra that he needed Tilly to attend a business engagement to talk to overseas clients about the development of the sugar plantation. Petra agreed it was a good idea, but was not convinced Tilly was the person for the job. Lord Wrexham persuaded her otherwise, you know, money talks and all that! Quite shallow really. Tilly was obviously overjoyed at the opportunity, but unfortunately the love affair was rekindled.

Lord Wrexham and Tilly, quickly became more infatuated with one another, they were supposed to be meeting in secret, but there were a few sightings by the locals. By now, wherever they met and whatever they did never mattered, to them it was all about being connected. Those that saw them say that their exchanges were littered with more than just romance. It spoke of the love that lay there, unspoken, the gentle gaze of their eyes, the relaxed nature of their faces, they appeared deeply in love and nothing could or would change that.

Lord Wrexham knew that he could never let go of Tilly, she was beautiful, charming, strong, independent, everything Lady Wrexham was not, he needed her, her loved her. He was also fully aware that Lady Wrexham could make things very difficult if she found out that the affair had been rekindled, he would not be able to convince her legal advisors again. He had to do something in order for him to remain a notable pillar of the Island and keep Tilly.

Lord Wrexham explained this to Tilly, at a secret rendezvous one night. They both came to the conclusion that their only way forward was for Lady Wrexham to meet an unexpected and unsuspicious death. Over a bottle of rum they plotted her demise, he needed her death to be quick and painless, but be sure that her life force would definitely depart this world, Tilly did not want to be involved in any sordid murder. It needed to look like her death was as a result of a desperate depression and an inability to cope with life and her failed marriage. So they planned her suicide.

CHAPTER 19

So, to the plan, Lord Wrexham would continue with his usual rituals. Every evening at eight in the evening, he would head to the kitchen to make his wife's hot chocolate, all milk, with two heaped spoons of a mixture that contained real cocoa.

Lady Wrexham had become dependent on drugs to help her sleep, she often injected Diazepam into her thigh, sometimes when she felt too weak, Lord Wrexham would administer it for her, she still trusted him to do that. So he would help her into bed and after taking her night cap, he would tell her she was too weak and he would inject her with a syringe of pellucid emerald liquid, but this time it would be a lethal dose. Once she was asleep he would suffocate her, that way she wouldn't know anything about it, she wouldn't wake up and she wouldn't suffer, she would just be in a never ending dream. He would make sure she looked comfortable in bed, just like she was sleeping, he would then leave the house and go to a party which Tilly would organise, meaning he would have an alibi. On returning home, he would find his wife dead in bed, it would look like death from natural causes or that she had given herself too much sedation accidentally, or as a suicide but without a note.

The Caribbean law enforcement being one of corruption itself, meant no one was likely to question what had happened, there probably wouldn't even be a post mortem. Lord Wrexham could then give his wife the funeral she deserved and lay her to rest, not feeling guilty because she would appeared to have died with dignity. He would have her gravestone expertly engraved, a monument to a beloved wife! No one would suspect anything and he would regain his status on the Island as a grieving doting husband.

Winston shuffled uncomfortably and wiped his nose on his sleeve, then took another sip of the left over dregs of the warm drink, " Don't stop now" I said, like an excited child being told a story, he swallowed hard. "Ok, but can we sit on the bed, it will much more comfortable?" We both got up off the floor like two old age pensioners, we had been sat there a long time.

He continued. The day of the deed came all to soon, Lord Wrexham spent the day with his wife as normal, they feasted on their usual elaborate meals and spent the evening together before she bathed ready to retire for the night. Lord Wrexham made her the nightcap and took it to her in bed, exactly as usual. The plan was going swimmingly well, nothing out of the norm. He prepared the syringe and without any resistance from Lady Wrexham, he injected her with the Diazepam overdose, she apparently even told him to do it as she felt too weak, it couldn't have gone any better. As he kissed her goodnight, she sighed before closing her eyes, her body unknowingly being dragged into a shadowy world of forever blackness and she fell asleep in an instant without suspecting or feeling anything.

Lord Wrexham sat on the bed beside her watching, her features were much softer when she was asleep, the lines that usually creased her brow were replaced by a youthful appearance, she looked so peaceful. As her breathing became more shallow, he donned on a pair of gloves, then tightly squeezed the pillow and applied pressure over her face. Her death came swiftly in the most kind and gentle manner, she never put up a fight, never stirred, just literally died in her sleep.

Lord Wrexham removed the pillow and put it back under her head, then he kissed her silver dashed hair, as the tears rolled from his eyes. She lay their, tucked in as if it mattered, totally perfect. He got changed and left his dead wife looking just like she was sleeping, there was no greyness, simply a lack of the usual pink colour to her cheeks. She looked peaceful, his hand found hers one last time without thinking but he recoiled just as fast. It wasn't her anymore, just her body. He left her there alone and went to Tilly's party in order to been seen, following their scheme to the letter and giving them both solid alibis.

Winston paused for a short intake of breath, he licked his lips as if to moisten them. My mind was still a surging perplexity, I knew I had a puzzled expression my face. "I still don't understand why I was abducted and why I'm being held captive," I asked. He stared into thin air, his face lacking any mobility for a moment, before he adjusted his gaze to rest on me for a bit longer than I would have liked, it made me feel a bit uncomfortable to be honest. He must have sensed it, he smiled. "Sorry," he uttered before he continued with the story again. "Jaz, you know the letter warning you off, you knew it was wrong, yet you continued to dig deeper regardless. Every time you were told to leave it alone, you still grabbed every opportunity to try and find out more information, they both got scared, what would they do if you worked out what had happened.

You had to be stopped so you wouldn't scupper the plan, but it started to go wrong, when you announced in a loud voice that you wanted to see Lady Wrexham. Lord Wrexham panicked, he had to silence you, otherwise all the other media toffs that were with you would cotton on that she had not made an appearance and would have made things very awkward for him. So you got yourself locked up, initially whilst Lord Wrexham rang Tilly and they could hatch another plan to deal with you, they just needed more time. I'm not defending them, they just wanted you to stop asking questions, so they both agreed that if you were locked up for a short time, they could get rid of their guests, you would fear for your life and in turn they would gain your silence, ridiculous, I know, but it did work.

I shifted uneasily on the bed and looked down at my hands, I noticed that my knuckles had become a white colour from clenching my fists too hard, I could feel myself grinding my teeth, anger was boiling up inside me. I am the steam in a pressure cooker, waiting to explode, I have to find a way to let it out safely, I have to search for my inner peace, otherwise Winston will bare the brunt, Poor Winston. "What a complete and exaggerated sense of self preservation on their part." I said, he nodded agreeing with me, which was a good move on his part at this present time. Right now, I hated Tilly and wanted revenge for Lady Amélie Wrexham and for me too. But this wasn't the way, the more I let the hatred overtake me, the more it would only guarantees me more enmity, more pain and that is not sensible.

A heavy silence settled over us, there was an uneasy tension in the air. Winston shifted himself uncomfortably on the bed, he obviously felt very awkward about what had happened. It still hadn't explained why he was mixed up in this, but there was still more to tell. "Jaz I really am sorry, do you want me to go on?" I nodded tentatively, unclenching my fists as I got off the bed and propped myself up against the door.

Winston began. So, back to Tilly's party and the night Lady Wrexham died, apparently a good time was had by all, but the police were called because the locals complained that music was too loud, they described it as thunder. This was even more perfect for them as they chatted to the police, they had now been seen together by the police, nothing would be suspected. Lord Wrexham returned home after midnight, then he would execute the second part of their plan, to report finding his wife dead in bed to the authorities. However this is where it all went completely wrong, even before you became involved. "How?" I asked, curiosity building like a cat fixated upon its prey.

When Lord Wrexham returned home from the party he went upstairs to where he had left his wife 'sleeping,' but when he walked into the bedroom, she had gone, she was not lying in bed all neatly tucked in, she had vanished! Lord Wrexham was really spooked, the bed had been remade as if no one had ever been in it. Shear panic overwhelmed him, did she play dead, did he actually kill her, was she alive somewhere, lurking ready to get revenge for what he had done to her?

His brain went into overdrive, he became trapped in his own psychosis, a living nightmare playing on his deepest fears. Frantically he searched the house but there was no sign or any evidence of Lady Wrexham. He became so unnerved that he phoned Tilly explaining what had happened. Tilly, ever adaptable to changing situations, told him to face his fear with courage, it's the precursor to bravery, it wakes you up to what needs to be done. She ordered him to drive back to her house where he spent the night. They would return to Iberville the following morning with a new plan if needs be.

After a restless night, they both retuned to Iberville, only to find exactly the same as the previous night. Lady Wrexham had completely vanished, she was not in the house or in the gardens. When the service staff were questioned as to her whereabouts, they all thought she was in her art studio, but she was not. To make matters worse, her personal maid found an envelope tucked under Lady Wrexham's pillow, which she handed to Lord Wrexham and Tilly. When they opened it, they were quite shaken up. They both put on an act of being unconsolable, so as not to raise alarm bells to the staff, but really they were both extremely scared, the envelope contained a blackmail letter;

I know what you have done, you murderers, revenge is sweet, it is just simply matter of time. Your greed, selfishness, vanity will be the death of you both. I will be your psychological control, responding as the soft everyday-cruelty you have dealt to others. I am worthy of respect, keep looking over your shoulders as one day I will be behind you.

Fearing that Lady Wrexham was in fact still alive, a sense of panic engulfed them both, neither of them knew what to do next. They told all the staff that, Lady Amélie Wrexham had gone away for a few days to a friends in Paris as she needed to 'find herself'. The letter worried them both, they had to get rid of it, if it was found it was evidence that something had happened and could be traced to them, so they did the first thing that entered their heads. "Which was?" I asked, Winston shrugged, "Burn't it in the fireplace, now there was nothing that could incriminate them, or at least that's what they thought!

Exactly one week later Lady Amélie Wrexham's body was caught by Blot and the rest is history, or so the saying goes.

You have probably put together by now everything that followed. I gasped, the air suddenly felt cold, I shivered. Oh my god, I was right, it was Lady Amélie Wrexham's body that was netted on the beach. Winston sighed again, as he ran his hands through his mop of black hair, "I shouldn't be telling you all this, I could get us both killed, I don't want to put you in any more danger." "Well, you've basically told the whole story already so you might as well finish, I'm sure we can both go into the incredible hulk mode if necessary." I took his left hand and squeezed it tight, trying to put him at ease, he gripped my hand in return and almost in unison we gave our shoulders a wiggle and lolled our heads in a circle, we were both so tense. His eyes moved around the room with the alertness that came from the heavy stress he was under, his right hand remained clenched by subconscious demand.

There was a rustle from outside the door, we both stayed very still, scared for our lives, there was no plan for this bit just our biological reason and purpose for being fearful, our only mechanism to keep us both safe, part of our natural intuition. There was complete silence as we quickly processed our feelings and let our higher brain switch back on, enabling us to make the real choices about what to do next, to make a real plan with a viable solution. Luckily the noise stopped and no one else came.

Winston stood up and anxiously looked at his watch, he was nervous and rightly so, because to him, he was doing what mattered, he wanted to get it right and get us both out of here alive. "Jaz, we need to get a move on, start changing out of that raggedy dress and put the clothes on I bought you whilst I finish telling you, I don't know how much time we have left before I am missed." I did as I was told, I didn't care that I would bare all to Winston, I just stripped myself out of what was left of the dress, it didn't take much anyway, put on the black trousers and hooded sweatshirt, then laced up the old trainers which were quite a bit bigger than my delicate feet! But at least I could still walk in them, they would do, beggars can't be choosers.

Thank goodness there was no mirror here I thought as I looked down at my attire, the sleeves of the sweatshirt were all patched and it was too long in the arms, the trousers were also too long in the legs, I looked like some battered old clown in big baggy trousers, but the clothes felt warmer as they greeted my skin with their gentle touch, like an aspect of a protective nurture. I began to turn up the sleeves and trouser bottoms, Winston laughed and was quite astute, as he pulled some string from his pocket. "Just to help keep the trousers up." We both giggled nervously as he helped me tie the string around the waist of the trousers. Never in my life had I been dressed to look like a hobo, Oh well, at least I still had my life.

CHAPTER 20

As I readjusted the clothes, Winston stood next to the door, "Where was I? Ahh yes, he muttered and started to explain the next piece of the puzzle. "So as I said before, you started to dig into Lady Amélie Wrexham's death, obviously not knowing it was her, but you began to get too close, you even tried to speak to Candice. Tilly knew how close you two were and was even more aware that Candice liked a good gossip. Lord Wrexham and Tilly thought that she would tell you about the police and mortuary technicians being paid off in order to silence them about the body on the beach. They then paid for someone to get close to Candice and gain her confidence in order to influence her actions, a sort of functioning hypnosis so to speak.

However Tilly and Lord Wrexham realised that Candice might try and be smarter than they had expected, they became even more paranoid and used their contacts to increase the pressure on her so she was left with no choice but to obey orders. She became absolutely petrified of Tilly, she wanted desperately to help you but couldn't without risking her own well-being. In order for Tilly to get you out of the way, she had to get you to come here, to Iberville. It then became easy because you tend to enjoy yourself and often drink a bit too much, so it was a pretty sure bet that you would do the same at the plantation experience, especially when the drinks were free and plentiful! Luckily for them, you went one further and fell over, hurting your knees, which gave Lord Wrexham the opportunity to escort you to the washrooms. When you fell asleep in the chair, they both moved you, a simple task as you were almost anaesthetised from the booze and obviously everyone else was still soaking up the atmosphere.

Initially you were put in one of the downstairs rooms to avoid any suspicion, as Robin kept asking if you were ok, they just told him you were sleeping it off, it seemed to pacify him. Then, still out for the count and without anyone noticing, you were moved here, to a stone cottage right at the back of all the other buildings, out of sight out of mind type of thing. Tilly's plan was to keep you hidden until both she and Lord Wrexham managed to get away from the Island before any suspicions were raised and then you could be released not knowing what had happened.

I was absolutely flabbergasted. "Apart from blackmail, how do you and Candice fit in to all this?" Winston went silent and urged me to do the same as the sound of approaching footsteps clip-clopping, became apparent, he pulled me with him so we were hidden from view if the door was to open. We held our breaths as the clattering noise came to a halt and the door creaked open, Winston looked at me and held his hand over my mouth. Candice entered the room and closed the door behind her, she grabbed hold of me and hugged me tight, grinning from ear to ear as she uttered "Kool fashion, Mi hav missed yuh." "Just telling Jaz everything" Winston said. "Ok, ok Mi wi cova fi yuh hurry up ar wi will all git caught." With that she blew a kiss, "Get tuh guh before dem suspect anyting. Wi will bi free very soon." Then she was gone, her clip clopping fading into the distance. I knew she would come through, but I didn't want her or Winston to put themselves in danger for me.

It did help raise my spirits from the depths of despair when I saw her, she was not perfect, or neat and tidy, but she had enough love in her heart to fight for and defend for what is right and good. Both she and Winston did, it didn't matter that they had frayed edges and scratches, because what counts is that they hold a steady rhythm within.

Winston looked at his watch once more then stuttered. "Jaz we have to finish this quickly if we are to escape." I nodded and circled with my finger as he began once more, but this time at a much faster pace

Candice and I met on the bus, we were both going to work, I had never noticed her before but she boarded wearing these dreadful lime green leggings and a bright yellow t-shirt with a matching headscarf. Anyway the bus was full, and I made some derogatory comment, rather too loudly, that she looked like a budgerigar, she heard me and came over, we ended up sharing one seat between us. By the time we got to town were chatting like we had been old chums for years. Tilly met us as we got off the bus, not sure why, but told us both to meet her after work in the disused armoury two streets away, she had information for us. We questioned her about the meeting and why it involved both of us, but the more we interrogated her, the more she ignored us and began to fly into one of her rages, so we made our excuses and left her, agreeing we would see her later.

Anyway, we both met her after work with a sense of pure fear and trepidation. When we got there, she was staring at one of the armoury walls that has been crumbling for years, looking at the graffiti, old paint and dried weeds. She was holding a candy bar and I noticed her hand tightened involuntarily making the wrappers crinkle as we approached.

She turned to face us, Candice was for some reason hanging off my arm and she stretched up and whispered in my ear, "Don't let her good looks fool you, she can be an evil bitch." Tilly looked different somehow, it was as if we were looking in a magical mirror, showing a representation not of her, but what she had built herself to become. I remember noticing her eyes were filled with so much bitterness and hate. I went to say something, can't remember what, but before I had time to respond, she grabbed me, pushing Candice to the side away from me. I felt the knife on my neck before I saw it. She held it precariously against my skin, soft enough not to pierce, but hard enough to enforce her intended message, Candice stood frozen to the spot for a second.

In the next instance, Candice was trying to grab the knife, yelling at me to get away. Tilly turned into this whirling dervish and soon had control again, both of us pinned against the wall, petrified, unable to move from fear and the excruciating pain of her betrayal. All I could do was stare lifelessly into her brown eyes that gleamed with a terrifying coldness I had never seen in her before. She threatened us both, I know bravery sits between cowardice and foolhardy, but in our dangerous situation we made no moves at all, that was the brave choice and the right choice. We just stood there like she had this psychological control over us. She had turned into Satan's warrior. She made it very clear that if we did not obey her, she would have us killed, she had power, she had contacts.

She told us about what had happened and her next plan, which involved you including the role we would play in the charade. Fearing for our lives and far too scared to resist, we did as we were told, but later when we were on our own we secretly plotted to help you. We couldn't tell anyone, but we agreed to visit you frequently, bring you food and drink and make sure you were ok, whilst we tried to fathom out our timings in order to free you. We would never have let any harm come to you.

As he talked, there was kindness, a gentleness to him, I had never really got to know him before, he was just Winston the Alise courier. I now realised that he was more in depth than that, the kind of person who lived how he believed people should live, no malice in the world. I liked him, I believed him, I could trust him.

Lord Wrexham organised the sugar plantation open day as he really did want to help move the Islands economy and status forward, he also needed to keep everything normal. It was Tilly's idea to send you and Petra agreed, without knowing the infinite details. They thought they could confuse you and silence you without you cottoning on to their plans. Unfortunately, you found the painting on the easel, they didn't reckon on that, you thought it was a self portrait of Lady Amélie Wrexham, but it was actually a painting of Tilly painted by Lady Wrexham from memory. If you had been given the opportunity to see it, in its entirety, you would have seen she had her throat cut. Lady Amélie Wrexham's way of showing revenge, I suppose, she couldn't get to her for real yet, so she would convey what could happen in a painting.

They both became even more spooked with that and what with you yelling questions at Lord Wrexham in front of everyone as to the whereabouts of his wife, they had to shut you up there and then. What I'm not sure is how (or if) they planned to return you to civilisation without you saying anything, I know they would be long gone, but you would definitely put something in the Alise and cause a stir.

Candice and I were supposed to slip some sleeping powder into your drink whilst you were in the gardens, we were dressed as butlers, once you had fallen asleep, we were to take you to the Keepers house, make sure you were safe and then leave the party and become Tilly's runners, doing whatever she needed us to do. As I said, it all went wrong so Candice and I were not needed for that part, Lord Wrexham took over. You made him so cross by your incessant yelling he moved you and imprisoned you here in this stone cottage. The more Winston revealed, the more I could feel my blood beginning to boil, how evil could they be, I always knew there was another side to Tilly, but never thought she would stoop as low as this!

Winston sighed once more, this time the breath escaping from his lips was slow, a reset button for his emotions, allowing a response to come that has the benefit of both empathic and logical thought. His gaze caught mine, "I really am so sorry, I feel dreadfully guilty for what I have done to you, I like you a lot, always have had a soft spot for you, it has been a living nightmare for Candice and I. If only I had defended myself sooner, this may have never happened, he cocked his head to one side, Jaz, you know, sometimes, when I am not feeling very good, just the thought of your name lightens my mood, you have always had and always will have a place in my heart."

God, I wish I didn't blush so fast, in an instant my cheeks were rosy and he could see my embarrassment, I wish I had some ability to keep my emotions hidden. He grinned at me before continuing. "We managed to persuade Tilly and Lord Wrexham to let us bring you food, as they certainly didn't want another murder added to their crime, despite Tilly thinking you deserved death by starvation, anyway they agreed, however what we didn't anticipate was you trying to escape and stabbing me in the process.

It caused a few issues with Tilly and me, as she told me I was an idiot for leaving a butter knife with you, she wanted to kill you there and then and get rid of me. Candice was quite sly and managed to persuade her once more that she could square things, she also sorted my wound out. Tilly agreed, but Candice never let me live it down, that you stabbed me, she thought it was quite amusing, she described you as strong willed, well that's the polite version.

I was hearing what Winston was saying but had no idea that Winston secretly admired me. Was I the centre of his romantic fantasies, or just a pleasant distraction in his head? He looked at me and grinned, I stared back beginning to feel lost in his eyes, we both leaned forward as our lips met. What were we doing? We were supposed to be escaping, not messing about kissing each other, however, in the heat of the moment, it felt like we were in each others protective cocoon, our pure and vulnerable selves on show. I pulled away quickly, he looked slightly dejected, "Jaz, it's ok." He uttered in a reassuring manner, taking hold of my hand and then hugging me tight. "Jaz, we have to get out of here." In that split second, his hug gave me a new found confidence. We both stood near to the door, the small stone room hung with a heavy air to it. "It is time, my friend, Candice and I will follow you separately, we will meet you at the edge of the rainforest," Winston said, I nodded and then he gave me specific instructions as to how to find my way out, carrying the tray with the hood up on the sweatshirt, giving the impression I was him in case we were being watched. He showed me how to walk like him, I copied him and got it down to a fine art quite quickly, it wasn't difficult., I could act when I needed to

Once outside, I was to leave the tray by the wall for Candice to collect. To the right of the building was a worn grassy area, I was to follow it straight until I came to a path that veered to the right, at this point I was to follow the path which would lead me into the rainforest. From there I should continue straight and should be able to find my way back to the safety of the shoreline. I was to leave the big wooden door slightly ajar in order that Winston could still get out after me, he didn't really have a concrete plan for this bit, but he assured me it would all be fine.

Winston checked I still had the pocket knife and torch, telling me not to show the beam until I was a safe distance away or if I could leave it until I was in the rainforest, even better. He picked up the tray and handed it to me. "Let's make haste before it gets too dark." I put the torch and pocket knife into the trouser pocket, took the tray from Winston, he kissed me on the forehead and whispered, "Keep yourself alert," as I made my way out of the door for the first time in a while. I glanced back, hoping he was about to follow close behind, but instead he was already on a mission, removing evidence, stuffing bits of paper into his pocket, "Winston" I said, he turned to face me, flicking his hand at me, "go Jaz, go, there is no time for goodbyes, I will see you soon." I felt very overwhelmed, I wanted him to come with me. I took a step forwards, my heart was thumping really fast in my chest, I took another step forwards, still I could hear my heart beat echoing in my ears, but I needed that confidence to come back, I had to do this.

I moved to just outside the door leaving it ajar just as he told me to. With every step I took, I became more and more terrified, my hands trembling, I felt hot and sweaty, the air was silent, nothing there, just darkness. I have to escape its my only chance. I continued clumsily forward, putting one foot in front the other, trying to walk as Winston had shown me, quickening my pace as I got more able to use my legs again. I did believe Winston that this would work, but I just couldn't shake the feeling that something wasn't right.

The corridor had a cold darkness to it, only a small ray of light showed the rough walls dwindling as it snaked away. I shuddered, my brain desperately trying to see the way out. I felt as if I couldn't breathe properly, as if the air was choking me, all I wanted to do was call Winston, then he would come running and save me, my knight in shining armour, but he wasn't going to do that, he would follow me in a bit, that's what he had said, but it was just me. I had to be strong, I had to do this. I felt sick to my stomach, but swallowed hard trying to replay in my head the instructions Winston had given me.

Quite quickly I came to the entrance of the stone building, I never realised that there was more to these buildings than meets the eye, I thought they were just huts, not huts that resembled bunkers. For the first time in over a week, I felt the warm air beating down on my skin, I squinted as the light streamed into my eyes making them water, I had not been used to so much light. As my eyes began to adjust, a sense of serenity and a peace seemed to want to invite itself into my soul, slightly odd feeling given my current situation.

I glanced back at the corridor, little stars seemed to bounce off the walls from the light, I hoped to see Winston's shape following behind me, but he wasn't there. I was startled by the sound of voices, which didn't seem too far away. In my bid for freedom, I placed the tray by the side of the building, adhering to my instructions, then, my heart still pounding, I began to run, run for my life. The trainers held me up a bit, each step, a mammoth undertaking, they were too big and my feet kept slipping out of them, maybe I should have taken them off. Having said that, they did have the most incredible bounce, as if they had tiny 'space hoppers' inside them. I kept running awkwardly, gasping, panic trembling throughout my body as I followed the path until I could see trees in front of me, this has to be the rainforest surely. It seemed closer than Winston had explained.

I came to a small opening in between the trees, I stopped for a nano second to catch my breath, turning around to see if anyone was chasing me and hoping to see Winston hot on my heels with Candice, but they weren't. Still very aware I was not at all free or safe yet and fully aware that I could be captured at any given time I had to keep going. My legs wouldn't move, they felt like jelly as the adrenaline surged so fast I almost vomited, the saliva thickening my mouth to a rancid paste. I wanted the hammering in my chest to quell, I have to keep running.

I was brought back to reality by the sound of gunshots resonated like a loud fire crackers hitting something hard. Every shot I heard fired ripped right through me, making my whole body feel numb. Any one of these shots could be the one to silence me and dull my eyes, taking me to a higher plane, a brutal reminder of what could happen if I was caught. Could these gunshots be the arrival of my heroes, Winston or Candice, or was it sound of them being slain. Oh my no, not the latter please, I was trying hard to convince myself that the sound had not caused a murder, a brutal shout from the coldest of lungs.

I hesitated, a deathly silence followed, as if everything around me was collaboratively holding its breath waiting for its next move. They had found out I had escaped, they were coming for me! I turned towards the rainforest and ran, it was my only chance of survival.

I was exhausted, my throat was so uncomfortably dry, my skin was roasting, and thick salty beads of sweat rolled over my skin more than ever. The once baggy clothes now clung to me in a wet hug, my legs were unsteady, shaking and painfully sore. I was stumbling instead of running, I was losing control, everything felt disconnected, the only reason I wasn't dead right now was because I hadn't been caught yet.

CHAPTER 21

Nightfall had graced the sky with its ambient deep hues. I took the torch from the pocket of the trousers. I pressed the button, feeling a reassuring clunk under my thumb as a beam powered into the night. The solid pure beam cut right through the darkness into the trees and beyond, but I then had second thoughts, if they were still out there searching for me, they would see the light, so not the best idea for now, I turned it off and replaced back in the trouser pocket.

I carried on as best I could but without any light, it was getting increasingly difficult, I couldn't really see where I was going and my body felt like it was being sucked by some colossal leech draining all my energy away, every one of my muscles seemed to be giving in to gravity, is this what it feels like to be a zombie?

Gnarled tree roots began to dip in and out of the ground their finger-like extensions grasping at the earth, making it even more treacherous under foot. I looked up briefly at their twisted branches rough with age, worn down by the moss that adorned them as they disappeared into the darkening sky. Amid the trees, small openings let the stars shine brightly through, like sugar spilt over black marble.

Darkness is supposed to be a strong protective arm, holding us close until the promised dawn, however this darkness just became confusing, robbing me of my senses and replacing them with a paralysing fear. I was so tired, any shadow made my brain create frightening magical beasts with jaws that were home to razor teeth, moving in all sorts of unnatural ways all ready to kill me with a sudden pounce. Gosh, there's a certain level of tiredness that really does equate to insanity, for me so much so, I'd like to temporarily dislocate my spirit from my body and just rest.

I had to listen to my body, I could run no more, I took a mis-step on the uneven ground and turned my foot over, twisting my ankle. Ouch, it was really painful, I could feel it beginning to swell up like a balloon and every step I took after that caused an unbearable pain to surge through my aching body. I had absolutely no idea where I was or where I was heading, there was no sign of the clearing Winston spoke of, the rainforest was intent on getting more and more dense. As my brain was on five percent battery and I was so physically exhausted, I had to rest, but my head kept reminding me that I wasn't free yet and had to move on for a bit.

Despite the air still being warm the darkness was suffocating me, like a damp, musty, thick blanket, clinging to every inch of my wet skin. Tears began to stream down my face, cascading into a waterfall, I was completely alone and lost and there were even more dark hours ahead of me. My feet were so sore and I began to tremble from fatigue, I needed this to end, I needed to see the opening and be free. The constant hammer of fear in my head tried to keep me alert telling me the fear will evaporate just like water, I just needed to keep going with confidence, fear is just an illusion.

I began to pant heavily and my mind continued to conjure up all manner of things. The rainforest was transforming itself into a lethal weapon, tree branches stretching out in front of me forming a cavern of distorted limbs, reaching out just far enough to grab me, clinging tight to my clothes as if to stop me in my tracks. I put the torch on, I felt far enough in now for the beam not be seen and it would help make everything I was imagining less distorted.

I looked down, shining the light at my feet, here come the ants, flowing over the earthen trail like some great celebratory procession might, splashing over my trainers, heading up towards my trousered legs. They were nothing like the harmless black ones we have in England, by comparison the ants in the Caribbean are weaponised, possibly the product of some evil genetic engineering genius. They are armour plated with large sharp mandibles and robotic legs which move almost too quickly to be tracked and then they take offence at everything around them, at this moment in time, that included me. I felt their sting as they fed on me for their dinner. What with these little blighters and the nights mosquitos, I was a bug magnet, a yummy morsel of food for their delight. The bites began to itch and irritate as they turned from tiny red dots to huge cratered volcanos that itched even more.

I couldn't cope any longer, every part of me became a melting pot of vulnerability. Before I could stop myself and not meaning to, the air became alive with my yells and pleas for help. I do realise that loss of control is a weakness, but my yelling came as an auditory version of tears as I was all cried out. I stamped my feet on the spot, like a child having a tantrum, trying to shake off the bugs, brushing at them with my hands while my feet crashed noisily on the carpet of leaves beneath me making my ankle throb even more. My chest had a heavy band around it from all yelling and crying, in fact every single muscle in my entire body had given up. I started to limp onwards for a couple of hundred yards, each step a negotiation rather than an order, wincing every time I moved, my ankle!

Then a sudden loss of concentration caused a miss-step and one of my trainers got caught in a tree root that was sticking out of the ground. I lurched forward loosing my footing and tumbled head over heels, managing to slide down an embankment in the process. As I put my hands down to try and break my fall, thorns pricked into my skin scratching it as if more evil flesh eating insects were out to get me.

Tears came again as if my pain had been condensed into a deluge of rain, pelting my skin like tiny hailstones. I looked at my hands through my watery eyes, blood seeped from the ripped flesh, the thick fluid mixed in with earth. I stared at the blood, numbed by the pain for a few seconds, until an intense burning pain hit me before momentarily passing out.

When I came to, the sound of cicadas was still buzzing and clicking, multitudes of them amplifying the noise into an overpowering high pitched hum, little frogs croaked to each other, the rainforest was alive with differing layers of sounds echoing around me, a choir of life. The noises were irritating all I wanted was to see blue sky and space again, my shack, not these virescent arms and lofty limbs of trees that groped at the sky. So in this noisy darkness, I sat, barely able to move, every muscle has seized up, my body's way of telling me it is struggling to recover, to repair the damage. This must be what prey feel like, having to stay still with an overwhelming paralysing fear.

My ankle felt like it had swollen to twice it usual size and was really throbbing, unable to move with any grace my movements were quite jerky, but I managed to move my blooded hands to the bottom of the trousers and then using every ounce of energy and strength I could muster, I ripped off a small length of material and wrapped it around my ankle for support. I heard the screams in my head as my hands trembled, they were so sore, as if they had shards of glass embedded in them, I don't know which was more painful my ankle or my hands. Gently I picked at the tiny cacti thorns that were still embedded in my ripped skin before cautiously wiping my hands with a semi wet leaf wincing as I did it.

I shifted uncomfortably on the earth beneath me, my throat was dry and sore, every lungful of the warmish air I inhaled felt like it drained more water from my already dehydrated body. There is a stake being hammered into me, it's strike radiating pain in a way that completely shatters me into tiny pieces, or at least that's what if feels like. I didn't want to move again, so I stayed still, breathing shallow, I had never known such pain in all my life and now there is now a pain at the back of my head threatening to grow into a powerful migraine.

My stomach gurgled frantically, crying out for sustenance, I picked up another wet leaf and began to lick it at first and then took a bite from it. It was disgusting, but I didn't care anymore, I just needed something to ease my thirst, I took another bite but the bitter taste just made me gag and almost vomit, I wanted to die!

I don't need to find the gateway to hell because I am already in it, I shuddered and whimpered pathetically to myself, I couldn't move without a plant or tree touching me. Having said that, the sheer denseness of the foliage around me made me feel weirdly cosy, but how on earth could a rainforest make you feel snug?
I can feel my heavy eyelids try to close, sleep wanting to come like a falling axe, but I have to try and fight it with

every last bit of energy reserve I have, if I fall asleep, I will be completely oblivious to my surroundings and defenceless to whatever the next few hours may bring, I have to stay awake, I feel utterly wired until I can't fight it anymore. Suddenly sleep is as instantaneous as it is unwelcome, dragging me into the shadowy world of dreams.

I'm not sure how long I slept for, but I woke suddenly, my brain already on the alert, my eyes scanning the surrounding area, becoming aware of a thin ray of light trying to squeeze its way through the trees. I still felt very afraid and alone, a constant vice squeezing with just enough pressure to be an unbearable pain, the fuel of my nightmares, the reason I struggle to breathe when I am awake. Where is the limit, when does the help begin? I need to know the answer, I really need to know.

The air was beginning to feel quite a bit warmer, almost reminiscent of a sauna, without a doubt I know I've slept too long. I began to panic, my chest began to burn, it felt like I had drunk something too hot and too fast, if only! I could smell ice cream melting in a cool glass of milkshake as my tongue gnawed at the roof of my parched mouth, this craving was unbearable, I really needed this to end now, who cares if they actually recaptured me, who cares if they killed me, I couldn't do this anymore.

I blinked and shook my head at the same time, ouch won't do that again in a hurry, every muscle ached so much. No longer was I a cohesive machine of blood and bone. They are my enemy, decaying and angry. My eyes fell again to the ground in front of me, normally inconsequential, but not now. Before my feet begin to move an inch, I can feel my jaw clench in anticipation and already I am resigned to the discomfort that will follow.

As I was about to try and move awkwardly, I became aware that I was no longer alone, there was a hooded body laying quite still at the bottom of the embankment, they were laying face down, not more than three feet beyond the radius of where I was. Whoever it was lay lifeless like a rag doll discarded onto the ground, limbs at awkward angles and head tilted forward in such a way that they were not sleeping, they were going to be dead. Cast aside as an abandoned shell left to rot in the open stagnant air of the rain forest.

I inhaled, I had to move from this position it was going to hurt , but I had to do it. As I breathed in, the air had a sickly, sweet odour a bit like a butchers shop, I hadn't noticed it before. I managed to crawl over in a lot of pain and with some trepidation. I touched a hand that was nearest to me, they were cold, stone cold, any life that had once dwelt within them had gone. I crawled a bit further and then with all my body weight managed to roll them over onto their back, it took some doing!

OMG! Winston, he was ghostly pale, his lips already bluish, his eyes staring, pupils exploded, he was now in some other place, perhaps in the arms of angels. I shook him, "Winston, wake up, stop messing." I wanted him to laugh, giggle or even say that this was all a big joke, but no such luck, his heart that used to beat with love was still, he really was dead. I began to cry again, well it was more than crying, it was desolate hysterical sobbing, an emotional pain that just entered me like a tsunami. "Oh, Winston, why, Why?" I sat next to his lifeless form, sobbing and sobbing until there was nothing left to cry, only a raw emptiness nibbling at my insides like a hungry rat. My eyeballs hung heavy in their sockets, my entire body felt bruised, in the same way as with a physical bruise. My grief felt so strong I could feel myself being swept away, letting it remove me from the real world.

The sun seemed to filter through more broken areas between trees, helping them to reach for the blue above, they will grow so tall, as if they knew they were born to become giants in this world. But not Winston, the birds were singing in bursts of melody, but he could not hear them, for him there was no beauty left in this world, just a blackness. Winston had put his life in danger for me, had he now died for me as well? A conflict of emotions flushed through me, guilt, regret, anger, all of them trying to protect me from the overwhelming pain and emptiness I felt. I had failed myself, and Winston, what about Candice, where was she?

I was sure Winston had been murdered, left to be consumed by the animals and insects of the rainforest, slowly giving up his flesh to the soil, bearing his bones to the sun, all because of me, he has departed, left for a new life, a new existence. I laid on my side next to him and kissed his head, lightly stroking his black hair, willing him to wake up and speak to me, when really I needed to bid him farewell and get to safety, If they had killed Winston, they would still be looking for me. I couldn't help Winston anymore, but I could still help myself, I sunk my teeth into my lower lip, so many questions going through my mind, why did they do this, was he alive when they dumped him? If only I hadn't fallen asleep, he would still be alive, wouldn't he? Where is Candice, are they watching me?

I decided that despite possibly putting myself into more danger, I would stay with Winston for a while, I know it seems weird but I needed to do the right thing by him, I wanted him to feel loved, I didn't want him to be alone. I rested my head on his chest, I closed my eyes willing his heart to beat once more. Blackness filled the edges of my vision as the only thing I could hear was my own heartbeat. I patted his chest and whispered "Winston, I am so very sorry, it wasn't meant to be like this, please be at peace. This is only the end of one chapter, my friend, your spirit is still alive I can feel it, we just have to connect in a different way." I looked up and closed his eyes, kissing his blue, cold lips.

Slowly, I moved from his lifeless body and began to haphazardly gather some fallen leaves, cutting larger leaves in half with the penknife, the pain in my hands was nothing in comparison to my heartache, I wanted to do this for Winston. I placed his penknife back in his hand, just in case he needed it for his onward journey, then covered his body in a blanket of warm leaves, kissing him goodnight once more before covering his face. I couldn't dig a grave, but I could do the next best thing for him.

I patted the top of the leaves ensuring he was tucked inside his cosy blanket and whispered, "I will come back for you Winston, I promise, you won't be alone for long." Then, with all my might I managed to roll a rock I found nearby and half-buried it in the ground next to him before looking around to ensure I would actually be able to trace my steps and find him again.

A gentle breeze came to whisper the story of a powerful passion and the sun shone even more brilliantly through the trees with more virescent colours, Winston's soul was alive, it still didn't remove the greyness of my emotions, I was still struggling to hold back the grief and my tears were still ready to flow, but in time I will let the good memories flood in and allow smiles and warmth and those funny or sweet things that were once said, but for now everything was too raw. I will seek justice for him.

CHAPTER 22

I put one hand and leant against a tree, my fingertips gripping into the crevices that ran through the bark. Under my trainers the leaves seemed as noisy as the static in my head, nothing was making sense anymore, Winston was gone, there was no reason for the world to exist anymore. I willed the world to dissolve around me, just melt away, yet I could still feel the sadness through the gentle breeze that refused to reflect the howling pain, that tore through my body. I had to muster the strength to leave Winston and carry on, no one said this was going to be easy, I should be the one lying there dead, not him. I will definitely make sure he would have a proper grave and a joyous celebration of his life, I owed him that much.

I started to hobble, trying to gather some momentum and continuing to glance back a few times, I still felt uneasy about leaving and also hoped I would see Candice, I needed a friend right now, but she wasn't there, so the only logical thing to do was to save my own skin and get justice for Winston, this was the only way. A continuous excruciating throbbing from my ankle reminded me that this was not going to be an easy task. I had forgotten about it when I was with Winston, but now, I felt so unwell again, headache, many aches and pains everywhere, hunger, thirst, no energy,

I felt like I my body was about to self destruct, well if I am going to die out here, I want it to be swift and in the most kind and gentle manner possible, in the end it isn't dying that scares me so much but a long lingering pain and being alone.

As I continue to make slow progress forwards, everything looked so big, the leaves, the insects, the imagined predators, I know it's just my mind playing tricks on me, I am simply very disorientated in this rainforest, it is like being dropped far out into the ocean, only it is not blue but I am submerged in a million subtle greens. Every moment I am here passes untreasured until I can get back to my shack and a steady supply of food and drink.

I never knew that dehydration was so painful, as I limped on I couldn't turn off my thoughts, of a tall iced glass of water. I couldn't suppress the wanting for a drink, its my number one item in flashing neon light. I felt a white paste upon my lips as I touched them with my finger, they felt withered to crinkled versions of what they should be. Even the corners of my mouth ached, my skin made less flexible by dryness and it hurt so much to swallow or yawn, it was going to be like this until I had the chance for a substantial drink.

I licked my lips, I couldn't see any obvious way to go, I was trapped in what felt like a cage that was closing in around me, sealing off any viable exit. Lianas, a type of English bindweed had taken on the appearance of slithering snakes and every shadow from the awakened sun resembled a crouching jaguar. I hobbled a few more paces forward, my senses on red alert, my head alive with thoughts that I really needed to release rather than let churn around inside and scare me, I had to focus. I couldn't stop thinking about Winston's killer, were they lurking, waiting for me? How I would I manage to fight back if they jumped out on me? Well, probably with some horrible, abject, overkill and brutality that they deserved, but in reality there was no way I was strong enough for that. For goodness sake, I had to get to safety, I had to do this for Winston.

Despite the now oppressive heat, I continued to struggle on for what seemed like ages, limping awkwardly as I tentatively put one step in front of the other, wincing from the pain, perspiration adorned my skin like condensation on a window pane and dripped from my hair. I felt so hot in these clothes, everything stuck to me like a second skin. I could feel nausea rising up from my stomach ready to lurch forward at any time, my legs felt like they didn't belong to me, they struggled to hold my weight.

I felt as if I was going mad, imagining the worst nightmare I have ever had, unable to wake up from it because I am already awake. I am an extinguished fire, one that used to know happiness and a future, now my mind is dark, subsisting on the burnt tinder of who I was. All I can do is, live from heartbeat to heartbeat. I feel like the world isn't really there at all, it has been stolen and replaced with something empty, photoshopped, fake. All I can do is flounder in this never ending void.

One of the hundreds of hanging vines brushed against my skin, I shivered as if I had a fever, I need a cool breeze to pass over my skin, I need to drink, I have to get water, my throat is now so parched that the burning sensation that is growing steadily stronger is harder to ignore. This was the unbearable delirium of dehydration. I wanted to scream but needed to conserve my energy to hobble on. I stopped momentarily to catch my breath and try to find some sort of bearing. There is probably more life here, per square metre than anywhere else on the planet.

Bugs zipped in and out in front of me, humming and buzzing their little annoying songs, landing on my exposed skin and making their way into my torn clothes their bites causing more small mountains of itchiness to go with the existing ones. I waved my hand in an attempt to scare them and slapped at my sore skin, killing a few more.
My irritability levels increase ten-fold and my logic decreases as if locked into some inverse relationship, I am completely lost and disorientated, Candice has not made it to me, was she dead as well?

I stared in front of me, the more I stared, the more the foliage seemed to break formation and open out to a small clearing. The trees seemed to unfold and become nothing more than vibrant strains of colour, revealing pure sunlight,

was this a mirage, was I seeing things? Whatever it was, a
new warmth invited my lips to produce a tiny smile of hope,
I had made it, well nearly. A new surge of endorphins
seemed to release a new energy, making me move forward at
a faster pace, my pain momentarily disappearing as the trees
continued to separate further apart and give way to a new
type of music from the beach ahead, a percussion section of
waves performing their soft rolls from the stoney seabed
below.

As the ocean came into view, some of the woody overhanging
branches of the vines continued to try and hide the sand
from sight, crawling onto them as if to try and take it
hostage. I almost broke into a hobbled run, ignoring the
surging pain that had now reappeared. I caught my footing
in one of the vines and fell forwards onto the sand, landing
on my knees the sand was the softest golden hill ever, its
grains offering a steady warmth from the grains. The beach
stretched out alongside the water, these constant friends
chattering as the water came in reassuring me. This was the
gateway, the place where two different worlds collided and
where mine began to feel a little more familiar and possibly
dare I say it, a little bit safer.

I laid down on the sand, the suns rays warmth in their
brilliance, reflecting a shimmer from the ends of my
eyelashes, inviting my eyes to rest. I let it seep into my skin,
as my heart took on a steady ambient rhythm soothing me,
from water to sunlit air, the briny aroma has all the callings

of home. A gentle ocean breeze wrapped itself around me as if to cosy me in the warmest of soft towels and I began to feel myself fall asleep.

All to brief I was awake again, my body jerking into action, my "on" button had been pushed by a new electricity circulating through parts of me it didn't before. I sat up feeling the adrenaline pump through me, a sort of funfair ride taking away my chance to rest. I looked around me and began to become lost in watching the waves coming in and out, transient yet always there, rising and falling, scattering the light, the hue of the water ever changing yet always that familiar turquoise blue. As they crept towards me before running away, those loving rascals, sun-warmed and sweet, repeated their ebb and flow in a cycle that caused droplets of salty water to spray onto my now bare, sand-encrusted feet.

Beyond the magical waves was something even more amazing and breath-taking, the colours of the sky, beautiful smudges of coral, lavender, turquoise, and a fiery orange ball blended together to create a sight so astounding that momentarily, it swept me away from all of my worries. A warm feeling of security began to overwhelm me as I realised that if I kept to the shoreline, my shack, my little place I called home would eventually be within my reach, I was almost there, "A stones throw away" as my mother would say. This vast ocean in front of me would keep me safe and be my guide home, to a place I would be safe and free once more, no one could get me there, could they? There was that doubt again. I couldn't sit back on my laurels just yet but I did have a bit of relief beginning to wash over me.

I crawled forward on my hands and knees and let the water lap around me, fizzing and bubbling for a moment longer. The shoreline was such a graceful arc of sand, I felt comforted as I shifted my head slowly from side to side letting the gentle breeze caress my face once more. I crawled a bit further, moving like my knees were hinges, wobbling to and fro as I made it into the blue-green water. I let the salty brine flow over my skin, the water moving around me in swirls, creating a buoyancy and sense of freedom for my sore and aching body. I cupped my hands and drank some of the salty water, it felt so good in this heat, the greatest luxury on earth. I felt a chill surged through me and my head made an involuntary shake as if to feel disgust at what I had just done, followed by a numbness, then I vomited back up the water.

I made my way out of the water with some difficulty, it felt like treacle sticking to me. Exhausted I fell back on the warm sand, melting into the soft golden blanket beneath me I picked up a piece of seaweed that was next to me and took a bite, I was so hungry anything would suffice at this moment in time, goodness only knows what I was thinking, I had just been sick and the salt was not welcomed by my stomach, so I was sick again, I wanted to drift into a world of sleep, wake up and be at home, but I couldn't not yet.

I looked to the left of me, familiar mangroves stretched out across the flats and shallows of the shoreline, if I am not mistaken, I think I am on the other side of the Island, I am sure Mogsey had brought Candice and I here in his boat a while ago when we wanted somewhere quiet to sunbathe if you catch my drift. If I am right, I think I can just about muster enough energy to stumble the rest of the way to my shack, it would take me a while but I could make it, I'm sure, well I don't really have any other options.

I hauled myself drained, stressed and what felt like too thin a body to cope with life's storms anymore to a sitting position, my stomach ached, my chest felt tight but I had to make it. I hugged my knees with my hands and rocked back and forth gently, I yawned, it's simply a level of worn-out-ness that makes my body hurt I will finish, I am nearly home, I told myself.

My brain begged me for rest but it would have to wait, I took once last look around, there was a haunting solitary beauty to the gnarled trees behind me which I had never noticed before, then with my last energy reserves and a lot of concentration, I adjusted the torn hoody cloth around my ankle and stood up discarding the trainers on the beach, thankfully I could walk barefoot the rest of the way. I took a couple of awkward steps forward, but it was quite difficult, as the sand shifted, so with every motion forward there was some backward motion, just like walking in fresh fallen snow. Yet unlike the crystalline blanket of white bequeathed by the winter time in England, the fine Caribbean grains under foot gave me warmth.

I had only taken about four steps before I had second thoughts about leaving the trainers on the beach, my conscience got the better of me. How many whales and dolphins would choke on pollution or die with stomachs full of garbage before effective action is taken? I didn't want to be part of that, so I picked then back up and carried them by their laces. I suppose because of my recent thoughts, my eyes were taken in by the elegant ocean once more, the waves rolling in, white tipped, spreading themselves like fine lace over the beach after they arrive at their destination in their soft way. It is beautiful to watch as long as we don't become complacent, the ocean does not care who it takes.

I stepped off the sparingly loose sand and onto the sandy sponge sand next to the waters edge, thinking it would be easier to walk on, clearly I was wrong, as my feet were absorbed and enveloped by this sandy sponge, sinking in with every step. Every now and again, it got a little bit more challenging as the finger like roots of the mangroves stretched into the water, making it even more of an effort to lift my legs over them. Despite my overwhelming tiredness, my eyes could still act like a camera, catching every corner of the landscape, blinking, staying alert, my radar scanning the whole time.

Sooner than I could possibly have imagined, I caught a glimpse of Blot's tin shed where he stored his nets, in the not so far distance not much further now I kept telling myself. I stopped again to catch my breath, I couldn't stop too long in case I ceased up. I fixed my gaze firmly ahead, squinting a little, then it came into view, there it was, my home, my place of refuge. I felt all my fears diminish, as a she warrior inside me broke free, a feeling of inner courage surged through my body, empowering me. I could do anything, I was fearless, unstoppable, nothing could hold me back from reaching my shack now, I had made it.

I took the deepest breath I could and spurred myself on, heaving my legs, feeling like I was wading through sticky glue, my eyes so tired, they could only squint letting in just enough light to navigate, there was no way I was going to slacken my pace now, even the rainbow flame in the evening sky as the sun began to set wouldn't stop me. I kept repeating "keep going, each step will take you closer to home, each step will take you closer to home."

By the time I did eventually reach my shack it was enveloped in a blanket of semi-darkness, the deck lights had come on and the familiar yellow glow made it feel warm and welcoming. A sudden wave of panic hit me, I had come so far, but how was I going to get inside, my bag was taken, with my keys inside. Candice had a key, but where was she? Then I remembered, I usually left the back door unlocked, a bad habit I know but it was safe enough around here, if anything was tried, they would have the coals to answer to. I relaxed a bit before the next wave of panic hit, what if the killers were here in my home waiting for me, what if it had been burgled?

I walked around the side and twisted the metal doorknob of the back door with ease, phew! It was still warm against my palm, so made me release quite quickly as it burnt my prickled skin causing me to yelp. Opening the door slowly, I peered inside, the lights had come on and on the surface, all looked ok, nothing touched, I felt a sudden comfort as I went inside, I fell into a heap on the floor completely drained and totally exhausted. I was a tortoise retracting into my shell, trying to evaporate recent events from my mind, at last, nobody was here, I was safe in my sanctuary, my cocoon and place to rest.

CHAPTER 23

I was utterly relieved, at last, my homestead, the teddy bear of my emotions, my walls are my embrace and my protection. I resembled a clockwork soldier, so tense, I ached and hurt so much, it was as much as I could do to pick myself up off the floor. I tried to gently loll my head in a circle, but I became dizzy and nauseous so thought better of it.

I managed to haul myself up onto my couch and luckily for me was able to initially take some comfort in drinking half a small carton of juice I had left on the side table. I turned on the radio and rested my head back trying to relax to the music, I closed my eyes and let the music soothe me. Despite needing something more to drink and something to eat, I just needed to rest for bit, my body telling me so very powerfully not to move anymore unless I wanted to be sick. Before I knew it, I was asleep.

When I woke, the radio had stopped, I had been meaning to change the batteries for ages but never got around to it, I needed to drink, eat, wash and then sleep more. It was all I could do to put one foot in front of the other but I somehow managed to make myself a cup of tea, eat a biscuit and run a bath, before heaving myself into the tub.

I slid down into the water, trying to block out all sounds and thoughts and instead relish the calming peace of escape that is my bath, but that is easier said than done. Soaking in my warm and fragrant bubble bath was shear bliss but extremely sore on my skin, it hurt when I dabbed the bruises and cuts. Maybe from my bubble bath cocoon I can emerge as an energised butterfly and awake, from past events being only a dream, some hope! Eventually I managed to find the use of my legs and get then to heave my body out of the bath, I patted myself dry, applied as much Savlon as I dared and took an aspirin to help ease the discomfort. Exhausted and too tired to eat anything more, I fell into bed, my linen sheets were my heaven, I loved my bed so much, even more so now, it gave me a sense of my mother's hug, so much so, I fell asleep again in an instant.

I awoke suddenly, as if there was an emergency, as if sleeping was actually a dangerous thing to do, I know I had been dreaming of Iberville, but was I still there. My heartbeat ponded in my chest and my brain instantly buzzed trying erratically make out if I really was in my own home.

In the few hours I've actually slept, I must have woken up six times, not for that long each time, but enough to break my sleep into unrefreshing chunks, that with every disturbance cause a new nightmare. Slowly and reluctantly I peered out from under my soft duvet, blinked and blinked again as streaks of sunlight penetrated the bedroom window trying to blind me. I sat up slowly dragging my feet off the bed and rubbing my sore knuckles into my eyes, Ouch! Dare I try to stretch my arms above my head, probably not. My muscles felt as though they had been flash-burned with acid from the inside to out, replacing them with ageing rubber bands, thick and twisted. I yawned instead and watched my legs dangle above the floor as I tried to summon the energy to go any further.

I managed to make it to the window and drew back the curtains. Through the glass was the ever changing art of the sky, the clouds that brought infinite images of beauty. There was something in that feeling of gratitude, for being able to spend a moment gazing into the blue, I watched the cloud patterns change as they flowed across the sky.

I managed to side step with a lot of concentration across to the mirror on the dressing table and plopped myself down in preparation for what I would see, I hadn't been bothered last night. As I looked in the mirror, what a sight to behold, my eyelids were droopy, drunk with fatigue, against my ghostly skin were purple welts that will only deepen over the coming week, they look grotesque, but I know I am lucky not to have any broken bones. I looked positively cadaver like, my spirit left snuggling under the duvet. Why couldn't this be a magic mirror showing the beauty within me, rather than the zombie it was reflecting? I couldn't be bothered too much about my appearance, I needed something to drink, my limbs felt far too heavy for me and my ankle was swollen beyond recognition, it was all I could do to hobble slowly. As I managed to take tentative steps, it was as if I was having a personal struggle against my own gravity. I would wobble every few steps before correcting my balance and moving on, holding tightly onto any object in the vicinity in case I fell.

After overcoming that challenge, I reached the kitchen and made myself something to eat and drink and took more aspirin to ease my throbbing head and ankle and sore heavy limbs. I moved back to the fridge, consuming yet more food as if it was going out of fashion, cramming it in thick and fast, a way to nurture myself to show my body that it was worth the effort of nutrition.

I sat at the kitchen table, drinking my third cup of coffee and listening to the random sounds that came sailing by the open window in the gentle breeze. The sounds of the creative and loving universe, birds, sea are the tuning fork of my soul as I sat there staring ahead at nothing in particular. I know it's lazy, I'm always lazy when I'm tired, tired in brain or body, its a form of protection, yet in reality there are jobs that need doing and I'm the only one who can get them done. So, lazy feelings or not, I have to get back to putting a few things in order each day and get back to a routine. First I needed to process everything and rest some more in order for me to regain any sense of tranquility, I still felt conflicted and bitter, I needed to resolve this inner battle of me vs me?

Just as I was about to come up with the answer, a wave of nausea came from nowhere, I retched and my stomach lurched as I just about made it to the kitchen sink before my expulsion happened. Yuk! I rinsed my mouth round, cleaned up the vomit and slowly made my way into the lounge and sat down on the couch to rest. I needed a distraction and some love, well for now anyway. I picked up my house phone and dialled my parents number, I wanted to hear my mum's warm voice more than anything. I also needed to be able to lie convincingly to her, for now so that she wouldn't panic, when she asked lots of questions about my lack of phone calls to her.

I stared vacantly into space whilst it rang, thinking of a tangible excuse, one, two, three rings and there she was. "Hello, hello." No matter how big I was, mums voice always had the magical power to be my shelter, my guardian, always with an open door and a love that is so huge it embraces you into a virtual hug. She seems to love most things I do, praises me, listens to me and makes jovial conversation, but most of all show me unconditional love. I'd swap every possession I ever owned to keep my mum if I needed to.

Right now, I needed her to be my refuge from the craziness of my current life's storm. "Mum, it's me" I replied. "Jasmine, darling, thank goodness, my darling girl we have been worried sick, me and your father, didn't know what to think." Then came the questions. Where have you been, did something happen? We haven't heard from you in a while, we got so worried, dad even tried your work but couldn't get hold of anyone, are you ok?" I sighed having some difficulty trying to process all the questions being fired at me all at once. "Slow down mum, I'm sorry, I didn't. Mean to worry you both, I'm ok, really." I paused again for a nano second, but not long enough for her to sense anything was wrong. Should I tell her the truth now? No, not a good idea, not yet anyway, they were a long way away and I didn't want to worry them unnecessarily and I needed to sort it all out in my head first and feel better. "Jasmine, you sure you are ok? You sound a bit hesitant." She said. "Sorry, sorry mum, I'm still a bit preoccupied with work, I've been on an undercover case, reporting about." Mmhm, what should I say? "Murders and got carried away with it, I lost all sense of time, I didn't mean to worry you, work couldn't speak with you if they had answered, breach of confidentiality and my safety, etc." I said hoping that would be enough of an excuse. "Well, a phone call to let us know you were safe from them would have been helpful, we have been going out of our minds. I was going to call the police, but dad said our boys in blue wouldn't be able to do anything." "Sorry, I will speak to work." Was all I managed to say before mum screeched, "Did you say murders? Tell me all about it."

She sounded so excited, if only she knew the real truth, she would soon, but this is not the time. "I can't, not yet mum, I need to get everything signed off first and run it past Petra, then I will reveal all, in our next phone call, I promise." By the sound of her voice, I could tell she thought it was all a bit dubious and her sixth sense told her I was not telling the whole truth, but she didn't push it further. Instead, for the next hour, I felt calmer and better in myself as we chatted about aunties, uncles and their antics, the state of the village, what was new, what she was cooking for tea, etc. Just the sound of her words seemed to anchor me, forget my troubles, regardless of where I am, she makes me feel comforted.

I do love our conversations, always have, yes we have our ups and downs like all mothers and daughters, probably because we are so alike, neither of us can run our brains in nihilistic thought patterns, instead we just chat with the freedom and any direction it takes us in. Most of our conversations usually feature at some point, topics of the day, either here or in Sussex, news, family, money and odd goings on in the village, I had missed this so much. Out of the blue, I thought I better let mum know that I didn't have my mobile. "Um mum, must tell you, I have managed to loose my mobile so can we chat via my house phone until I get another. I will call you so its not so expensive if that is ok?" So many questions were fired off again, did I know where was it, how did I manage to lose it, did I need money for a new one, would the number be the same?

Luckily we had to end the call abruptly due to an unexpected knock at the door, which saved me from any further interrogation. I had started to relax, but now a panic began to flow through me, growing stronger by the second as my mental faculties gave way to my emotions. I started to shake absolutely terrified, I felt like jumping out of my skin and join the ether, anything to avoid what lay in wait for me. Already I felt as if I couldn't draw a breath in, as if concrete had been poured into my airways. The panic and lack of air drove me to start gasping, panting as if the oxygen had been sucked from the air around me. I doubled over and sunk to my knees, one hand on the ground to support my weight and steady myself. My thoughts were becoming jumbled as the panic swirled inside me, it was them, they had come for me, they were going to kill me, I had no time to alert anyone.

Terrified, I managed to move slowly towards the door and then tried to peer through the slit at the side of the door to see who it was. I was going to be murdered, this was my fate, I expected to cry yet in truth I felt nothing at all, maybe after all I had gone through I would never feel anything ever again, but of course that was not true, it was just a stress response really. Iberville would be difficult to reverse and will have long lasting consequences, but I do need to take back control. Relief overwhelmed me, as the figure through the door slit happened to be Blot, cautiously I opened the door, still wearing my pjs. He looked me up and down before saying, "Yuh bac den, Wi missed yuh, Hab yuh hear seh Winston Hav bin fine dead uppa Iberville." My brain stuttered to a halt for a moment, as I stood thee motionless, unable to move or say anything until my thoughts caught up. His name bounced around inside my head, I tried not to show any emotion or even that I knew, but it was not easy.

I hesitated before replying, trying to hold back the tears, all I could manage was, "Err, w-what, no, how?" "Nuh kno details

Jus wondered eff yuh kno A wuk wid him an all dat Did tink yuh shud kno Si yuh." With that, Blot turned, waved and meandered back up the road without looking back, I wanted to shout after him and get him to come in for some company, but he was never one to visit people, meet him at the bar and he could talk for Britain, well, Caribbean anyway, but to chat in someones home was a big no, no in his book.

I stood at my half opened door staring into space, before realising my attire and quickly closing the world off from me again. Sadness reappeared in my eyes as I thought of Winston, my heart became really heavy, a true ache, Winston had died for me and I had left him there alone, I was supposed to be getting justice, not wallowing in my own self pity. An awful hollowness, a wave of wretchedness threatened to engulf my mind, body and soul, as I mumbled, "Oh Winston, you should be here, I miss you, why didn't I figure it all out and save you?" I hobbled back upstairs to the bedroom and fell onto the bed, grief comes at such random moments, but the feelings are so strong I felt like I was being swept away, before they are replaced feeling of normalcy and those familiar tears. I must have cried myself to sleep.

The next few days and nights seemed to all roll into one, every night I tried to fall asleep but I found it was near impossible. My head was constantly filled with thoughts flooding my unconscious, making it work overtime, replaying every little detail, looking back in hindsight, thinking if only I had.... Eventually I would doze off about half past four in the morning, leaving me two and a half hours until the glare of the sun woke me once more. My eyes were bloodshot and defined with heavy black creases, I was exhausted from lack of sleep and stress, I hadn't answered the phone and post must have been piling up in my mailbox as the mail man had now resorted to leaving it outside my door. I felt like I was going insane, but deep down knew that most forms of mental illness only arise from ongoing stress.

I actually hadn't left the house for anything, not even food shopping, since I had got back, I was too afraid to leave my safe sanctuary. I was down to my last few rations and would completely run out by tomorrow, I had to pull myself together, surely I would be safe now and I owed it to Winston, if he could lose his life for me, I could get my life back and get justice for him.

I had never felt so alone, so lost, so incapable of doing even the smallest tasks, after several long days of being alone, I hoped the pain would ebb, but I was wrong. I needed to confide in my mum and talk to work, but I couldn't, not yet. In my situation such as this it would be odd to not have anxiety and I know what I am going to have to face is going to be difficult, but realising why I am anxious means at least I know I am in a cage and I need to find the door and the key, well, it's a start. Right, today is the day that my state of simply existing as a matter of will power will turn into bravery. Mum always says that you come out of bad experiences stronger and wiser, I guess that's true. I'm still the same person, I have a loving heart, I am a good person I am proud to say, I'm just a bit battered and need to find my idealism and courage again.

My first step in my bravery mission to conquer was to get dressed and turn on the computer. I would go food shopping later. I think I made the wrong decision as flashing messages from work appeared, one after the other, asking me to contact them urgently, what was going on, I had made no contact during my trip? Confused by it all, I actually opened one email from Petra, it appeared that Tilly had told her she sent me to France to cover a story on some 'Revolts.' However in another email Petra said she had been confided in and knew everything and seemed genuinely concerned for my well being. I was very aware I had to reply, but not yet, just one more day that's all I would need. This was stupid, I was supposed to be finding my courage, I couldn't let fear rule my life. I could hear my mother say, "Jasmine, Don't put off until tomorrow what you can do today." I had to call Petra, I had go out, I needed food.

Right I would definitely conquer the food issue now, I took a deep breath, gathered my keys from the bowl near the door and plucked up the courage to leave the sanctuary of my shack for the first times in days. As I stepped outside the door and closed it behind me, panic began to fire off inside me like a cluster of spark plugs, I felt the tension grow throughout, making every limb, every feature of me hurt, my breathing became more rapid and shallow. I closed my eyes and gripped the door handle tightly, willing myself to let go and move further away, but I was frozen to the spot. Somewhat reluctantly, I managed to gain control and was able to release my grip on the handle, I took a deeper breath and opened my eyes, the softening sun stroking my skin with a slight calming effect. Looking up, squinting, I noticed a few clouds had gathered, they were a brilliant white against the blue sky. I could still hear each of my breaths rasping but I had to do this. I put one foot in front of the other and luckily for me the rest of me seemed to follow, scanning the surrounding area as I went.

As I limped down the street to the local store, which was actually a small wooden shed, selling all sorts, I began to relax slightly, this wasn't so bad, the old houses still stood dishevelled, windows long shattered in the weakness of their structures, families still sitting outside their homes that looked abandoned, waving at me. The locals still passing the time of day 'limin' propping up fences, smoking joints and gesticulating as I strolled by, "Hey Jaz," just like nothing had ever happened. Very weird! Surely they must have noticed I had not been around for a while.

All too soon the store came into sight, I amazed myself that I seemed to have reached it in record time, especially with my ankle. I was quite proud that I had managed to claw myself out of the mire of dysfunction I've been lost in and had managed to make this simple task feel quite easy. Nothing had happened to me, I was going to be safe, no one was after me.

The local store was wedged between two taller houses and still had the old sign hanging outside, but some of the letters had become illegible as the paint had peeled off in the heat of the sun. I walked in, there was Agwae, sat just inside the door taking on his usual stance, I mean doing nothing. "Waa gwaan" which translated means "what's up," "oh nothing, just my usual shop" I said trying to avoid eye contact, "Yuh hear seh bout Winston he did murdered body all did messed up buried alive he did." A hollowness, a shell, holding in a thousand oceans of tears wanted to erupt once more, luckily, I managed to quash them as I stood there. I'm sure Agwae could see the sadness draining through me, travelling through every cell until it reached the ground. "Er yes I heard, so very, very sad" I replied.

I know it sounds quite barbaric but I moved to the back of the shop and tried to busy myself, gathering food and sundry supplies. I didn't want to be outside anymore, my bravery was fading fast, I needed to return back to the shack as quickly as I could, without engaging in anymore unnecessary conversation. I know it sounds selfish, but even if it is, to hell with the rest of the world and their opinions, they didn't know what I was going through, they didn't know I buried Winston, I can't deal with this. I paid and left, scurrying back down the street like a frightened mouse.

CHAPTER 24

Once safely back in my shack, I packed away the food and made myself some ackee and salt fish, I must admit, I did feel better after venturing out, making myself food and eating something more substantial. I know I shouldn't have, but I then opened a bottle of my favourite wine, it was quite early to partake in alcohol really, but needs must. I sat down at my desk staring at the computer screen as it slowly whirred into action, it gave me enough time to find something to put my foot on to help reduce the swelling, I hadn't realised how black and blue it was. Eventually the computer sprang to life, a stack of e-mails flashed at me, "Great." I made the decision that I would answer the emails and ring work, then I would go into the office tomorrow. I took a sip of the wine, dutch courage, it did help.

I scanned through, deleted most of them which were advertising sites I had looked at before, a couple from my parents with photos of the new library in their village and details of their days out to some familiar places, whilst trying to relive their youth. The messages that looked important, I pulled up one by one and read them, I had to respond to Petra at the Alise as there were several e-mails, all of the same content, asking me to contact her urgently. Initially she still thought I was investigating France's struggle to quell revolts on the Caribbean Islands of Guadeloupe and Martinique, amid fears that strikes and street protests could spread to other French overseas departments. Thats what Tilly had told her. The last ones were where she was genuinely concerned, Winston and Candice had spoken with her and she was doing what she could. There were some from Goldie too, asking if I was ok, she wanted to come out to me in France but Tilly had told her it was too dangerous.

It's now or never, another sip of wine and I picked up the receiver, dialling work, Goldie answered. "Hello" I uttered, trying to sound measured and controlled, "Jaz Weh a yuh Tilly did tell wi yuh anda cova eena France Afta finding sinting out. A yuh bac yah now? Petra waah yuh too Shi a a bi a try tuh reach yuh everyday." There was something in the way Goldie always spoke, that gave her away, a keenness to seek out information, coupled with the fact that she had made up her own language and very few people actually understood what she was saying. "Jaz, Wah deh a go pan, Wah mek didn't yuh call mi?" "Um sorry Goldie, I'm ok, just need to get myself together, I will come into the Alise tomorrow and tell you everything, I promise. I need to speak to Petra." By now my confidence was beginning to waver and she knew that. "Shall mi cum ova now?" I wanted to say yes, in truth I needed her, but, I wasn't ready, so instead replied, " Goldie I'm ok, really, no need to come over, I will see you tomorrow." With that she made me promise to call if I needed to talk and then put me through to Petra saying, "Ok sure ting girlfriend, wi will si yuh first light."

You could feel the relief in Petra's voice, "Jaz, thank God, I was about to go to the local authorities if I hadn't heard from you by end of play today. I know what happened, it will be ok." I never really knew Petra, she was the boss and that's all I needed to know, I started to explain a few bits but it was so garbled, how she understood was anyones guess. As time went by, it became an easy conversation, she listened and replied with words that had a heartfelt kindness to them, her concern was genuine, so natural. She asked if I needed anything or her to come over and after declining on both accounts, she told me that she would send Goldie to collect me the following morning and bring me to the office, she gave me her personal telephone number and made me promise to call her at any time if I needed to, but for now to rest a bit.

By the time we had finished our conversation, I had been on the phone for most of the afternoon, which was good to make it fly by. I hadn't even noticed how hot it had been or felt the sun shining through the windows. I had spent the whole time absorbed by the computer and talking to Petra. I closed the computer down and lolloped onto the sofa grabbing the remote as I went. I switched on the TV as the news came on. I had forgotten about my ankle, until a twinge reminded me, I sat forward, rubbing it with my handed then put my feet up on the sofa. The swelling had gone down quite a bit, well I hadn't really walked on it very much, so that had helped. As I looked at the television screen a photo of Winston stared back at me, smiling, a photo taken a while ago, he looked so handsome, if only I had noticed him before at work, to think I was his secret crush and he would do anything for me, well he did the ultimate thing for me, died!

The news reader continued, "A man's body has been found in the rainforest grounds of the Iberville Estate. It is believed to be that of Winston Ristil. He had been reported missing on Sunday, his body was found after an anonymous tip off by a member of the public. He had sustained gunshot wounds to the head, it is not yet clear as to why he was there or why he died. A full investigation has been launched"

I didn't hear the rest of the news, as tears started to form which then grew and turned into hysterical sobbing, it was still so painful, so much heartache. I grabbed a cushion, hugging it for support as I shook uncontrollably, my tears were an unstoppable tsunami. I cried until my head throbbed and no more tears would come, my eyes felt red and sore. I screamed, like a child, my primal mind crying out for the love that evolution has taught it to expect and made my head throb more in the process. There was so much anger behind my sadness, just go to show how fragile we humans are.

I switched off the television and made my way upstairs to the bathroom, I stared in the mirror, my gaze caught its reflection, I didn't look like me, so ghostly pale, bloodshot eyes with dark bags underneath, my smile had disappeared, leaving my face completely expressionless, my gravity-drawn shoulders painted a picture of how my heart felt. My brain has built some new walls and I am lonely on the other side. I was a void of nothingness. I need to take those bricks down and start to feel myself again, bright, my eyes expressing happiness and freedom. If I shine lights on the sad times, I can discover me again. With that thought in mind I finished my ablutions and dragged myself to bed.

I tossed and turned but didn't seem able to find the right position to be comfortable. A lingering haze of sleep sat somewhere at the back of my mind, too far away to reach, as an icy discomfort blossomed in my chest as I took long deep breaths trying to make myself fall asleep, but they just caught in my throat. This is going to be a long night, I go to bed tired, I get up tired, I want to feel refreshed, not deprived of sleep. This sleeplessness is my torture, whilst the rest of the world embraces their dreams, their eight hours of rest, I am still chasing white rabbits. Why is my night a futile tussle of conflicting thoughts, the more chance of sleep I have, the better tomorrow will be. The usefulness of my thoughts left long ago, leaving fatigued neurones to fire almost randomly, flailing without direction. I want so much to not to think at all, I want to be absorbed into the darkness that the night promised me hours ago, but instead there is a tenseness to my muscles that makes me more like a mannequin on my soft mattress.

Even when I do drift off, the trauma to my brain is worse than being awake, a violent whirl of stupidity, trying to organise the chaos in my life. My conscious brain knows all this but my subconscious remains stubborn in its attempts to protect me, to ensure my survival. Ironic really, because what I really need to survive tomorrow is sleep.

The following day after another restless night, I showered, made myself presentable, ate breakfast and prepared to go into work. Goldie was going to pick me up, but first I needed to go back to where all this mess started. I opened the door and that wave of panic came at me once more, this demon still gnawing away, I retracted inside quickly as a metal lid clattered to the floor and skidded towards me, but it was just one of the locals falling over a dustbin.

As my heart pounded in my chest, I heard my mother's voice sounding in my head "You can conquer this evil. Fear is wisdom in the face of danger." She used to say it a lot, "It's a good thing to be tuned in enough to feel fear, but figure out why it's there and what to do about it; that's what bravery is." I stepped forward biting my lip hard, making it bleed a little.

As I tentatively let go of the door handle and closed the door, my first mission of the day was to go to the beach, hopefully Goldie would use her initiative and find me there. I had to do this as a start to heal these painful memories and prove to myself that I could move forward from this. I took a few steps further forward with my thoughts churning around all the reasons not to go back to the beach just yet, but I tried really hard to ignore them and instead sent them a blanket invitation to go as I continued on my quest.

CHAPTER 25

It was only a short stroll to the beach, but my thoughts continued in overdrive, I was so anxious, paranoid even, my hands were sweaty and I was trembling inside, if I back away now I will have to do this all again another time. I can let my thoughts leak into the ether and remain in control, or let them get the better of me and swirl me into a vortex of stupidity. This feeling of anxiety needs to become a kind of background noise, as if it were traffic on some unseen road. I have a responsibility, a mission to accomplish, I need to achieve my goals, I can still see my shack, so, I wasn't that far from home, a bit of security at least. I had to do this, I just had too.

I sat down awkwardly on the warming sand and stared ahead. It was just like any other day, Blot was in his usual place fishing for bait, waving at me and yelling "waa gwaan" at the top of his voice, his way of saying hello, I waved back and Mogsey was 'limin' in his fishing boat waiting for Blot to come to him armed with bait. I felt safe, despite everything this still felt like my serene space of infinite potential where I can create the new and tempt it to follow me into reality. The beach has always been my go-to place, some people like their fancy coffees, some like their cakes, but me, I love the driftwood that comes in on the buoyant waves like tiny rescue boats, the seaweed, the flora of the salty waves as deeply green as any high summer foliage, in fact I love just being next to the water.

I allowed myself to lay back, stretched out both arms and legs to look like a starfish, I felt a smile come over me as my anxiousness seemed to diminish. The sand was a gentle hue of gold, the humble star of the scene with its co-star, the blue cloudless sky. All the torment in my mind actually fell quiet for the first time since I had come home. I closed my eyes momentarily, listening to the waves pulse on the shore in a steady rhythmic beat.

In my quiet contemplation I thought about love, the people I cherished and what was right with my life, until an unexpected but familiar voice echoed along the beach. Despite recognising the voice as Goldie's, you always heard her before you saw her, she always had a million reasons to shout. I sat up, frightened, vulnerable, my logic suddenly abated, "Goldie," I uttered as she arrived next to me and leaned over, like some towering giant. She grabbed my arms and pulled me up off the sand, as I landed in her arms she squeezed me so hard I thought my insides were going to explode. I was so glad to be with someone I could trust, I think, there was that niggling doubt again, I never used to be like this.

As she spoke, there was a kindness in her smile, a gentleness. "Gud tuh si yuh Mek wi taak." she said as she released her grip but still held onto my arm. "Petra waan tuh taak tuh yuh, Winston dead and Tilly resigned from do paper, yuh tell mi whappen." She said without pausing for breath. I sighed deeply, I suppose that was some solace in itself, Tilly deciding to resign. She began marching me across the beach to her wagon, usually she never broke out of a stroll, but today she was on a mission. "Git eena cyar Mek wi guh." she said as we arrived at her distinctive wagon. It had somehow hauled its way around the Island for years, she patted the dented and rusted bodywork. "Cum pan, Git eena." She said, as I lost control of my senses and blurted out, "Goldie, I've ruined and lost your dress and my phone," She just smiled and slapped my back, "Wi a guh sort ih out empress Nuh ya worry."

The short drive to the Alise enabled Goldie to babble nonstop at me about what had happened since I had been away. It felt like I had been held captive for months rather than a couple of weeks. Beneath her chat was the love, the gentle glances of her eyes and the relaxed nature of her face. I just listened as she helped me to relax, before my question and answer session that was to come from Petra.

On arrival at the Alise, I pulled down the sun visor to check if I looked ok, I'd been biting my lip so badly that it was now bleeding even more and it seemed to have grown a lump as well, Goldie handed me a tissue to dab my lip with. 'Yuh luk gud empress." She uttered trying to put me at ease as I clambered out of the wagon. I had managed to cover the fading bruises on my face with make up but I still felt a little worse for wear. I stood, staring at the building that loomed in front of me, I clenched my fists tightly until my nails dug into the palm of my hand and caused me to wince, they were still sore from all the thorns and insect stings. My heart throbbed against its enclosed cage of my chest. Goldie took my hand,"Yuh a guh bi fine." She smiled reassuringly, " Cum pan."

We walked up to the office door, as I touched the door handle, goosebumps rose all over my body, I shivered, I can do this I reprehended myself. I took the biggest breath in I could and pushed the door open, stepping inside. Everyone was there, they all stood up and clapped me. I felt embarrassed, I turned as red as a beetroot, you could feel the heat radiate off me, you could have cooked a three course meal on my face, I wanted the earth to open up and swallow me, I didn't deserve this, I was no hero. A smile quivered across Goldie's face as she said. "Wi a all glad tuh si yuh." She nudged herself towards my side and giggled, she knew how to make me feel more at ease.

Petra now stood tall and proud in front of me, with arms open, she beckoned me to move forward, "Come into my office Jaz, she took my hand, back to work the rest of you" she clapped her hands and everyone obeyed the order instantly. I began to tremble, suddenly feeling very apprehensive, I knew I was safe with Petra and Goldie. But there was a feeling inside me that said, "No, this is a trap." I want this inner battle of me vs me to be fully resolved and my inner conflicts to vanish, I need to fight to find the courage and do what is right. If I choose to be brave instead of being a puppet of fear everything will get better, surely. So I'm going to make the choice that's right, the one I believe in. Petra and Goldie will understand, they will help me, this is the release valve I need.

Petra closed the office door behind us and embraced me, before patting me on the back and indicating to me to sit down in a rather comfy looking chair. She returned to the other side of her desk and then on her intercom summoned for coffee and biscuits to be brought in. Goldie pulled up a chair and sat next to me, as close as she dare without sitting on my lap, notepad in hand, eyes as big as saucers. Petra leaned forward and in a professional manner said, "How are you, Jasmine, I am aware something very sinister has happened. Tilly has now resigned before I terminated her contract. I promise you will be safe, you will be protected no matter what." She smiled as we continued to chat in general, trying to make me feel at ease. The coffee and biscuits arrived during the conversation, which 'wet our whistle' so to speak. The conversation was littered with smiles, it was not just words that were spoken, but an underlying love that was there between us all, never seen before, it felt right, it felt like they were my friends ready to help me, the best doctors and medicine combined.

Once Petra had decided I was sufficiently relaxed, she nodded to Goldie who took my hand and squeezed it tight. "Enuh Winston is dead." "Err yes, I know, I was there." I whispered biting my lip once again, she squeezed my hand harder, "Candice is too." "What" I said, leaping out of my chair, "shh" Petra said as she made her way to where I was standing and held me tight with Goldie, a group hug I think they call it. Goldie repeated it, "Candice is dead too." As I processed what she said, a single tear began to slide from my eyes, followed by another and another, until a steady stream of salty tears flowed down my cheeks and dripped silently onto my arm.

Petra moved her chair next to mine and Goldie's, we all sat in silence as they gave me time to think about what had been said, it was a complete shock. After a few minutes and in between the tears, I managed to ask "How, how, why?" I looked at Petra, than at Goldie who passed me some tissues, she held my hand so tight it was beginning to feel numb. I took the opportunity to shake it free as I blew my nose and dabbed my face. I squeezed the tissue tight in my hand and looked at Petra whose eyes were also welling up. "Jaz, I'm so very sorry, I know you two were close friends, but we had to tell you, it is better to find out from us than the local gossip vine." She was right. "One of the locals found her on the road side, near to Ziggy's bar, her face was badly bruised, her ribs had been broken, her stomach lacerated and her skull broken. She was alive when they found her, but she passed away soon after the ambulance got to her before reaching hospital. They did everything they could, but they couldn't save her. "Oh my God, poor Candice, she was beaten up because of me, I knew it, two people dead and it's all my fault." I sobbed as Petra put the box of tissues on my lap.

I felt so much anger, I didn't want to be friends with anyone, I can't trust anyone, it'll be safer that way, no-one else will get hurt because of me, but how much of this is really to do with sadness and my scars that just won't heal. She was the best, the one I could rely on no matter what. She even walked tall when they beat her down, she never gave herself up, I'm glad of that. I'm sorry they stole your life to advance their own.

Petra replied placed her hand on my shoulder, "Jaz, that's simply not true." I nodded and wiped my eyes, my inability to think clearly soon followed as I replied, "Yes it is, I want to see her, I need to see them both, they died because of me, it's all my fault." Goldie pulled my hand up in the air and shook it gently. "Jaz, Jaz, Calm dung tap blaming yuhself." I glanced at her kind eyes and started to picture Candice's smile, her voice, in fact lots of memories came flooding back in a nano second. Petra rubbed my back in a circular motion, "We can go to the morgue so you can see them if that's what you want." She said. I hesitated for a moment, before replying "um, yes, I think I would like that." I wasn't convinced this was the best idea I had ever had, but it might help me bring some closure to this. Petra handed me my coffee cup and smiled warmly, "It will be ok, trust us, we will be with you every step of the way, you will get through this. Look at it with a different perspective, they knew they could loose their lives, they wanted to die to save you, they loved you that much."

I took a mouthful of the warm coffee and tried to compose myself, what on earth must Petra think of me showing all this emotion in front of her! Petra's voice was soft and calming, I looked at her and then Goldie, I felt like a void, a dark empty void, a hollow plastic doll with a painted face revealing no emotion nothing left to offer.

Both Goldie and Petra gave me all the time I needed, I felt my walls that had held me up, trying to keep me strong through the last few weeks begin to collapse, until the bricks just tumbled down completely dissolving to a pile of rubble. "It really is all right Jaz, come on, you can talk to us." I must find my calm core and stop crying, Winston and Candice will never come back, I will never see them again, but I can do the next best thing by them and get justice, help their souls to rest peacefully. I sniffed and wiped my eyes as began to reveal what had happened. Goldie scribbled the details down as furiously as she could, shaking her hand at times when her fingers ached.

CHAPTER 26

For the next three or so hours, I recounted events as best as I could remember. Luckily they understood as every word I spoke seemed to be pitched higher than the last and at times quite garbled, everything that was bottled up inside just came out. Despite my desperate attempts to stop crying, my tear-rimmed eyes and watery streaks still fell down my face. My cheeks were now blotchy and mottled, I ran my fingers through my hair and smoothed it, as a type of comfort and in the hope it would soothe my nerves. It didn't, it just reminded me of how bad it looked and felt, as wild as a jungle, untamable and unruly.

I had started at the beginning, with Blot ensnaring the woman's body on the beach and then told them about the anonymous note, Goldie interrupted at this point to say that Tilly had seen it and wanted it, how she knew this I don't know and I was so wound up, I forgot to ask. Anyway, I explained that none of the locals or even Candice herself, would talk to me, it was obviously a cover up. I talked through the events that occurred at Iberville leading to my captivity, my escape and Winston revealing all and his death, and actually if truth be known Candice's death too.

As I continued to talk about how Winston helped me to escape, I found myself reliving the moment that I found him lying at the bottom of the embankment near me. I paused as my fear inside had an overwhelming desire to overpower me, I couldn't gain control and just like that, the floodgates opened again. My chin trembled like I was a small child, my shoulders heaved up and down with all the weight in the world on them, I felt like I was dying inside.

I managed to explain, how I covered him in a blanket of leafs to keep him safe, promising I would return for him and get justice. I paused once more, only to blow my nose and drink some more coffee which had been replenished whilst we had been talking. I munched on a biscuit before continuing to describe how I managed to find a way out of the rainforest, onto the beach and eventually back to my shack, all alone, scared witless and fearing for my life ever since. But, one question I did have; why did they believe Tilly when she told them I had gone to France? I would have been contactable after all and how did they find out what had really happened?

By the end of my epic saga, I realised that Petra and Goldie had also shed a tear or two. They wiped their eyes and smiled at me awkwardly, I felt uneasy, I hadn't meant to upset them as well, I couldn't get anything right at the moment! Petra stroked my face, "Jaz, I'm so sorry, I wish I could turn the clocks back and take away all your pain, I wish I had done more." Goldie looked up from her notepad, all the pages nearly written on. "Poor, poor ting, we try tuh find yuh" she said. I tried to smile, she didn't mean to patronise, but all I managed was a fake smile that simply said I am still scared and uncomfortable. It felt like a black mist had settled over me and was refusing to shift, no matter how bright the day was outside, it was weird because I also felt relieved for getting everything out in the open.

Petra, ever the mother figure, drew a deep breath. "Jaz," I looked up at her, she spoke so softly, "Did you know it was Candice who spiked your drink at the Iberville luncheon." I found it quite unbelievable, shocking really, my mind was sent reeling, unable to comprehend or process what Petra had just revealed, I was at a complete loss for words. Not in my wildest dreams did I have ever image Candice would do such a thing, I thought we were good friends. I banged my fist on my lap and the used tissue lurched from it in slow motion, coming to rest on Petra's lap, I had so much anger and confusion that wanted to escape at the same time."You have to be kidding me, why, the hell would she do that to me? I think you have it wrong, her and I go back a long way, you can't disrespect the dead." I barked. As Petra calmly put the tissue in the bin, I realised what I had said as I took control of my faculties and apologised to them both at my outburst.

Goldie pushed my hair away from my face and handed me another tissue, just in case, "Dem mek har dweet Yuh get tuh lack Shi didn't put as much eena yuh drinkz as dem did tell har tuh. Jus enuff fi yuh tuh sleep fah ah bit." Roughly translated, Candice was forced to spike my drink, but she didn't use as much as she was supposed to, just enough for me to fall asleep so she could get me out of there. The shock brought a quietness inside me, a moment to feel my emotions change gear and calm down a bit. I think I understood, she did make sure no real harm came to me after all with Winston's help.

Petra moved to the filing cabinet and handed me a piece of paper. "Tilly has resigned, she came in one night after the office was closed, left a note on my desk, quitting with immediate effect, no reasons given, cleared her belongings and then disappeared, no one has seen her or heard from her since." Petra smiled. "Good in a way, but I wanted the satisfaction of terminating her contract and letting her know what I knew. She thinks she's escaped, but in truth, we will hunt her and Ed down, we will get justice and they will get what they deserve.

My head now throbbed from crying so much, I delved into my bag to retrieve an aspirin as Goldie thrust another cup of coffee at me. This was the last thing I needed, the more coffee I drank, the more I became wired. "Is there any water please?" I asked as yet more beads of water started to fall down my cheeks, why couldn't I stop crying? I had never cried this much before. Petra handed me a cup of water and I used to take the aspirin, then Goldie pulled me close to her chest, both of our chairs wobbled a bit as she stroked my head like I was a cat until my crying subsided. "Jaz,please nuh bawl nuh muh Mi nuh lakka eh wen yuh a vex." It was a welcome relief that I didn't have to hide behind a mask, it didn't matter that I was struggling to cope, I could be honest and get heart felt advice, I really am safe and amongst new good friends.

Petra had now moved her chair back behind her desk, she leant forward and with her elbows resting on the top as she explained her side of the story. "Initially I believed Tilly about sending you to France, I felt awful about that. I only found out about everything after Candice and Winston confided in me. They both became scared for their own life when they couldn't find the money to meet the original blackmail plan. Lord Wrexham found out and, according to Winston, was going to hire a contract killer to eradicate me if I said anything to anyone or tried to help Winston, Candice or you, printed anything or went to the authorities. I tried different ways to get to you, but Tilly always blocked my paths."

She paused and helped herself to a cup of water, "Lord Wrexham had a disturbed mind, an emotional indifference if you like. I knew that if I did anything too radical to get to you, we would all loose our lives and what they had done would remain undisclosed. Winston and Candice promised they would keep you safe until I could figure out a plan to free us all and hand Tilly and Lord Wrexham over to the authorities. They both tried to keep me abreast of the situation, but Tilly found out about Lord Wrexham's note, hiring a contract killer and panicked, she knew that she had to do something to shut us all up. Luckily, getting to me proved more difficult than she anticipated, so she took revenge on the easier targets, those being Winston and Candice."

I have to transform hate into the positive side of emotional indifference, otherwise it will be my poison. I'm not going to like anyone that goes out of their way to harm me and my friends, they had killed three innocent people and their families will suffer forever. There isn't a place they can hide, I will find them and destroy them both. I don't care how it happens, I just need them to suffer, extinguish them from this universe. You may think this is an overreaction, but I don't. I can't even think of him as gentry now, so from here on in I will refer to him as Ed.

Petra shifted in her chair, "When Ed returned home after murdering his wife, the last thing he expected was to find her missing, completely vanished. One minute she was there and the next she was gone, it was as if she had dissolved into the very air itself and blown away in the nights breeze. Tilly had previously confided in Candice about Lady Amélie's murder as she needed her on side when the body went to the mortuary, to ensure nothing out of the ordinary was found." "A cover up, you mean, " I sniffed, "exactly, however, Candice being Candice hatched a plan of her own to scare them both. She knew the date and time of the murder, all she had to do was move Lady Amélie's body single handedly, without being seen, casting it into the sea further down the shoreline and then wait. We all know Candice considered revenge to be a much believed concept, she always served people exactly what they truly deserved in life, this kept her happy and serene." That was true, she would just smile, and then when you weren't expecting it, something would happen, the odd nail in your tyre, etc, I am glad she wanted Tilly and Ed to suffer badly for what they had done, but not at the expense of her own life.

There was a knock at Petra's door, "Come in," she answered, it was Colby, "Can you look at this for me?" He asked nodding and smiling at me. "Yes, of course," was all she said as he made his way out of the office and closed the door behind him. Petra shuffled the papers and placed them in a pile to one side of her, then continued, "When Lady Amélie was washed up on the beach and found by Blot and you, unfortunately you told Tilly as you thought it would make a good story for us. In order for her cover not to be blown, Tilly told you to investigate it, but knew she had to work quickly to cover their tracks. Ed of course, could use his power on the Island by buying everyone's silence, but she was scared it wouldn't be enough." "What about the note that came to my shack?" I interrupted. "That was from Candice warning you to stay away, she had already been threatened with her life by Ed and Tilly, although at this point Ed and Tilly weren't aware it was her that had moved Lady Amélie. She wanted to protect you, give you a clue, she loved you like a sister."

Petra stood up and stretched a little, I glanced at my watch, without realising it nearly the whole working day was coming to a close and the rest of the office staff were packing up ready to go home. Petra opened the top drawer of her desk and removed three shot glasses and a bottle of rum, placing them on the top of her desk, before pouring a generous splash for each of us.

She handed us a glass each and took a sip as she sat down, "The trouble was you didn't stop digging, so the only way they thought they could buy your silence was to invite you to Iberville on the pretence of the luncheon, initially to keep you out of the way until they could escape. However when you caused a bit of a stir, they wanted to kill you to silence you, Candice got wind of this and was there disguised as a butler, she spiked your drink to help get you out of there earlier than the other guests. Unfortunately Ed got to you first and took you inside. When you came out from the washroom and sat down in the chair, Candice sized the opportunity to get you out of Iberville, she went to get Winston to help her, she thought you would be safe for a minute. However, when they arrived back, you had gone, the chair she left you in had been moved and a tall urn full of decorative flowers stood in its place, they didn't know where to look for you without being found out. They did try looking but things got tricky for them when Ed caught them in part of the house they should have never had access to."

I nodded, I do vaguely remember plonking myself down in a chair, but I don't remember Candice. "Tilly and Ed took you to one of the stone buildings on the estate, that was yet to be converted, they needed you alone and then they could kill you later when the guests had all gone. No one would be any the wiser and then you would just disappear, they didn't even think about you being missed. They dealt with Candice and Winston by threatening them. If they didn't do exactly as they were told they would meet their demise as soon as their services were no longer required. Candice and Winston managed to persuade them not to harm you and get Ed and Tilly to agree to them bringing you food and water until Ed and Tilly escaped the Island, then they would let you go, this was a better plan than killing you. Ed and Tilly agreed that this was a better option for now.

As far a I was aware, the last part of the plan had not been discussed, you would still remember the event and would still report what had happened, but they hoped to be far away out of the country by that time, I think. Unfortunately, both Winston and Candice devised their own plan to release you and expose Ed and Tilly, that's why they were killed as far as I know."

We all knocked back another shot of rum, ahh, I shivered as it made its way through me. Petra poured yet another, I did try to cover the top of my glass with my hand, but Goldie just moved it out of the way. I have to say, one shot was all I needed, I could feel the battle of heroes begin, being drunk is the fools anaesthetic, its just a couple of happy drinks, the tonic I had needed, a drink with my colleagues, well now my friends, it was an updraft to raise my spirits.

Petra took another sip of the rum for dutch courage as she continued. "All went swimmingly until Winston had a huge row with Ed, I don't know what it was about, except Ed became really angry. As a consequence, Winston decided to tell you exactly what was going on and help you to escape. Ed found this out after spying on Winston, he watched and let you escape and then shot Winston, probably those were the gunshots you heard as you were running towards the rainforest on the edge of the estate. Winston was gravely wounded but wanted to make sure you were safe, he tried to seek you out, he got to you, but died from severe blood loss. You found him and the rest you know." I knew it, I should never have let myself fall asleep, I could have saved Winston!

"What about Candice," I questioned, Goldie raised her eyebrows and knocked back the rest of her rum. Petra smiled awkwardly, "You know Candice had her fingers in many pies and she knew a lot of people on the Island. She was in on Winston helping you escape and was supposed to follow, but after seeing Winston shot, it became too dangerous. She let the dust settle and then secretly got together a search party hoping to find both of you, but she only found Winston. She involved the Caribbean Law Enforcement Foundation, despite knowing that Ed had paid the police to keep silent, they told him. Tilly also found out and hired a gang of drug dealers to beat her up in order to silence her. What Tilly didn't bargain on was Candice retaliating and stabbing one of the gang leaders, so they killed her and left her for dead."

I could feel the anger as it boiled inside me again, hot lava, churning around, followed by even more hatred, all I wanted to do was focus on getting revenge. I am pretty sure Petra and Goldie felt fires of fury smouldering as well, but coming up with lots of justifications for revenge, wasn't the answer, we would just stoop to their level, we needed to be better than that. "Where are Tilly and Ed now?" I asked, "In hiding I assume, too ashamed to face their punishment and as most of the locals now know what happened through their gossiping at Ziggy's bar, Tilly and Ed must know they will not be safe if found." Petra replied.

I wanted to scream, my terrified soul wanted to unleash a demon, I swallowed hard in order to try and contain it. I needed to find my inner peace, a physical activity usually helped me, well I was lifting a glass of rum so I could class that as some form of exertion, now all I had to do was be able to release self control, do that and I have a winning combination.

Petra stood up and put the papers from her desk into her bag, "Jaz, I know we haven't really spoken much in the past, as friends I mean, but I promise I want to get justice just as much as you do, you can trust both of us, Goldie and I, if we work together we can lay Lady Amélie, Winston and Candice to rest, find Tilly and Ed and put an end to this, its what you want as well isn't it?" I hesitated, a conspiracy theorist would rather hold a gun than form a trusting bond, they would find trust more scary than bullets, but that's their irrational behaviour and a warped perspective. I nodded, "Yes, Yes definitely Petra." I did trust them both, after all I had spent the whole day explaining everything to them, I had come this far.

CHAPTER 27

I sat back in the chair, my head throbbed even more telling me it was time to rest some place quiet and ride out the storm in my brain. I felt nauseated and my eyes were still red and sore from crying, when I sniffed a sharp pain flew up between my eyes. I will blame it on the rum, but it's probably a combination of everything if I am honest.

Petra walked over to me and embraced me again, it felt warm, protective and for a moment my tormented world stopped still on its axis, there was no time, no wind, no rain, my mind was at peace. "Jaz, let's get you home, you need to rest," she whispered. "Goldie will take you and we will come for you in the morning, we will all see Candice and Winston together if that's what you still want? We can then sort things out after that, ok?" I looked at her like a child in their mothers arms, she had warmth in her eyes, a look of real sincerity. I nodded and glanced over at Goldie, who was also smiling. "Ok, thankyou" was all I could say, I did feel emotionally and physically drained.

Goldie took my arm as I left Petra's embrace and escorted me to her wagon, this time we drove back to my shack in silence, both of us having our own thoughts. Goldie escorted me inside my shack and poured me some juice then she gave me a peck on the cheek, "Si yuh first light empress sleep well," I nodded as I kissed her back. Home is my serenity, my comfort, my familiarity. I am at ease being vulnerable and real here, this is my place where I know I will be all right.

I walked upstairs into the bedroom, I walked to the window and opened it, standing alone with my thoughts for a second and heaved a huge sigh. I was so tired, but I knew I would probably be in for another night of futile tussles and conflicting thoughts. My head said, "I don't want to sleep, not yet, but wait, I have just spent the day awake, I need to sleep," then a second voice chastises me, "the longer I lie in bed the more chance of sleep I have." But all I know is that between now and the return of daylight are my zombie hours, when I am mostly awake but dozing in fitful spurts. Six hours feel like sixty, then I get up just as exhausted as I am now.

To try and solve this problem, I walked back down to the kitchen, ignoring the juice Goldie had poured and instead chose a glass of Red Label, not a good idea on top of rum shots. I sat on the sofa just staring inanely at the glass, I could feel myself beginning to doze off, my head lolled as my eyelids finally decided to close. At some point I must have curled up on the sofa and let my body go limp. Maybe I could finally sleep without the complex workings of my conscious mind.

Alas my sleep ended abruptly, as I woke back to the world of reality by some dustbin lids clattering outside. The noises of the street are a good heartbeat of the place, yesterday, I would have become anxious thinking someone was coming for me, but now, I just laid calmly on my couch hoping to fall back to sleep but this was not to be.

I felt so fatigued, I needed matchsticks for my eyes and I ached from head to toe. I let out an exasperated yawn, groaning as I rolled off of the sofa, what time was it? Eight thirty, great! I hauled myself to a standing position and dragged myself up to bed, I might as well have been wearing heavy armour for all the effort it took me. Let's hope if I snuggled under my duvet I would now be able to get a decent nights sleep.

Once again I tossed and turned for most of the night, unable to get into a comfortable position, a lingering haze of sleep sat somewhere at the back of my mind but was too far away to reach. Everything about me, from the muscular aches to the emotional pull toward lethargy, the fatigue made me feel like I was on a treadmill and couldn't press stop. I tried to will myself to fall asleep, I wanted so much to not to think about anything at all, I just wanted to be absorbed by the darkness that the onset of night promised hours ago. I want to wake up refreshed to streaming bright daylight, unaware of the hours between then and now. I began to count sheep, one, two etc, the more I counted the more I struggled with what numbers came next, I gave in.
Eventually, my thoughts must have given way to sleep as I woke to the steady patter of rain on my window which

brought a calmness to my mind, a soothing melody, a natural lullaby. It wouldn't last long, before the sun would come to life again and drive away the rain, it was always short but predictable showers here.

I got up slowly, dressed and poured myself a glass of water, my head felt like it was about to crack, possibly a bit of a hangover from the rum, wine and drama of yesterday. I found myself staring out of the window at the brilliant sun that was now streaming through, daydreaming a personal movie with myself as the main character, a simple whim and a plot that could change direction, dramatically or swiftly. Which ever way you look at it, I was lost in my own enchanted world of make believe.

It was quite weird, I was looking at the sea but holding a coin, old and covered in dirt, the engravings were worn and the kings head was tarnished I held it in my left hand, watching the mud dirty my skin, when I saw my right hand there was a new spring leaf in my palm, but then I turned back to the coin, the image of the king had freed himself and journeyed over my hands to land on the leaf.

It wasn't long before Petra and Goldie arrived, bringing me back to reality. We walked outside to the deck and sat there for a bit, chatting and sharing laughter. In this easy-going camaraderie we all knew we had ignited a kind of friendship that will remain forever, it began to restore my faith in human kindness. I made some coffee for us all to go with some warm Johnny cakes Petra had brought with her. A late breakfast watching the fishing boats and water taxis nip back and forth amongst friends seemed to allay my headache.

Our banter was easy, I felt relaxed in their company, I knew I would not come to any harm, I might even go as far as to say I felt a little bit rejuvenated. The sun began to turn the whole sky into a beautiful blue blanket with its brilliance, my mood lightened even more, my battery was recharging from all this solar power. At last I was unburdened, except for the bit about me visiting the morgue, it felt an impossible task to achieve. I know I didn't have to do it, but I needed to, it was the right thing to do and with their support I felt sure I could accomplish it.

When I felt ready, we climbed into Petra's car, Goldie sat next to me, holding my hand all the way, giving it little squeezes now and again. For the short journey, we continued to bounce remarks between ourselves like a kid's rubber ball, predominantly to keep my mind off of what was to come, but also we just clicked, we brought a sense of playfulness out in each other, it was great, the medicine I needed right now.

As we drew up outside the morgue, Petra helped me out the car, I felt a shiver run through me and I looked at the sky where two puffs of white magic in the form of clouds sat in the acres of blue right above my head, Candice and Winston. "Are you absolutely sure about this?" She asked. I smiled, "Yes absolutely." I replied.

We walked inside and were met by a petite bronzed lady who led us down a sterile corridor to a metal door at the end, it was freezing cold. Petra and Goldie stood by the door as it opened and I was ushered to go in, I hesitated before managing to put one foot in front of the other. I stopped in my tracks and turned, "Will you both come with me?" I asked Goldie and Petra. "Of course," they both replied together. I had never liked seeing dead people, not that I had had much opportunity, except on television. Their deathly white skin, with an odd sheen and tinged blue seemed to have shrunk tight against their bones, eyes all black staring back at you. I shuddered, quite unsure about going any further, but I had to do this for them, I needed to say a final farewell, they were dead because of me.

We all walked forward, arm in arm holding on to one another for moral support. We saw Candice first, lying so still, she looked like she was fast asleep with a hint of a smile on her face. She was beautiful, peaceful, perfect in every way. I put my hand under the sheet covering her body, to find her hand, but recoiled it just as fast, she was icy cold. I expected to cry and feel numb, yet in truth, where there was pain, so much pain, it has now been replaced with a sense of joy and pride for who we were and what we achieved together. I bent down, stroked her hair and kissed her forehead, whispering "sleep tight princess, I love you, you will always be with me, Candice." As we turned to walk back out of the room something made me glance back, I could have sworn she winked, she didn't, it was just my mind playing tricks on me.

All three of us then went into the room next door where Winston lay, he also looked so peaceful, such a handsome man, his life cut short, for an honourable self sacrifice. I stroked his head, then kissed him on his blue lips hoping he would respond, he didn't obviously.

A chill breeze reflected a howling pain that tore through my body without warning. I felt my insides become wooden, my face become passive in its expression. How I wished I could wave a magic wand or go back in time and take a different path, but that was impossible. There was no way back, I had to go forward. Petra was right, there was only one way to make this right. Get justice!

I stood staring at Winston for a moment longer, everything is recycled, the atoms of one thing become those of another, energy from one place becomes energy in another. I have no idea where Winston's soul is now, or what God has asked of him, but I am sure he will be by my side, loving me in the ether. At least they are both somewhere safe from the perils of this world and that's what matters to me.
We all said our goodbyes and were escorted out of the morgue with compassion. Petra then drove us all back to my shack, letting our emotional health speak the most clearly in the silence.

Petra and Goldie came inside for about hour and we sat on my deck drinking juice. We smiled and laughed as we reminisced, thinking of all the good memories we could keep safe and alive in our hearts. The happy times happened, they were real, now we have to pack our mental suitcases with only the best of memories so we can fly with them, anyplace we want. I felt a warm breeze caress me and as I savoured its gentle touch, it made me think of the times when Candice and I laughed and told silly jokes. I think I have come to terms with what happened and gained new perspectives on it in the process, it is time to set myself free.

We watched Blot catching fish as we laughed, it was good to feel this bond of friendship, trust and security. Petra suddenly dug into her pocket and pulled out a phone. "Here Jaz, I almost forgot, for you." I was completely taken back, I didn't expect this. "Petra, I can't take," she cut me short. "Jaz, just take it, you can stay in touch with me then, I have put my number on a speed dial, Goldie's too. Any time you need us, call us, we can all get hold of one another now, so no arguments."

Reluctantly, I took the new smart-phone from her, actually relieved that I was now in touch with the outside world again. Petra helped me download a new crime reporting app, which meant I could now send information to the Police Federation authorities completely anonymously if I wanted to. It also gave me the option of a panic button if I felt unsafe and needed help instantly. I'm not sure instantly is a word I would use here, but it was a nice touch. Goldie also told me to contact the British High Commission in Bridgetown, they would give me help to report what had happened and to complete the necessary forms. Petra was keen for me to do this, then they would come with me to explain the events face to face and finally seek justice.

Both Petra and Goldie needed to go back to work, we agreed that I should have a couple more days at home to write the events down and get some more rest before coming back to work. I wanted to get back and take my mind off of things but Petra was right, I did still need to sort myself out. In time Petra also wanted me to write a spread for the Alise, she thought it would flush out Tilly and Ed, if the media got wind of what had happened then globally they would be on a wanted list and eventually captured for their crimes, It would also help me moving forward. Mmhm maybe, but I'm not entirely convinced. Both Petra and Goldie reassured me, they would be in touch with me daily, but I was to call them at any time day or night if I needed anything.

After seeing them off, I went back out to my deck and just lazed, enjoying soaking up the sun for the rest of the afternoon and trying to keep my mind free of any useless thoughts that might stop me from getting a good nights sleep.

Apart from getting up for food, drink and to cool off inside now and again, I enjoyed spending the rest of the day in quiet contemplation thinking about the people I cherished and what was right with my life. Despite the heat I was almost frozen in place, being calmed by the ocean, as I watched the waves rolling in white-tipped, spreading themselves like fingers over the beach after they crashed in their soft way. There is nothing noisy about them today, just a soothing sound.

CHAPTER 28

I slept extremely well that night and woke up feeling refreshed and at peace for the first time in ages. I poured myself a glass of water and munched my way through two apples. I felt alive again and ready to fire up the computer, I began to type, at first I had some difficulty as all my emotions seemed to flood back in, but this time instead of crying and feeling sad, I opened my minds' front door and showed those emotions the exit. I am going to get the job done, I am going to get justice, embrace my future and move forwards with a new found confidence, I couldn't turn back the clock and bring Candice, Winston and Lady Amélie back, but I can certainly change the future.

I was unstoppable, I frantically tapped away on the keyboard which I admit had seen better days. What was once a metallic shiny silver colour was now a grimy brown colour stained with bits of dirt that clung tightly to the greasy finger prints embedded on the keys. My stomach growled and I squirmed in my chair in an attempt to silence the rumbling, I hadn't even noticed that it was now beginning to get dark outside. I glanced at the clock, it was seven in the evening. Blimey! No wonder my stomach was complaining, I'd been here all day.
I hit the save button, turned off the computer, made myself something to eat in the microwave and turned on

the television. I tried to keep my eyes open, I really did, but it was so hard and I was so comfortable. My eyelids became heavy as I drifted off to sleep, just me and my dreams. When I came to, the debris of last nights meal still surrounded me and the sun was once more warming my face as its rays stretched through the window. Another brilliant nights sleep but I needed to get back to some sort of normality, a routine, I couldn't just eat, sleep on the couch and repeat.

I showered, had breakfast and brought the computer to life again. I spoke with Goldie then emailed Petra and the British High Commission with everything I had written the previous day. I also emailed myself a copy for safe keeping so I could upload it via my phone onto the crime app, when I had the courage, well, one step at a time.

The post plopped into my mail box, at the same time, my phone also sprang to life making me jump about twenty feet in the air! It was Petra, talk of the devil, "Hi Jaz, you ok, do you need anything, can I come over later?" she said. "No, I am ok thanks, I have written everything and emailed it to you and yes I would like that." "Well, done my friend" Petra replied. "Goldie is on her way over to you now, she is going to take you to the Police Enforcement Federation, they will listen to you, I will join you both as soon as my meeting here is finished." I really liked Petra, I had never really got to know her on a personal level before, she was just Petra, the 'boss'. As a new friend, she was sincere, calm and trustworthy. "Um, I'm not sure I am quite ready to do that yet," I stated, beginning to feel myself quiver. "Yes, you are, come on, Candice and Winston want justice, you can do this." Came the stark reply, gosh I daren't back down now, no matter how I felt. "Ok, I'll do my best, thank you so much, see you soon." I replied and with that, the phone fell silent.

Goldie arrived a matter of minutes later, her gold jewellery gleaming in the bright rays of the sun. "Hi empress, ready tuh guh" she said, luckily I was about there, just the last few pages to print off of the computer. Putting the paper into a folder for safe keeping, I tucked them under my arm, grabbed my bag and phone and we made our way to her wagon. It was non stop chatting with Goldie, a sort of verbal dance, beautifully chaotic, but also one that made you laugh, she spoke so fast when she was excited that you really had to listen intently, she had made up her own language which got worse as she talked faster and was also prone to go off on a tangent, so I didn't always manage to keep up with her conversations, but it was a welcome distraction right now and it made us both giggle as we drove to the offices.

Walking up the path to the Police Enforcement Federation, I felt fear loom over me, as if I was the criminal here. I dragged my heels reluctantly trying to stop myself from going in, for Goodness sake Jaz, stop now. I gave myself a silent reprimand. This fear is my challenge and my demon to slay, the only way out is to order this brain to function, by demanding solutions instead of this crazy making circling anxiety. I know it feels as if my bones have no more strength and my muscles are all out of power, but I have to choose to fight. Goldie must have sensed my trepidation, as she took me by the hand and led me in.

Inside a policeman stood behind a rather low desk, wearing some overly large 1970s sunglasses, hoping to stop the glare of the sun no doubt, his gun hung idly at his hip, he looked fit, his muscles were proof that he could overcome adversity and rise, proof that he valued himself. As he stood there staring into space, cigarette in hand, he was either going to be helpful or unpleasant. I cleared my voice to get his attention, Goldie leaned forward and poked him gently in the stomach, I pulled her hand away, we didn't need to get arrested on top of everything else. Luckily he was too deep in thought to feel anything, probably planning his next 'limin' break or whether to move anything other than very slowly in the heat. The police here are a breed like no other, there are good police and bad, they can be honest, courageous, corrupt, devious, malicious, altruistic, cunning or stupid. And that's just my short list, they are like chameleons, blending in with those around them, saints and thieves alike.

The Police Enforcement Federation are supposed to pride themselves on being top notch and are feared by everyone including the Island police. I cleared my throat again, I was trembling, Goldie put a reassuring hand on my shoulder. He looked at me, nudging his glasses higher on his nose with one finger. "Yes, sorry ma'am, how can I help you today?" He grinned as he said it and poked Goldie back, she giggled. Tentatively, I gave a brief synopsis of why we were there, he pulled his sunglasses down slightly and peered over the top of them. "Wait here one moment please ladies," he said before disappearing into a back office.

Goldie and I looked at one another and laughed, it was a way to release our nerves, anyway before we could say anything he returned and beckoned us forward into a interview room behind the desk.

The room was small but quite hot, it had some floral touches of verdant foliage. It looked like it had once been an office with filing cabinets standing proud, but now it just had marks where the cabinets had been and its walls were a faded teal colour with some grey wicker chairs scattered to the side and a table. A jug of water and some glasses were brought in and placed in the middle of the table for us to help ourselves to. Goldie played mum as I was trembling too much.

A few minutes later we were greeted by two policemen, one of whom introduced himself as the Commissioner, both were smartly dressed, wearing their uniforms with pride. We stood up, like two soldiers standing to attention and politely they shook our hands, and gestured for us to sit down. Goldie took my hand and squeezed it tight, smiling, "Gwaan Ih will bi ok." She said.

I took a deep breath, handed them the file of papers and began to recount recent events including the murders and naming the killers. Both policemen listened intently without any interruption, the Commissioner thumbed through the pages as I spoke, making the odd facial expression. About half way through my explanation, the door opened and Petra was shown in, the two policemen stood up and shook her hand too as another chair was brought into the room. Petra sat next to me and took my other hand, it was as if we were all glued together. I continued to explain everything and Petra recounted her side of the story from what she had been told by Winston and Candice.

When we had finished explaining everything, the Commissioner stood up as did the other policeman. "This is a valuable and concise account of everything, we need to process what you have told us today and do some investigations, then we will be in touch, can I keep this as evidence?" The commissioner asked. I nodded, it was then that I noticed there had been another female officer sat at the back of the room behind a small table, tapping away on a typewriter, compiling their own accounts of what was said. Politely they thanked us and escorted us outside into the sunlight again. I turned to Goldie, I was cross, I expected more questions, were they actually going to do anything with this information. "What a waste of time." Petra winked at me as Goldie replied. "Dem will sort ih Truss m." "How can you be so sure they will sort it?" I asked her trying to calm myself. "Dat shawt policeman wi spoke tuh Im fi mi uncle." I was completely lost for words as I stood there processing the enormity of what she had just said. I had no idea that Goldie had family in high places or how she got her uncle involved, but brilliant. "Lets go for coffee" Petra said, "as a celebration, what you have achieved today Jaz, is credible and incredible all at once, So proud of you." My blushing was a pink perfection.

As we walked the short distance to the cafe my phone bleeped with an email, it was from the British High Commission, thanking me for sending the email, they had already been in contact with the Police Enforcement Federation and were taking this very seriously. They needed to carry out some investigative work of their own and would be in touch again with their decision and forward proceedings very shortly. Goldie peered at my phone and giggled "Si did tell yuh fi mi uncle wud cum tru." I looked at them both smiling back at me, I let the happiness I felt soak right into my bones.

As we arrived at the cafe, jazz music poured out of it along with the aroma of fresh coffee, it had a good vibe about it. It wasn't a true cafe, more of a marquee right in the middle of the town square and was overlooked by two large stone lions. Around the edges were food vendors, it was market day, the atmosphere was brilliant, from the old to the young, a gorgeous invasion of smells. We grabbed a table and began to people watch as we waited for the coffee to be served. It hit just the right spot, a rich and dark amber liquid with a creamy oat milk topping, its perfect accompaniment was the yam cake served with a sweet glaze. Rich and moist with a flavour that was hearty and solid, it was a popular food choice here on the Island.

Suitably full we strolled back to the office, Petra wanted to talk to me some more, she guided us all into her office and shut the door. "Take a seat both of you." She said pulling the chairs next to her. "Jaz, I have read everything you have written, it's brilliant but I have edited it a bit by way of taking the emotion out of it and keeping it more, factual, hope that is ok? We just need to read through it together before it goes to print." The sun streamed into her open window, soothing me, I wish there was a word for the feeling it brings, for now I'm going to call it "sunjoy." I know for sure that today will be better than yesterday, this time we are the winners. "Yes, yes, that's fine, sorry I didn't mean to do that, I just wrote from the heart and not my head." I replied. Petra and Goldie laughed. Goldie stood up, stretched and then excitedly said, "Cum pan Wah a wi den wait fah Mek wi dweet lets duh di final edit now." So that's exactly what we did, for the next few hours we edited, designed fonts, laughed and giggled until Petra was satisfied with the final article and announced "Its done, it's going to the print room, a brilliant front page spread for tomorrow." She hit the send button and with a shhhhhhh, it was gone, whizzing off into the ether. Within minutes, Colby was on the phone, saying it was running.

Petra's smile extended from her eyes to her cheekbones with an honesty that was so pure. "Jaz, I want you to be careful over the next few days as this will cause a bit of a stir when the rest of the media world get hold of it, they will want interviews and photo's. Please don't do anything without me." I nodded as she held out her arms, initiating a group hug. There is an energy to our hug, as if the matter from one of us powered up the others. I felt I had a true Caribbean family again, people I could really trust and call my friends.

Petra released her hold, "Goldie, it's been a long day, please will you take Jaz home and make sure she is ok." Goldie nodded, there was a certain sense of warmth circling me, a fullness in my soul, I was so thankful to Petra and Goldie for all they had done to help me and believe in me. In the next moment, I don't quite know what came over me, but I gave Petra a kiss on the cheek, before the embarrassment at the realisation of what I had just done set in. I stammered " Sss.orry, thank you so very much for everything." "You are most welcome, I will call you tomorrow unless you need me first," she beamed.

Goldie was excited that at last it would all be in black and white in the news tomorrow. She chattered all the way back to the shack as if she had a sort of verbal diarrhoea, I didn't really mind. If I'm honest, I felt relieved, it was as if a huge weight had been lifted from my shoulders, I even joined in with her banter. She stayed with me for a bit, just clowning around for the next couple of hours, I needed it, my social doctor, healer. We giggled and rolled about my lounge like a children's spinning top, vibrant and heart warming. Our laughter came in fits and bursts, loud to soft to nothing at all and back to loud again and at absolutely nothing in particular. It was as if there was an invisible feather tickling us, we laughed so freely, until it became late when we parted until the next day.

CHAPTER 29

The following day I was awake early, sitting on my deck and enjoying watching the pelicans dive for their breakfast. Goldie appeared on the beach in front of me and climbed up the decking posts like some demented monkey, until she stood with me, don't ask me why she couldn't use the back door on this occasion. She thrust the crumpled newspaper into my hands, beaming from ear to ear. "Luk Luk Eh deh front page." Apprehensively, I stared at the page, yep, she right, just as Petra had promised, there it was in large bold print. A whole front page spread showing the faces of Ed and Tilly with the story which continued onto the next page.

Identity of Triple Killers in St Kitts Revealed
How long can they hide?

Jasmine Tormolis
Journalist Alise

I began to read and became so absorbed in it, I completely forgot Goldie was still there, until she had helped herself to the ingredients of my larder and plonked a couple of glasses of rum punch, a plate of butter, bread and cheese and pate down on the table by the side of me. Startled I looked up, she was still grinning. "Criss a nuh ih, lets celebrate." She handed me a glass, "Sorry, I didn't mean to, " she cut me short, putting her hand to my lips and holding up her glass with the other one. I became aware that a few of the locals had also gathered at the bottom of my deck, with quite a few excited questions and comments. "Jaz, Jaz, Fi wi hero cum yah." Goldie giggled as we both leaned over the deck to talk to them."Yuh di bess Jaz Yuh gaan tru suh much Wi waah fi shake yuh by di hand Mek wi fine dees two horrors an bring justice. Winston an Candice didn't need tuh drop out lakka dat."

Loosely translated for the non-Caribbean speakers amongst us, they basically told me I was the best, their hero. They were shocked about what had happened and how and why Dicey and Winston had died. They wanted justice and wanted it now, they wanted to take matters into their own hands. I was quite taken aback at their reaction to want protect me and find Tilly and Ed, no matter the cost, they had killed two of their own and wanted them to suffer. After some gentle persuasion and translation by Goldie they seemed to understand cold retribution was not the way forward, but they didn't get the English metaphor, "Revenge is a dish best served cold." They were adamant, revenge and punishment would be done.

It was quite an overwhelming feeling, at such sense of camaraderie. I knew I had been welcomed here, but I didn't realise they thought this much of me, there is nothing more human than the feeling of love, and do you know what, the more love we all give, the more we all have, it's the most awesome magic trick in the world.

Petra called around to check I all was fine after seeing the spread in all of it's glory. She managed to convince the locals that, as much as I appreciated true friendship and was grateful for their support, I had been through enough and needed some space. They understood and retreated, clapping me as they dispersed. As nice as it was, I was grateful for Petra's intrusion, I hadn't wanted to seem rude to them. My phone pinged, it was two emails from The High Commission and Police Federation. They needed to speak with us again to clarify a few things but were abhorred by what had happened and had set wheels in motion to flush out Tilly and Ed and ensure they did not leave the Island, along with the added promise that they would bring justice to those who had lost their lives and help me lay my demons to rest. They would contact me with convenient dates and times for us to attend their proceedings, but for now this was an update.

Satisfied that I was of full mental capacity, Petra took Goldie back to the office, they both needed to deal with the sudden onslaught from the mass media since this had now gone viral and wanted to protect me as much as they could. I must admit as much as Goldie was fun to be around, I did want to shy away from society for the rest of the day and re read the article.

Goldie however, did come back unannounced late in the afternoon, but this time she was not alone. She had brought Mr Fedett with her, a friend of her fathers, a well respected lawyer. He looked like he had come from a monochromatic world, even his skin was the colour of dirty snow. He wore black rimmed glasses which hid his grey eyes, if they had ever been any other colour in a former life, they must have somehow been bleached out along with his humanity, he looked very severe. Maybe this was a bit harsh. 'Never judge a book by the cover,' as my mother would say.

After the initial introductions he sat down glancing at his paperwork and then smiled at me, probably trying to placate me, I am so pessimistic! Goldie had already explained the events to him, so after making sure I felt fine to go over everything again, we were able to finish up in record time. He said he would be honoured to represent me and would put up a good fight, he would definitely get the deserved justice but it would help my cause if they could find Tilly and Ed first.

I explained that I didn't think I had enough courage to attend the trials, especially if Tilly and Ed were found, I wouldn't be able to face them in court and go through all the emotions it would stir up again, it would not bode well for my mental well being. Mr Fedett said this was unusual for a prime witness, but he understood and would ask the Judge and see if I could be granted special circumstances, although he couldn't add any guarantees as I was a crucial part of the prosecution case.

My house phone rang as they left, it was mum, she was always one for surprises, each day a multitude of different things, this time she had seen the papers, the story had reached England and was all over the BBC news, apparently, it was even in the local Sussex News. She was so proud of me but also very concerned about what I had been through, why I felt I couldn't confide in her and what I was still going through with a possible trial, did I want her to come out to support me? We chattered for over an hour, she wanted to know everything, she was really concerned and slightly irked that I hadn't told her. She told me that she would move heaven and earth for me, she loved me and if she didn't have the power, she would find it. She felt bad that she was thousands of miles away and I wouldn't let her help.

After hopefully, allaying all her fears and telling her just hearing her voice helped me so much, she seemed to be a bit calmer. I explained how Goldie and Petra, my boss, had got involved and were keeping me safe. Reluctantly she agreed to phone again in a couple of days rather than daily. I loved my mother and my friends but I did want some time to myself, we said our 'see you laters', as she hated saying goodbye over the phone, she said it sounded too final.

Talking of final, both Candice and Winston's bodies had been released and their funerals were to be in two days. It was to be a celebration of their lives and we were to dress in the most colourful clothes we owned. My wardrobe was not vibrant in any way, just pain neutral colours. However I did still have an orange lace top and green trousers Candice had leant me months ago and I had forgotten to give them back. Would that be too weird for me to wear to her funeral? She would probably be laughing at me and saying, "What the hell do you look like?" I expect Winston would have a laugh at my expense too, he only used to wear black and grey.

The day of the funerals arrived all too soon. Petra and Goldie arrived at my shack, both dressed in the most vibrant attire they could find and we all travelled together to the church on the hill, as we all stood together in our multi-coloured outfits, we resembled a selection from a liquorice allsorts box, but we weren't alone. Hundreds of people had turned up, I hardly recognised any of them. As there were too many of us to go inside the church, we joined those gathered outside, they opened all the church windows and doors so the service could be heard.

The sun shone brilliantly, on this particular day and brought a glow to the foliage, the grass, to every garland of bloom. It shone from the insects who flew, as if each were a star of the daytime air. It brought a warm lightness to the heads of the birds, a shine to their feathers of all colours, it brought cheerfulness to an otherwise sad day. I watched a hummingbird in a nearby flowering shrub, so tiny, so busy, a rare treat.

We managed to stand next to an open window, I wiped my eyes as the tears began to form. I didn't want to cry, but I wasn't ashamed that I did shed a tear. I loved them both dearly, but I wanted them to be proud even though they were gone. Goldie put her arm around me, "Eh ah celebration Dem a a watch wi Suh wi betta bi happy." I smiled, she was right, I looked at Petra, "Lets celebrate them Jaz." So that's exactly what we did.

The service began with the preacher's messages of love, his warmth was a hug to the congregation. The singing commenced led by joyous upbeat songs from the gospel choir. Very different compared to our English choirs, they didn't sing dull hymns, but rich harmony music with hand clapping and foot stomping as a rhythmic accompaniment. Our voices all joined together like angels with multiple layered harmonies, high notes soaring up over the clouds, hands clapping, dancing on the staves, as we praised the Lord, Winston and Candice. The music was the tuning fork of our community, it silenced the fear and brought all of our thoughts together into a steady rhythm. For today, that familiar beat in the heart of the village turned a thousand souls into one. Rest in peace Winston and Candice.

The service ended with a private burial for close friends and family. Their two graves had been dug close to the lane that ran the length of the cemetery. There was a sense of serenity in the cemetery which seeped the love of those passed on to the angels who will now protect and guide them both. We all threw flowers onto the coffin, someone also threw a packet of cigarettes in for Candice, it did make me smile, she would have appreciated that.

Over the last few weeks, I have had so much sadness, so much anger as my companion, but after today, it has lessened. Where it once was, I now have lots of happy memories, joy and pride for who they both were and what they achieved. They will always have a place in my heart. So whilst I have no idea where they both are right now, they will always be with me and that's what matters most of all to me.

CHAPTER 30

Over the next few weeks, we all went back to our daily routines and life seemed to return to normal in the village. Lady Amélie's body was flown to France where she was buried in Père Lachaise Cemetery, the first garden cemetery of its kind, quite near to where she grew up and where her parents were also buried. Apparently it takes its name from the confessor to Louis XIV, Père François de la Chaise, I read up on it, not sure why, curiosity probably!

I managed to completely take stock of my life and get a grip on reality, turning my negative emotions into positive ones, I think returning to the Alise helped me a lot, gave me a sense of purpose. Petra, Goldie and I became very close friends, spending a lot of time together in and out of work. My mother went back to ringing every week for an update and to ensure I was still all right, no mental breakdown had occurred or unusual blemishes broken out! Her words not mine. I had taken heed of her nagging and started to eat a little more healthily, I have to admit, I felt better for it. Goldie insisted on cooking for me once a week, well it was supposed to be teaching me to cook but I was more of a hinderance, anyway, it was just a bit of fun. I had almost forgotten about the trial that still needed to be endured once they had found Ed and Tilly. I had spoken to the High

Commission again with the information they needed and life was good, they were very supportive.

Then one day, out of the blue, just when I thought I was on top of everything, Blot arrived at my door, pounding with his fists as if he was going to break through. He had heard, although it could just be gossip, but apparently, Mogsey had been told by someone at the bar, he couldn't remember who, that Ed had been found hiding out in an abandoned storage barn somewhere on the Island and had been arrested by the Police Federation. They were holding him in jail for questioning and pending trial. Tilly was not with him and Ed was refusing to talk to the authorities even with the Island's solicitors present, he wanted his own.

Mogsey told Blot to come and tell me, it all seemed very convoluted I must say. I'm not sure how I actually felt at that moment, an emotional indifference maybe. I was glad Ed had been caught, if the gossip was true and he would be made to talk, he was scum of the earth, he had lost all credibility, respect and his social status on the Island. He wouldn't be able to bribe the police now. I know this sounds evil, but I hoped he would hang for what he did, then he would get exactly what he deserved. According to Mogsey, the Island's lawyers had frozen all assets associated with him and Iberville when they found out the woman's body was Lady Amélie Wrexham. How he obtained all this information I have no idea, but if anyone had their ear to the vibe, it was him, everyone talked to him, he gave the impression he was stoned most of the time and would forget quite quickly, in reality he remembered everything he was told and used it to his own means, but only when it suited him.

I was grateful to Blot for telling me the information, I offered him a drink but he declined, instead he just replied, "Guh git dem gyal." I promised I would buy him a drink at Ziggy's and then once he had gone phoned Petra, repeating what I had been told before I strolled to the Alise.

As I neared the market, I paused to take in the smells, flowers, fruit, vegetables and hot food lingered in the air. I watched as the old and the young bustled about their business, laughing and yelling at the tops of their voices, each one desperate to be heard. I felt more confident today than I had ever done before, I was a girl with a mission, walking into my own destiny, which lay squarely and firmly in my hands.

Were my thoughts at that very moment to become visible they would have been like an explosion of crazy chaotic turns and twists of light, all merging together as my mind clears itself of the last remnants of clutter and becomes more resolute. I had almost reached the Alise office when I was stopped in my tracks by the sound of police sirens, coming closer, they were rarely heard on the Island. Most of the police cars were old, rickety rust buckets, never maintained properly, I suppose that was part of their charm, everybody knew they could never catch anyone in them.

Two cars veered around the corner and screeched to a halt outside the bank, half on the pavement, half off. A torrent of policemen and women bumbled out of the cars and blustered inside the bank with as much speed as they dare go, I never knew you could fit so many people in a car and the chassis copes.

I stood motionless, agog by the amount of police that were all congregated together in one space, I was intrigued as well, I wanted to see what was going on, as did everyone else. I retrieved my phone from my bag, I could take photos and voice record on it, but I would have to be slightly underhand about it, so as not to get caught. By now the market was crowded, people were hanging out of their windows above, all desperate to see what was occurring. Petra and Goldie appeared at the front of the Alise, they too had the same idea as me, was this another article in the making? They waved, attracting my attention and I went to walk over to them, but I wasn't quick enough.

I was held back by the crowd as an almighty commotion materialised, the bank doors were opened and the police emerged, ay back please, stay back." A young policeman, with strong a blossoming of confidence and fortitude walked out, he seemed to inspire great pride, cuffed to him was a woman. Was that Tilly? She had the right physique, the right hair, but I need to get closer for a proper look at her face. Goldie had made her way to me from the other side of the road and suddenly she pushed me forward. I nearly lost my footing, but managed to recover my stance without falling over. OMG! It was her, Tilly, wearing a flouncy short sleeved dress and supporting a large diamond necklace around her neck. I smiled contently, She was a killer, a she devil and now a thief. I really hated her, I wanted to put her in a pit and shovel dirt onto of her, until she was buried alive. I wanted to hear her cries for help, begging me not to do it, watch her as she suffocated, she deserved to suffer.

She looked sideways and caught sight of me briefly, standing proud, not on ounce of fear in me and with a stare that conveyed a bubbling hatred, she was quickly bundled into the car. I didn't get chance to get any photos, it all happened too fast, one minute she was there, a glittering gala and the next she was gone, a sad excuse for a person. Goldie clapped her hands together as Petra appeared, she calmly lowered them as Petra gave her one of her professional looks. "Not in public, there is a time and a place, Goldie." She did smile as she said it though.

We stepped inside the Alise, everyone cheered, they had been watching too. "Let the celebrations begin," Colby announced, gosh he had been released from the print room. Petra threw her arms around me and hugged me tight, Goldie lurched forward at the same time and nearly knocked us flying, we all laughed. I felt proud, relieved, "We've done it, justice will be served, they have finally got them both." I commented. Both Tilly and Ed would be behind bars now awaiting trial, awaiting their fate and then their life would be taken from them, just as they did to Candice and Winston.

I smiled again, at the thought of them trapped separately, in police cells with no windows, no one to comfort them, good, they would get their just deserts, at last. They will be given access to a lawyer from the Island, but they were well known for what they had done and had already been accused and convicted by Islanders before they were arrested, so they wouldn't even be able to try to corrupt their trial, I so wanted them to hang, but unfortunately this was not prevalent here anymore. Never mind as long as they got life without any appeals for the murders and kidnapping I will be satisfied.

As I have said before, nothing happens fast here and that includes court cases, it was not out of the norm for inordinate trial delays as had happened in the past, coupled with a frustratingly immobile criminal justice system. It was said to have meant numerous people were remanded in custody for sometimes, two to five years, but they were only petty crimes, the real criminals were dealt with rather more quickly as the High Commission and Police Federation were usually involved and they didn't want their reputation slated.

Local gossip stated that Lord Wrexham knew a friend of a friend who just happened to be a very good lawyer in

America. He had instructed him to fly over and help him, allegedly to create new evidence in order to negate the trial and ultimately quash their sentence, leaving them both to walk free. Surprising how money talks! The High Commission is alleged to have agreed to the lawyer coming over but due to the seriousness of the case, he was not able to apply for bail, instead he had to concentrate his efforts into representing them both at the trial.

The trial date was set and everyone here on the Island looked forward to the day, it couldn't come fast enough, they all wanted to see justice done. Before the trial Mr Fedett visited me several times with Goldie by his side, he also became Petra's representative as well. He assured us that they would definitely get a prison sentence, but wasn't sure for how long, possibly not life, we would have to work hard to get that, depending on the Judge. I was not given special circumstances and needed to attend to give my evidence. Unfortunately in Caribbean law, you have to obey what the court asks of you.

CHAPTER 31

The day of the trial finally arrived, it took place at the Caribbean Court of Justice (CCJ) for short. It is the only courthouse on the Island that settles disputes and criminal matters that have involved murder, they used to use the death sentence as punishment in years gone by. It takes pride in working closely with the High Commission and Police Federation agency, I'm not convinced it always gives a fair trial, but I didn't care, I just wanted Tilly and Ed behind bars for good.

I put on a smart dress, which I borrowed from Petra. Blue lace upon blue silk, it was cosy to my body, its touch on my skin felt light and soothing, I felt amazing, I could conquer anything in this. Petra and Goldie came to collect me so we could all go to the courthouse together, the mighty trio, we were going to be unstoppable together. They both looked amazing, Petra wore a light grey fitted trouser suit and Goldie was in a flowing orange dress.

I walked to the car trying to look feminine, strong and ready to take on the world on the outside. Whilst on the inside I was really nervous and anxious, but that was my protective mechanism cutting in. I always get nervous or anxious when I'm about to do something big, and overtime these emotions have become my markers for me to find my bravery and to move forwards, telling myself that I am worthy of success and that by doing so I can bring justice to others.

Both Petra and Goldie did a good job of reassuring me, it did help a little knowing that they would be with me all the way for moral support as well as Petra giving evidence. Petra announced she was going to run the trial in the paper each day so that everyone could keep up to date with developments, she had been given permission from the judge to do this.

Trial day one
I felt like I was wired up to an electric cattle fence, not enough voltage to kill but sufficient to create an uncomfortable buzz inside me. Tilly and Ed were seated behind a glass panel in the courthouse with an armed guard in their presence, they spoke only to confirm their names. Despite looking pale and thin, they showed no outward signs of remorse for their committed crimes. It was our day to explain events, Mr Fedett had spoken to us before we went into the courthouse and assured us all would be ok, as far as he knew their fate had been imposed automatically without any consideration to the mitigating factors in their cases or their individual circumstances. Petra was ushered to the witness box first and swore on oath before giving her evidence. She was really put through her paces by the defence lawyer and the prosecution, but she conducted herself impeccably,

remaining very calm and composed as she recounted the events of how Winston and Candice had confided in her. She explained she was threatened with her life when she tried to help, either by going to the police or trying to find a way to get the three of us to safety. The small jury sat quietly, listening and making notes as Mr Fedett and Mr Bonner continued to question Petra before asking her to stand down. We adjourned for lunch before it was my in the witness box.

I stood there, trembling, holding the bible in my hand. "I swear before the Almighty God that the evidence which I shall give shall be the truth, the whole truth, and nothing but the truth." I recounted my side of the events as clearly and concisely and as confidently as I could. Today I was a giant, standing tall, no more slouching or self pity. At one point, Tilly stood up and yelled, "You nasty little bitch, you are a liar, she's lying, they are all lying, its a conspiracy." My eyes wandered across to the jury to see their reaction at her out burst, she was quick manhandled back to her seat by two oversized policeman. I saw Ed shake his head, their cause was lost now, that's for sure. I felt a warmth, a satisfaction and steady determination. I felt like Candice and Winston were stood right next to me smiling, proud as punch. Once and for all, the healing is done, it is time to fight for others as others would have fought for me.

The Commissioner and judge smiled and nodded for me to continue. By the time I had finished giving my evidence and answering all the questions put before me, I felt mentally exhausted and exhilarated at the same time. The court adjourned until the following day when it would be the turn of Tilly and Ed to speak. Petra dropped off the days article for Colby to print and then dropped me home, tired, we said our goodbyes and would see each other in the morning.

Trial day two
Goldie decided we should all go to the coffee shop nearby before going to the courthouse, neither Petra nor I disagreed with her. The coffee shop wasn't too busy, it had tables covered with black and white check table cloths, white cups filled with black coffee and small jugs full of cream, with an ambience of friendly chatter. Here we can have our own seats, gain the feeling of being social, yet have the confidence that we can also enjoy our own contemplations if we want to at leisure.

We ordered a breakfast of soft pancakes and a selection of berries, it's one of my favourite breakfasts, but today it was even more enjoyable because I was with great company. We ate and chatted, watching the time, we didn't want to be late before making our way to the courthouse, each wearing the same outfits as the previous day with the variation of jewellery. We sat on the benches in the spectator area at the back of the public gallery, we were not expected be giving evidence today. I watched Petra frantically tapping away on her iPad as Tilly and Ed were put through their paces in the witness box. They were both expressionless and despite the obvious lies and flaws in some of the detail, they still protested their innocence.

The court eventually adjourned in order for the jury to make their decision, but after waiting for them to deliberate for a few hours, they were unable to agree on a verdict. The judge declared a hung jury and asked for the court to reconvene the following day for a verdict to be given. Tilly and Ed were led away for another night in the cells and as they were, I swear I saw a hint of sadness in Ed's face, eyes remaining dry, expression impassive. He knows that if he even lets a fraction out that the rest will follow, a never ending torrent of how weak he actually was underneath his persona. The three musketeers, as we now all referred to ourselves returned to the Alise to hand the trial notes over to Colby for a second day in a row. Apparently, the Islanders were loving it.

Trial day three
We were all at the Alise and just about to leave for the courthouse, when Petra received a phone call from the Caribbean Court of Justice, the judge had changed tact and had deliberated overnight, coming to the decision that as none of jury had any form of legal training or ever been in a courtroom before, for that matter, coupled with

the fact that they were struggling to understand his rulings on points of law, or explanations on complex rules of evidence, they were to be dismissed. Instead the final session of the trial would be completed by the Judge and High Commission only. He was able to do this under the current 'Gun Court Act,' which can be used if a murder offence involves a firearm or evidence that a second party was involved, eg hitman. We were not obliged to go to the courthouse for this part of the trail, unless we wanted to.

Petra went as a representative from the Alise, she needed to finish the trial write up for the newspaper, Goldie and I stayed at the Alise, researching and writing up other articles for tomorrow's news. The trial only lasted for three hours. The judge ruled that both Tilly and Ed were guilty on three accounts and were to be sentenced to thirty years in prison with no reprieves or retrials. Justice was served as they left the courthouse handcuffed to police officers. As they were whisked away to start their new life in prison, a massive celebration commenced on the Island as the gossip filtered through the verdict of guilty.

Petra wrote up the final article as the front page headline. Mr Fedett visited the Alise and was cheered for his part in proceedings as we all shook his hand, "I told you justice would be done." He commented with a huge grin on his face. There is an old saying here on St Kitts, 'You can live without freedom, you can sway in your own fantasies, you can create your own stories and your own fantastical realities, you can fly, you can soar in dreams and you can jump off the tallest ledges and survive-in your own imagination. But you can never escape, no matter how hard you try, you can never outrun your own conscience, it will always haunt you, yelling and screaming in the back of your mind forever.' How very true!

I phoned home to let mum know about the final outcome of the trial, she was elated, she screamed and whooped with delight. I was so pleased and so very grateful to everyone who had helped me and given me the courage to do and get through this. I looked out the window of the Alise office, two clouds of white ribbon made a half-spiral in the otherwise completely blue sky, fluttering in the lofty breeze. Candice and Winston also very happy with the outcome, it was their way of letting me know, they were peaceful now.

Goldie arrived at my desk, I hadn't even noticed she was missing with all the excitement that had been happening. She was laden with cartons of rum punch and the biggest pile of Johnny cakes for everyone to enjoy. At almost the same moment Colby arrived with the newspaper draft for Petra to complete the final sign off. It was almost there, The front page read;

Iberville Triple Murder Trial
By Petra Amwena

A "**CONTROLLING, ADULTERER**" husband suffocated his wife with her own pillow before attending a party with his lover. Subsequently they both killed two innocent people and abducted another. The biggest most exciting case in the Caribbean Court of Justice for many years.

Lord Edward Wrexham formally of the Iberville estate and his lover Tilly Colspur, who formally worked for the Alise newspaper as an Editor, eventually admitted manslaughter, saying their mental state at the time was such that they did not understand what they were doing, they denied murder on all accounts. The court heard that Lady Amélie Wrexham had been left dead in bed, before her body was secretly moved by Candice Jackson. Candice and Winston were initially blackmailed by Lord Wrexham and his lover and were subsequently killed for disobeying orders. The judge ruled that Wrexham was an evil twisted nobody who used money to get where he wanted to be, he gave not a thought to those who had suffered.

Lady Amélie's body was washed ashore leading to an unsolved investigation corrupted by the local Police. A newcomer reporter for the Alise, Jasmine Tormolis, became embroiled in this sorry saga, finding the body with a local fisherman and reporting on her death. She was later abducted and held captive, until she was helped to escape with her life but at a tragic cost to two close friends.

Showing no remorse for this despicable triple murder, both parties were sent to prison to serve a minimum sentence of 30 years, there is to be no reprieve or retrials according to Judge Conners.

It just so happened that on this particular day, it was also Election Day, locally known by the Islanders as 'corruption day.' Unfortunately in there Caribbean, it is widely accepted that our Politicians and Government are very corrupt, in order for a specified party to gain control and win the election, the candidates put undue pressure on voters to make them vote in a particular way. The voters are become so bamboozled and scared, that they do as they are told. The candidates also 'vote-buy' this can take various forms such as a monetary 'reward' or as an exchange for necessary goods or services.

I had made my way back to my shack with Goldie, leaving Petra to finish reading through what we had both reported on the election, she was going to join us later. As Goldie and I sat on the deck, chattering about the days events, Blot arrived underneath my shack and started shouting up at us from the beach. We both peered over two find out what he was concerned about. "Dem a gwine git out Wi need tuh tap ih ar ketch dem an queng dem." Goldie and I looked at one another, this cannot be true, Tilly and Ed had only just gone to prison. According to Mogsey, yet again, he had a new information source, who had told him that, the new candidate to be elected was a close friend of Mr Bonner, the lawyer. Apparently Mr Bonner had managed to call in a few favours and the candidate elect visited the Tilly and Ed in prison where some bribery is alleged to have occurred, money is always power, which means our society tilts towards destruction.

I am not really into the politics here, in my opinion, our Government advocate themselves on not keeping election promises but bowing to "money," they're corrupted before the ballots are cast. I read a good quote recently, "In the age of information, ignorance is a choice." However, I wasn't too worried by this, if Ed and Tilly were pardoned there was so much hatred towards them for their crimes, revenge would be had by the locals, they wouldn't get far or probably survive if they were let out of prison. The judge did make that clear. I wouldn't want to be in Tilly and Ed's shoes if they were freed, they would be hunted like dogs and not be safe anywhere.

Goldie took my arm, "Eh ok Fi mi uncle will nah let eh hap'm Dem will drop out eena prison." She said. I was actually reassured but I knew I would be ok, I knew that Tilly and Ed would be punished no matter what. I was in survival mode, cold and indifferent, I can't undo the trauma I've been through, but I am adapting and overcoming.

CHAPTER 32

Two years on and my life has changed somewhat. I still have my memories, good and painful, but they are now photographs, which means I can choose what kind of album I want to build. My negative memories still come now and again at a cost, but as addictive as they feel, once lessons are learn't there is nothing in them of value. The positive ones come as friends with a picnic baskets, they are good and nourishing, supportive and kind. So I let the bad ones wander off on their own and encourage more of the good ones to blossom and grow. This way I can remain confident, well balanced and in control of myself, appreciating every moment as a gift towards a positive future. It still feels strange not to see the people you once had in your life anymore, but it is true when they say time is a healer.

I live in my shack on the beach, still no boyfriend and with my occasional TV dinners. I say occasional as I have learned to cook, Goldie taught me, oh and I was promoted. I am now the boss at the Alise newspaper, Goldie has become my best reporter and I have employed a new sub editor, Rosie and an assistant called Jack, both are an asset to our team. I still haven't been unable to fill Winston's position on a permanent basis, but we get by with various temps.
Petra managed to conquer her dream of returning to England to rekindle her first love and attain her ultimate job. We are

still in touch on an ad hoc basis as her life has become somewhat busy, juggling a husband, a new baby and her job as editor for the Telegraph newspaper in London. We have vowed to meet up again one day.

My parents have eventually managed to get here for a holiday and loved my little shack and the Island, although I think they found some of the locals a bit on the dubious side. Unfortunately for them, they were given an Island tour with Mogsey and Blot whilst I was at work one day. I was really appreciative to the two fisherman to do this, but I think mum and dad were quite shocked at the complete disregard of any rules and regulations, thankfully they loved the sights. I don't think my mother will ever be the same again after being given a joint to smoke by Blot, she still talks about it to this day, always ending the conversation with "Jaz, be careful who you mix with." Well, she didn't have to smoke it did she?

Iberville is a memory of yesteryear, standing in all weathers, as if there is still a pride in its lasting, a sense of a strength, awaiting someone with a gift for seeing "what could be?" rather than "what is?" For the time being it is a ghostly estate, standing skeleton-like on the hill, a crumbled beautiful ruin of an era long past, it has chosen solitude for itself, alone and abandoned for sure, home only to the wildlife that shelters within, those tiny heartbeats and tiny legs are the only things to love it at the moment.
The locals refuse to go near it, they say it will bring bad luck and Lady Amélie's ghost haunts it. Apparently, local gossip is

that because she was unaccustomed to love in her living years, in death she is uneasy and is still looking for love and revenge, she is not ready to see heaven's gate yet, but no one has actually seen her ghost, so as per usual it's just idle gossip during a few pints in Ziggy's bar!

I was staring out of my office window, chewing on my pencil and still reminiscing when suddenly a news bulletin flashed onto my computer screen.

Commissioner pleads for help in order to find two fugitives, Ed Wrexham and Tilly Colspur, who have escaped from prison on the Island of Nevis, affectionally known as 'Russels Rest' where they were being held after being convicted of a triple murder and abduction charge.

A source told SEARCHLIGHT that they both escaped overnight from the maximum-security area where they were being held. It is thought they were assisted in their escape from a local drug Baron Box Defeux, who has now gone into hiding.

Whilst the St Kitts and Nevis Police Force (SKANPF) are seeking the assistance of the public to apprehend them, they advise the public to approach with caution and notify the High Commission or Police Federation immediately if they are sighted.

At the same time, the hotline phone rang, I watched from my desk as Goldie answered it, I took in a deep breath, got up and walked to my office door. I stood leaning against the door frame as I strained to hear the conversation on the other end of the phone. It ended with "Get ih." Goldie replaced the handset and turned to face me, looking quite startled. "Jaz, Dat did Blot Wi need tuh guh Ziggy's bar yah now Sinting a go dung." "Ok, you go, see what the commotion is about" I replied. "Nuh nuh dem waan both ah wi" She replied quickly. I felt a wave of panic wash over me, what us? Despite that I found myself grabbing my mobile, camera, jotter pad and my bag from the desk "come on then, no time to lose, if its that important."

Goldie and I hurried outside into the heat of the midday sun and clambered into the jeep parked outside. I started the engine and drove off, as we bounced remarks between us, trying to come up with what the commotion might be all about, just surmising really as journalists do, but nothing could prepare us for what we were about to encounter.

Ziggy's bar was only about a fifteen minute drive from the office and on arrival we witnessed a crowd of people gathering outside the bar, predominately locals, but intermingled with a few faces I didn't recognise. There was the usual arm waving and vocal commotion, but that was normal here for any incident no matter how small. Blot must have some sort of bat radar as he appeared from somewhere in the middle the crowd, I think. Anyway he pulled at my jacket. "Quick fight" he blurted out, before hurrying back in the direction he came from, dragging me with him as he held onto the edge of my summer jacket and yelling at us, "Yuh cum." We didn't have much option, so followed a short distance behind, pushing our way and jostling our cameras as we went through the crowd of pressed close bodies and heads, all straining for a view, good job we have elbows! As we got nearer the front, the crowd seem to part like the Red Sea, I think it was because Blot was yelling "Got the Alise, let dem tru."

Picking up on various excerpts of conversation we heard as we made our way through, two vagrants had been spotted by Bembe. He was a difficult unreliable teenager who had lost his way in the world, well known in the village, having got himself into numerous scrapes before now. He was impulsive, a pain in the preverbal, but deep down I think he just had a lack of understanding and a mischievous innocence about him. Anyway, Bembe spotted two people outside Ziggy's bar who he thought were Ed and Tilly, he ran to the beach and of course told Blot who commandeered Mogsey and it spiralled from there.

Of course a ripple of dissent then spread, the local gossip grapevine took hold and caused a crowd to gather. I have no idea why these two vagrants came to Ziggy's bar but if it was them, they would be in grave danger.

I found Bembe and questioned him, he said that he saw two people, a man sitting on the steps of an unused garage near to Ziggy's with a woman standing over him. She was dressed in untold layers of fragmenting fabrics, her hair tied back but clumped with grease, apparently she shuffled her head moving this way and that, unsteady like there was a personal earthquake beneath her inadequate shoes. The man had a mop of brown hair under a cap, not sure how he knew this, but anyway, he wore an old maroon t-shirt which clung tightly to his baggy trousers he was wearing. His arms were wrapped around his knees that jutted up sharply, as if to hug them.

I smiled, if it really was Ed and Tilly, they had fallen into the sub-human class that would eventually destroy them, vulnerable, fragile, downtrodden, well they shouldn't have escaped prison should they! A malice thought entered my head as I smiled again, the kind that comes as a knife in the back. I hated them both, let's hope that there was more enmity, more pain and a slow death ahead for them. Gosh this is really bad, I should be indifferent by now, I am supposed to be over the whole thing, I am better than this.

Once we got to the front Mogsey was there, his face looked hardened, he was opening and closing his fists rhythmically. In front of him and slightly to the side of him were the two vagrants, both barefoot. Mogsey grabbed one of them by the back of their shirt and swung at them, releasing them as they tumbled to the ground. Everyone gasped, as he turned his attention to the other one, who also ended up on the floor but not before putting up more of a fight. Everyone held their breathe as Mogsey went in for another round, but before he'd even taken two paces forward one of the vagrants was on his back tugging hard on his hair and shouting obscenities in a female voice. To the side, the other vagrant, who was definitely male from his stature, had already been knocked to the ground again and was lying injured in a crumpled heap, moaning. Both Mogsey and the female continued to fight taking handfuls of each other's clothing as they attempted to wrestle each other to the ground, punching the living daylights out of each other as they went. She was good, I give her that.

Suddenly, a surge of energy rippled through the crowd, a joy as the long awaited victory happened, the female vagrant released a hand-hold and started jabbing Mogsey hard in the ribs.That made him so mad, he was not about to be beaten by a female. He released both hands and grabbed at her hair, bringing her face down sharply onto his bent knee. Blood flowed from her possibly broken nose as she staggered backwards, before falling in a heap, defeated onto the ground next to the other groaning vagrant.

Despite his blooded wounds, mainly scratches and cuts, Mogsey raised his arms to the air, the victor winning his battle, short, violent but bloody, the crowd clapped and jeered as they surged forward almost crushing each other. Goldie and I moved out of the way pretty quick, to avoid the masses and being trampled underfoot. Well, ok that is a slight exaggeration, but we were all jammed together, jostling for a place to see what happens next. An unholy conglomeration of perfumes, body odour and over-applied cologne rushed up my nostrils in the over crowded area.

A police siren sounded, screeching towards us in the not too far distance, Goldie had called them. I walked over to the bloody mess on the floor, as Goldie joined me. The vagrants looked like grotesque gargoyles, already their eyes were beginning to swell, a bloody spit drooled from the man's slack jaws. The two crumpled bodies on the ground lifted their heads upwards as they managed to get themselves on all fours and then trying to stand as quickly as they could, helping each other, supporting each other.

Goldie held on to my arm as we made eye contact with them, they just stared back at us completely unashamed, there was a definite sense of familiarity to their faces. My heart started to hammer inside my chest like it belonged to a rabbit running for its skin, I felt quite sick. Surely not, they wouldn't be that stupid would they? I am almost sure it is, Ed and Tilly. I stood motionless, staring, shaking inside, Goldie gripped my arm tighter, "Jaz, A yuh ok Eh dem a nuh it?" She said, I nodded as I replied "I think so." Goldie smiled at me, I can do this, I whispered to myself as I took the part of me that was broken and made it a ghost, I'm strong, I can stand alone and take care of everything. I wrinkled my nose and took another step backwards, it was tempting to whisper something in their ears, but what was the point, at least these cockroaches would bare their scars forever.

I couldn't have predicted my next move, but I lifted my camera and held down the shutter, I am still a newspaper reporter after all and this was a story!

Books by Vanessa Wrixon

Book Trilogy

Iberville
Book One

Iberville is the first book in a murder mystery series. Small time English Journalist Jasmine Tormolis lands herself a new job in the Caribbean. From there on in, her life takes some twists and turns as she and a local fishermen discover a woman's body washed up on the beach. Despite the Authorities corruption and fraud, Jaz decides to do her own investigative work, which lands her in deep water and leads to a kidnapping and the murder of two friends.

Temptation
Book Two

Continues to follow Jasmine Tormolis, but now as the boss of the Alise newspaper. Her and one of her reporters land themselves in hot water once more, when they are dealt a chance holiday to another Caribbean Island. Here they try to become helpful accomplishes to a couple of secret agents they meet. Once again they find themselves being hunted down for revenge until their killers are killed or are they?

Haunted
Book Three

Jasmine Meyers formally Tormolis, now resides at Iberville with her new husband. Her and her reporter Goldie remain inseparable and help each other renovating their new abodes. Both try their hand at detective work, but it's not as easy as it looks. Lady Amelie Wrexham, having once owned Iberville remains there as a ghost, trying to perfect the art of haunting. However, failure to do this effectively gives her a chance opportunity to help Jaz catch and put her stalker behind bars for life. This is not without its problems when ghost tries to help.

Other Books by Vanessa Wrixon
Dark Nights
Camille Lavigne a French teacher at a secondary school, has arrived in England after a messy breakup. She finds her job frustrating to say the least. She becomes embroiled with a handsome man twelve years her junior, but despite a passionate steamy relationship, she is unaware of his dealings with the underworld and becomes the prime suspect in his murder, needing the help of her husband to bail her out.

Sowing the seed
Petra Defeu is on a stake out with her colleague. Having just moved into the area as a new detective, she hasn't quite got the measure of how things work and her colleagues can't yet get a measure of her. When she gets home from work one evening, her house has been burgled and there is a dead man in her kitchen. She then has to prove her innocence in a race against time before her colleagues or ruthless conspirators catch up with her.

Printed in Great Britain
by Amazon

11385443R00173